LEADER OF THE PACK

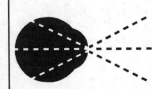

This Large Print Book carries the
Seal of Approval of N.A.V.H.

LEADER OF THE PACK

DAVID ROSENFELT

THORNDIKE PRESS
A part of Gale, Cengage Learning

GALE
CENGAGE Learning·

Detroit • New York • San Francisco • New Haven, Conn • Waterville, Maine • London

Copyright © 2012 by David Rosenfelt.
Thorndike Press, a part of Gale, Cengage Learning.

Thorndike Press® Large Print Core.
The text of this Large Print edition is unabridged.
Other aspects of the book may vary from the original edition.
Set in 16 pt. Plantin.

LIBRARY OF CONGRESS CATALOGING-IN-PUBLICATION DATA

Rosenfelt, David.
  Leader of the pack / by David Rosenfelt.
     pages ; cm. — (Thorndike Press large print core)
  ISBN 978-1-4104-5312-9 (hardcover) — ISBN 1-4104-5312-X (hardcover)
  1. Carpenter, Andy (Fictitious character)—Fiction. 2. Dogs—Fiction. 3. New Jersey—Fiction. 4. Large type books. I. Title.
  PS3618.O838L43 2012b
  813'.6—dc23   2012032082

Published in 2012 by arrangement with St. Martin's Press, LLC.

Printed in the United States of America
1 2 3 4 5 6 7 16 15 14 13 12

This book is dedicated to the
amazing members of
"Team Woofabago":

Cyndi Spodek Dickey
Mary Lynn Dundas
Cyndi Flores
Erik Kreider
Nick Kreider
Emmit Luther
Randy Miller
Debbie Myers
Joe Nigro
Teri Nigro

By the time Peyton Manning threw the pass, Richard Solarno was dead.

When Richard got up to answer the doorbell, Manning was directing the Colts in the no-huddle offense. Consistent with his style of play, Manning surveyed the defense while at the line of scrimmage, calling audibles based on what he saw before him.

As was often the case, Manning could do this for at least twenty-five or thirty seconds, until the play clock was about to run out.

Since Solarno had bet a lot of money on the Colts, and they were down by four on the Patriots' eighteen-yard line with thirty seconds to play, he wasn't happy about leaving the television at all. Chances are it was just a deliveryman, and he could deal with it and be back without missing a play. At least that's what he hoped.

That's not how it worked out. He opened the door, and managed to get out the words "what are you" before the bullet hit him in the chest, sending him falling backward.

There was a silencer on the gun, so the killer knew that no neighbors were calling 911. Solarno was technically still alive when he hit the floor, but likely dead by the time Manning threw the interception, effectively costing the Colts the game. But that was no longer Solarno's problem; he wouldn't be paying bookmakers ever again.

The killer heard a noise from the top of the stairs, so he entered the house, closing the door behind him. He then headed straight up the stairs, and within three minutes ended the life of Richard's wife, Karen, as well.

That had not been part of the plan, but it had to be done.

"So, what's on tap for today?"

Laurie's question, while seemingly innocuous, represents something of a problem, because my "tap" for today is not something she is likely to approve of.

"Well, I'm going to take Tara for a walk. Then I'm going to run over to the market for some beer, be back here by noon for the NFL pregame shows. I'll call my bookie, Jimmy Rollins, at twelve thirty to bet the games; then I'll order a pizza. At one I'll watch the Giants-Redskins game, switching to other games during time-outs.

"Then, at four, it'll be mostly San Diego against the Jets, again switching where necessary. That takes me to seven, when I'm hoping you'll have dinner ready. From eight thirty to eleven thirty tonight is Dallas-Philadelphia on NBC; then, if I'm lucky, you'll be in the mood for some sexual frolicking from eleven thirty until midnight."

That is what I would say if I had any semblance of courage or honesty, but since I don't, I opt for, "I haven't really done a tap check for today yet, but I'm sure I'll come up with something productive. Every day is a chance for a new adventure."

"Then let me guess," she says. "You're going to take Tara for a walk, get some beer, place some bets, order a pizza, and watch football all day."

"You make it sound really appealing," I say. "How did you come up with all that?"

"It's exactly what you did yesterday."

I snap my fingers. "I knew it sounded familiar. But yesterday was college football, today is pro. Apples and oranges."

"You're incorrigible."

"Actually, I'm partially corrigible. I'm not watching football tomorrow at all during the day."

"What about Monday-night football?"

"That's not during the day; it's at night. Hence the name. Oh, and I'm making the prison rounds Tuesday and Wednesday." Laurie knows what that means; I visit former clients of mine who were found guilty at trial and are in prison. I don't want them to think they've been forgotten.

"So what do you have on tap for today?" I ask, trying to pull the old switcheroo.

"I'm going running, then a spinning class, then Pilates, and then this afternoon I'm volunteering at the hospital."

"You know, I can't decide which of those things sounds the most awful."

"I've got an idea, Andy."

Uh, oh. Laurie's ideas often involve my expending energy by actually doing things, and today I really just want to plant myself in front of the large-screen TV in the den. I'm so looking forward to total relaxation that I bought a bag of already-popped popcorn so I don't have to deal with the microwave.

"I hope it's a long-range, down-the-road, futuristic kind of idea, because we're talking Giants-Redskins," I say.

"Well, it might be a way for you to really do something productive, something that you would also enjoy." She quickly adds, "But definitely not today; I understand we're talking Giants-Redskins."

My name, Andy Carpenter, is listed under "Attorneys" in the phone book, assuming phone books still exist. But since my desire to work is really low, and my bank account is really high, I haven't taken on any clients in almost six months, so I'm a little leery about what Laurie might be driving at.

"As long as what you're going to suggest

doesn't include judges, courthouses, depositions, or briefs, and if I can bring Tara, I'm all ears," I say.

"It doesn't include any of those things, and Tara's actually the key to it."

I relax the cringe I've been doing since the conversation began. Tara is my best friend, right up there with Laurie. She is also a golden retriever, the greatest one on Earth. My interest is officially piqued.

She continues, "I think you should take Tara to the hospital as a therapy dog."

This could be worse, but it ain't great. I know a little bit about the therapy dog process, and while I think it's a great thing to do, it's especially great for *other* people to do, with *other people's dogs*.

I can't speak, or bark, for Tara, but I'm not anxious to start spending time in hospitals.

"Doesn't Tara need some special training for that?" I ask.

She shakes her head. "Not this one; I've checked it out. All they require is a mellow disposition and friendliness on the part of the dog, plus human compassion. Tara is mellow and friendly, and she has enough of the human compassion part for both of you."

"Sounds great. But there must be a huge

waiting list for something like that. I don't want to cut in line."

Laurie shakes her head. "Nope."

"And I suppose you've already talked about it with Tara?"

She nods. "She was quite enthusiastic about it."

I look over at Tara, who does in fact seem fine with everything, and doesn't appear surprised. This has all the earmarks of a setup.

I'm not going to win this, so I might as well try to make it pay off. "How is this going to impact my life sexually?" I ask.

Laurie smiles. "I find the prospect of you doing this to be very erotic."

I return the smile. "My cup of human compassion runneth over."

If I hadn't seen it, I wouldn't have believed it.

I've been in the hospital room occupied by the very frail Mrs. Harriet Marshall for thirty-five minutes. When I got here, she seemed barely awake, and her mumbling speech was impossible to understand.

I told her who I was, and she showed no reaction whatsoever. I could have told her the room was on fire and I wouldn't have gotten a response. She was depressed, numbed, and mostly lifeless, sort of how I felt after the Redskins beat the Giants yesterday.

She had absolutely no interest in me, had nothing to say to me, and barely acknowledged my existence. In terms of dealing with females, it felt like I was back in high school.

Then Tara walked over to her, and everything changed. It took three or four minutes,

14

during which Tara sniffed her and put her nose against her arm.

Harriet resisted, until Tara pulled out the big move . . . the combination "lean-against nuzzle, with a slight lick and an adoring glance." In dog-land the move has a degree of difficulty of nine point seven, and as far as I know, there is no known defense against it.

So within five minutes Harriet was petting Tara with both hands. She was using a "reverse pet," which means she would stroke her head from front to back, and then from back to front. I know from personal experience that Tara is not a huge fan of that, but she was graciously allowing Harriet to do it.

The transformation has been amazing. Harriet went from silent and sullen to outgoing and borderline gregarious. In fact, I don't think I could shut her up if I wanted to, which I don't.

First, all she wanted to talk about was Tara, asking where I got her and whether she was always this sweet. I told her that I got her from an animal shelter seven years ago when she was two years old.

"So she's only nine now?" she asked.

Unfortunately, "only" is not the appropriate word. Nine years is starting to get up

15

there for a golden. "Yes," I said, "though in dog years that's fifty-two," I said. Many people think that each year a dog lives counts as seven, but that's not the correct way to figure it. The first year counts as twenty-one, and each one thereafter counts as four.

The entire concept would be depressing if not for the fact that Tara is going to live forever.

"Fifty-two? I've got stockings older than that." Then she laughed, and I was immediately glad that I let Laurie talk me into doing this.

She went on to tell me everything about every one of her relatives, and she has about thirty thousand of them. Her granddaughter Cynthia just won a regional spelling bee, but the region was in Seattle, so Harriet was bummed that she didn't get to go.

"Do you have family around here?" I asked.

"Yes."

"Do they come to visit?"

She shrugged. "They want to, but I don't let them. I'm too busy feeling sorry for myself."

"Because you're sick?" I didn't know what was wrong with her, so it was a question I probably shouldn't have asked.

"Because I'm old, and because things in my body don't work like they should anymore." She smiled. "I'm not afraid of death, but dying is going to be a pain in the ass."

We've talked for over an hour, and I really don't want to leave, but she's clearly getting tired, so I put Tara's leash on her to lead her out.

"Will you come back to see me?" Harriet asks.

"Definitely."

"And you'll bring Tara?"

"She'll bring me."

"I had a dog when I was growing up," she says. "Her name was Sarah. I remember everything about her." She laughs. "I can't remember a single boyfriend; hell, I can't remember what I had for breakfast today. But I remember everything about Sarah."

"Dogs are the best," I say.

She nods and pets Tara's head for the thousandth time. "And Tara's the best of the best. Just like Sarah."

I nod. "Exactly like Sarah."

The prison up in Rahway is maybe my least favorite place on Earth, with the possible exception of Lincoln Financial Field in Philadelphia. Actually, the two places remind me of each other. For starters, they're both enormous, often overcrowded, and serve mediocre food.

Rahway houses murderers and thieves, the lowest of the low, worthy of society's scorn and revenge. The stadium in Philadelphia houses the Philadelphia Eagles.

Six of one, half a dozen of the other.

I'm heading for the prison, as I promised Laurie, but keeping that promise is not my motivation. I have friends here, friends that rely on me. Unfortunately, relying on me is part of the reason they're here in the first place.

I've had a very successful legal career; you can count the number of cases I've lost on one hand. Well, actually it's more like two or three hands, and a couple of feet. But I know defense attorneys who can't remember the last time they won a case, and I'm actually on a winning streak.

But the losses bug me, especially in cases where I truly felt the client was innocent.

I'm financially independent now, and therefore able to pick and choose from prospective clients. Mostly I choose not to work at all, but if I do, it's only because I consider the person innocent of the crime they're charged with. In my older, poorer days, I didn't have that luxury, so sometimes I'd wind up with guilty clients, and, more often than not, the jury sealed the deal.

But Joey Desimone was different. He stood accused of the cold-blooded murder of a husband and wife in Montclair. The evidence was clearly against him, and I understood the jury's finding him guilty, but every instinct I had said he didn't do it.

Weighing heavily in the jurors' minds, though they would never admit it and the judge specifically told them not to consider it, was the fact that Joey is the son of Carmine Desimone, the head of an organized crime family in Central Jersey.

Joey was widely thought to have distanced himself from his family's "occupation," and I believed then, and still do, that he had

19

nothing to do with the criminal enterprise. But it was a mark against him, as was the fact that Joey was having an affair with the woman who died in the attack, Karen Solarno.

Public outrage at the crime was widespread; I was even castigated for representing him. The jury climbed on the anti-Joey bandwagon and gave him life without the possibility of parole. They would have given him the death penalty, but New Jersey doesn't have one. Joey's continuing to live actually became an issue in the next gubernatorial campaign, with one of the candidates pointing to it as a prime reason for a reinstatement of the ultimate punishment.

That candidate lost, and retreated to his previous post on Wall Street. Joey, in the meantime, spends twenty-three of every twenty-four hours sitting in a seven-by-ten-foot cell.

So I visit him. Not that often, maybe three or four times a year, and not for any reason other than to let him know he's not forgotten. Early on I could see the look of hope on his face that I was bringing him some news that might help get him out of prison, and then the disappointment when that obviously wasn't the case.

Now we just have easy conversations,

friends talking about whatever. He's managed to keep up to date on the news of the day, especially sports, so the conversation flows smoothly.

I don't bother asking him how things are in the prison anymore. The answer is always a shrug and "getting by." I know that he doesn't get hassled by other inmates, for a few reasons. First of all, he minds his own business. Second, he's a former Marine who can handle himself as well as anyone in the place.

Third, and by far the most important, everyone knows who his father is. Joey has often told me how distressed his father is that his son is behind bars, and that he was unable to prevent it. He is, however, more than powerful enough to have effectively put the word out that Joey is not to be messed with.

Joey is a football Giants fan, another mark in his favor, but he takes it to a level well past me. I know who the starters are, and am generally aware of their strengths and weaknesses. Joey knows everyone on the roster, including the practice squad, and he can talk at length about any one of them. Which is fine, because when it comes to football talk, I can listen at length.

I mention my experience with Tara, the

Therapy Dog, and Joey finds it hilarious. "So you bring a dog right into the hospital? Isn't that unsanitary or something?"

"Unsanitary? Tara?" I ask. "You start talking trash about Tara and it won't do you any good to smile when you say it."

He laughs, apparently not cowed by my threat. "Sorry, but I can't picture it. The world has changed a lot since I've been in here."

He probably doesn't know how true that is, but I decide that his comment is not banter material, so I don't try it. "I doubted it myself, but the first person I did it with, Tara really made her feel better. It's like she came alive."

His eyes light up with an idea. "Hey, does the person have to be in a hospital?"

"No, I don't think so. Could be an old-age home, even in someone's house. Wherever."

"Would you try it with my uncle Nick?"

There's pretty much no favor I wouldn't grant Joey, but bringing Tara to visit Nick Desimone is pushing it. "Nicky Fats," as he has been known to the tabloids, his family, his friends, police, and probably most of the people he has killed, has been Carmine Desimone's right-hand man since Carmine assumed control of the family.

Carmine has been known to be ruthless in stamping out his enemies, a throwback to the days when the accepted mode of operation was to shoot, stab, and club first, and ask questions later. According to the lore, Nicky Fats makes Carmine look like Mary Poppins, and apparently moves with a deadly dexterity that belies his three-hundred-fifty-pound girth.

"You want me to do dog therapy with your uncle Nick?" I try to make my voice sound as incredulous as possible, but I can't get it to the level that I really feel.

"You don't want to?" he asks.

"What if Tara sheds on him?"

He laughs again. "What . . . you think he'll kill you if she sheds on him?"

"Not necessarily kill, but 'maim' and 'torture' briefly entered my mind."

"Don't worry about it. Shedding would be fine; just don't have Tara pull a knife on him. But seriously, Andy, he used to call me all the time. Now I talk to him maybe once a month, and he's not like himself. Really down, you know? And not so sharp anymore. He forgets stuff; sometimes doesn't make sense. And it's getting worse."

In a courtroom, even under tremendous pressure, I can think on my feet and verbally and strategically react to anything that might happen. But in this case, talking about taking a dog to visit an old fat man, I freeze up like a Fudgsicle.

"Sure. Happy to do it," I say. In terms of level of truthfulness, that statement would rank with something like, "Damn, I'm going to be traveling to Saturn that day to go giraffe hunting."

"Great. I'll set it up."

"You're going to meet with Nicky Fats? And you're taking a dog?"

The speaker is Eddie "Hike" Lynch, the lawyer who works with me when we have a case to work on, which means we don't work together very often. He comes into the office pretty much daily to use the computer. Hike is cheap; he wouldn't buy his own computer if the store threw in the antidote to a deadly poison he had just taken.

Hike also takes pessimism to a new level, so I'm not surprised that he sees my upcoming therapy session as a disaster about to happen.

"It'll be a half hour, and I'll be out of there," I say.

"Really? What if you piss him off?"

"I won't piss him off."

"Come on," he says. "You piss everybody off. You're a really annoying person."

"Thanks, Hike."

"And speaking of pissing, what if your dog pisses on the floor?"

"Don't call her my dog, OK? Her name is Tara."

"What does that mean? She's not your dog?'

"She's my partner, and she's a trained therapist."

"Sorry. What if your trained therapist pisses on the floor?"

"There is no chance of that," I say.

"Oh yeah? If I was alone in a room with Nicky Fats, I'd piss on the floor."

My assistant, Edna, is not in because it is Tuesday. When we are not working on a case, Edna takes seven-day weekends. Tuesdays consistently fall within that window.

Her absence has left me with only Hike to talk to, which clearly is unacceptable, so I head for home. Laurie is not there; she's teaching her criminology class at William Paterson College. But Tara is, and she and I need to talk.

I grab the leash, which sends her barreling toward the door. We take the same walk through Eastside Park that we take every day, but as always she treats it like it's the first time she's been in this wonderful aromatic world.

26

"Tara, we're going to see this guy named Nicky; he's pretty old and probably still pretty fat. He's got a bit of a temper, so we want to be careful how we treat him."

She's not really paying attention, looking off toward a nearby tree. "You want to look for squirrels, or listen to me? Anyway, just be yourself, but follow my lead. Just do what I do, OK? For instance, don't lick him unless I do, and I definitely won't. Wagging your tail is fine."

Tara doesn't intimidate easily. I know that for a fact; we've argued over biscuit issues a number of times over the years, and the next time I win will be the first. She's either not worried about meeting Nicky Fats, or she's putting up a front. I suspect it's the former.

I may be worrying too much, and at the same time underestimating Tara's therapeutic powers. By the time she's done with this fearsome Mafia figure, he'll probably be a sensitive, poetry-reading, yoga-loving, introspective, mushy guy.

From pictures I've seen, he's got the mushy part down already.

Somehow, Nicky Fats manages to be simultaneously fat and frail. He doesn't seem quite as obese as the older pictures had made him appear, but I would still put him in the two-eighty-to-three-hundred-pound range.

But he's also gotten very old, which I suppose is an accomplishment for someone in his profession. He seems weak, and his face is drawn and almost thin, a weird contrast to the rest of his body.

So far the visit has been not as awful as I expected. Nicky lives in Carmine's house, which is on a nice piece of property just outside of Elizabeth, New Jersey. Two men greeted Tara and me at the door, but as security guards go, they were pretty lax.

I've been frisked by mob guys in the past in such a way that my private parts were made to feel open to the public. With these guys, I could have been carrying a bazooka, and I doubt they would have noticed.

They motioned me into a room at the rear of the house, which turned out to be a den. There was a large-screen TV, and Nicky was sitting in an armchair watching ESPN. Watching might be the wrong word; Nicky appeared to be paying no attention to it at all.

Nicky seemed to be expecting our visit, or at least he didn't show any surprise. All he said was, "The dog is here. What time is it?"

I introduced myself as Andy Carpenter, though I was tempted to say I was Hike Lynch, in case anything happened that would cause Nicky to order some kind of retribution. He didn't respond to that, or to my mentioning that Joey suggested I stop by, or to anything else I said.

But he sure as hell liked Tara. She went right up to him and he started petting her, occasionally laughing a weird laugh as he did so. This has now gone on for almost forty-five minutes, though it feels like next week will be two years since we got here. When one is with Nicky Fats, time goes in slow motion.

Nicky seems intermittently lucid, snapping back and forth from clear statements to borderline gibberish. But one constant is his petting and focus on Tara; she has got this therapy thing down really well.

Suddenly, Nicky looks up at me and says, "Who are you?"

I've mentioned my name a couple of times already, but decide that I don't need to point that out. "I'm Andy Carpenter. Joey suggested I come visit."

"Good boy, that Joey."

I nod vigorously. Nicky Fats is the kind of guy that makes you want to nod vigorously. I'll keep doing it until he says something like, "Stop nodding vigorously, asshole."

"Yes, definitely a good boy, that Joey," I say, since it seemed to fit in with the nodding vigorously approach.

"He coming here today?" Nicky asks.

Now, I know that Nicky has been in contact with Joey in prison, so it's not like it's been kept a secret from him the last six years. But if he's forgotten about it, I'm not going to be the one to rebreak the news to him. "No, he's not coming today," I say.

I swear, I can see his eyes, and behind that his mind, start to clear. "He's locked up," Nicky says.

I nod, less vigorously this time. "Yes, I'm afraid so."

"Who are you? How do you know Joey?"

"My name is Andy Carpenter. I am Joey's

lawyer."

"You lost the case?"

This time a slight nod and an involuntary cringe. "I lost the case."

"My fault," he says. "My fault."

I assume he's using the wrong pronoun, and instead of "your" fault, is saying "my" fault. I decide to be gracious and defensive at the same time. "It's nobody's fault."

"We shoulda hit the bastard ourselves, as soon as it happened," Nicky says. "I shoulda told Carmine. We should have been the ones to do it. My fault."

On second thought, maybe he's got the pronoun right. But whatever he's saying, it's so strange that I can't let it go. "What are you talking about? As soon as what happened?"

"The prick couldn't be trusted, you know? He was dirty; he had no honor. We shoulda hit him months before."

"Are you talking about Solarno? Richard Solarno? The guy they said Joey murdered?"

Nicky nods and seems to be getting agitated. "I knew the prick couldn't be trusted. I shoulda told Carmine."

"Solarno? Is that what you're saying? Why would you have to trust him? How did you even know him?"

Then something else seems to click in the

31

relic that is his mind, and he stares straight at me with very cold eyes. "Get out of here. Take the dog."

One more vigorous nod and Tara and I are out the door. I'm not sure, but I think she is nodding as well. Vigorously.

No one will ever have to put out an "All Points Bulletin" for Pete Stanton. The Paterson police lieutenant is always in one of two places; either he is on the job, or he is at Charlie's, the greatest sports bar in America.

Part of what I am saying is hearsay. Except for when his path crosses with mine on a case or at trial, I don't actually see him on the job. But he is a star in the department, and seems to be involved in a large number of investigations and arrests. He also knows virtually everything about any case the department is dealing with, whether he is assigned to it or not. So I'm assuming he works long hours.

But when it comes to Charlie's, I am an eyewitness. Pete, Vince Sanders, and I have a regular table at Charlie's. I'm not there every night, nor is Vince, but Pete's presence is a rock-solid guarantee. I think he

handcuffs himself to the table.

Laurie is the only other person allowed at the table, but for some reason she doesn't come by more than a couple of times a month. I'm not sure why; it's possible she doesn't care for the belching.

Pete's probably the only true sports fan among the three of us. Vince and I bet on the games, and therefore have a manufactured interest. Pete doesn't gamble, which in my view makes him a communist, but he will eagerly watch any sport on television.

Tonight is a perfect example. Because the four or five hundred ESPN channels each have to devour twenty-four hours of sports, they show games like Troy at Middle Tennessee State, which is on tonight.

I'm taking Middle Tennessee plus five points, while Vince has Troy. If I wasn't betting the game, I wouldn't watch it if you strapped me to the chair. But not only is Pete interested in it, he's spouting facts about the key players on each team.

At the half, Troy is ahead by two touchdowns. I don't mind that I'm losing; what bothers me is that Vince is winning. Vince is a terrible loser; he complains, makes excuses, and can't let it go. He's also a terrible winner; he brags, gloats, and is generally obnoxious. And tie games bring out the

worst in him.

"How could you possibly bet Middle Tennessee?" he asks. "Northern Tennessee I could understand. Southern Tennessee I get. But Middle Tennessee? They play chess and jacks in the middle of Tennessee, not football."

"You're an idiot," I point out.

"So you're down two touchdowns to an idiot?" he asks, a question for which there is no good retort, because it contains the truth.

"Currently I am, yes."

Satisfied with his rhetorical victory, Vince looks around the room, his customary frown on his face. "This place is turning into foo-foo land."

There was a time, early in our relationship, when I would have said, "What do you mean, Vince?" That time has now passed; he's going to tell me anyway, no doubt in a negative rant, so there's no reason to pretend I'm interested.

"Just sitting here, I can see eleven beer bottles on tables."

"So?"

"Of those, nine are light beers, and of those, eight are foreign."

"I repeat . . . so?"

"So if they don't like this country, and they don't want to be fat, why don't they go

35

to some health spa in Paris, sip wheat germ, and let me drink real American beer and watch football?"

There's no answer to that, and no reason at all to continue to talk to Vince, so I turn my attention to Pete. He hasn't said much during the first half, which is typical for him. For one thing, he's intent on watching the game. For another, it's hard to chitchat when one has a beer bottle in one's mouth.

For Pete, a beer bottle is like a pacifier. When he's complaining, or talking too much, you just stick one in his mouth and he starts happily sucking on it.

"What's new in the world of crime?" I ask.

"Why, you looking for some scumbags to represent?"

They've been verbally mistreating me like this for a long time, and I've suddenly had enough. "OK, listen, both of you. You are either going to talk to me in a civil, friendly, respectful manner, or you are going to buy your own beer and burgers." Since I am wealthy, and they're not, I am always getting stuck with the check.

"How's it going, my man?" Vince says to me, not missing a beat. "You're looking good today. You lose some weight?"

"Why would he need to lose weight?" Pete says. "The man is ripped. It's no wonder

Laurie is nuts about him."

This is even worse than the abuse. "That's enough," I say. "Now you're making me nauseous."

"Whatever you say, asshole," Vince says.

"I've fished bodies better than yours out of the river," Pete chimes in.

Back to normal.

"So I heard you were making the prison rounds yesterday," Pete says. "How's killer Joey doing?"

Pete was the arresting officer in the Desimone case, and his testimony at trial was credible and convincing. He never had any doubt about Joey's guilt, as he has told me on numerous occasions.

"How much do you know about Richard Solarno?" I ask.

"He's dead."

"Besides that."

"Read the trial transcript."

"I have, many times. I'm talking about beyond what came out at trial. How carefully did you check into him?"

He's quickly suspicious. "Why?"

"Because I'm buying the beer."

He shrugs his defeat. "Not that much. There wasn't much point; he wasn't the target. His wife was."

"According to your theory."

"Right. I've got to stop basing my theories on the facts and the evidence. I should use your approach and have my theories delivered to me from fantasyland."

"Any chance Solarno was involved in something illegal?"

"Like what?"

"I have no idea."

"Sounds like you're really getting somewhere."

"Just answer my question," I say.

"Yeah; he was into something illegal. He was a Russian spy. He also killed Kennedy and kidnapped Lindbergh's kid. Who's putting this bullshit into your head?"

"Nicky Fats."

Vince considers it time to jump in. "You talked to Nicky Fats? I hear he sits in a room all day planning to assassinate President Eisenhower."

"What the hell were you doing talking to Nicky Fats?" Pete asks. "Is he your next innocent client?"

"He's a misunderstood soul," I say. "But he had some interesting things to say about Richard Solarno."

Now Pete sneers openly. "Yeah? Why didn't he say them when Joey was going down?"

"Now that is a damn good question."

Nicky Fats forgot Carpenter's visit within ten minutes after he left. His short-term memory was unpredictable. Some things stuck with him for days, or even months, while others were wiped clean almost instantly. Were Carpenter and his dog to come back, Nicky would think they were visiting for the first time.

The deterioration of his mind had taken place slowly, and his family and friends had been just as slow to notice it. Of course, Nicky had never been surrounded by the most sensitive of people, nor those who were the most tolerant of weakness.

It was up to Nicky's brother, Carmine, to provide for his care. Carmine was the youngest of three brothers, seven years younger than Nicky, who in turn was born three years after Vincent Desimone. Vincent seemed destined to lead the family, but his ascent was thwarted by a bullet that spread

39

his brain matter over much of downtown Bayonne, New Jersey.

Of the remaining, unsplattered brains among the siblings, Carmine's was significantly superior to Nicky's. Since Nicky was far more prone to, and adept at, violence, the roles they adopted were the obvious ones. Carmine would be in charge, and Nicky would be his trusted enforcer.

Nothing much changed for many years, and the family ruled with only occasional challenges that they thwarted easily and ruthlessly. They've also been comparatively successful in fending off law enforcement. While other "families" have been infiltrated and had their top people taken down by the feds, the Desimone family has survived relatively intact.

To this day Carmine is said to be on top of his game, but instead of having Nicky as his enforcer, he has taken on the role of Nicky's caretaker.

Not that it's taken a lot of work. Nicky has been mostly content to sit in his room, watching television and movies on DVDs. He's not adept at working the remote control, but that hasn't been a big problem, because he doesn't really seem to care what he's watching.

Lately Nicky has asked to go out more,

even mentioning old friends that he wants to see. The fact that some of them have been dead for twenty years either is lost to his failed memory, or not enough to deter him from wanting to reconnect and hash over old times.

Carmine's primary custodian for Nicky is Tommy Iurato. Iurato is somewhat over-qualified for the assignment; he's been a top-level soldier in the family for years.

Iurato had given the OK to allow Carpenter and the dog to visit with Nicky. He figured that it would be uneventful, and might shut the complaining Nicky up for a while.

The other, more important reason was that it would serve as a test, to see how Nicky would handle himself when in contact with the outside world.

"Did you enjoy the visit?" Iurato asked when he brought in Nicky's dinner. It was the same dinner every night, spaghetti and meatballs, chocolate pudding, and a carafe of red wine.

"What?"

"When you saw the lawyer and the dog. How was that?"

"What the hell you talking about?" Nicky asked. He absolutely had no clue about having had a visit of any kind.

"Never mind. I thought someone was here today. Maybe I was wrong."

"Not only are you wrong, but you're stupid," Nicky said.

Iurato not only knew that Carpenter and the dog had been there, he knew every word that was said. He had seen it through the hidden cameras in the room, and heard it through the hidden microphones. Nicky was under constant surveillance.

Iurato didn't argue; he simply left the food, and then came back ten minutes later, when Nicky was finished. The old man still had a healthy appetite, yet had been losing weight regardless of how much he ate. It was the one thing about him that Iurato envied.

Iurato picked up the dishes and placed them on the table. He then propped Nicky up in his chair; he had slouched a bit and had a difficult time lifting himself back up.

Once that was accomplished, Iurato stepped behind Nicky, and in one motion, broke his neck. He did it quickly and expertly, in the same manner he had used with previous victims.

Iurato went into the bathroom and turned on the shower, then ripped the shower curtain and threw it on the wet floor. He then dragged Nicky into the bathroom, which was not an easy task, as Nicky now defined the term "deadweight."

Iurato placed Nicky on the floor, and then left the bathroom, closing the door behind him. The official report would say that Nicky had slipped and fallen in the shower, and no one would contradict it. No coroner in his right mind would believe that someone had come into Nicky Fats's house and killed him.

And no one could ever have imagined who ordered it, or why.

I am at my computer when I have a potentially life-changing experience. There, sitting in my e-mail in-box with far less important messages, is one with the subject, "Urgent response requested."

Never one to fail to respond to an urgent request, I open the e-mail and am shocked to find that it is from one Amin d'Amino, a bank officer in Ghana. He is writing to me because he has learned that I am a man that can be trusted to handle a sensitive matter with great discretion. And this is clearly a sensitive matter.

It turns out that there are twenty million dollars sitting in this particular bank, needing only a destination to allow Mr. d'Amino to send it to. And he has chosen me! From a country full of people! Obviously the Andy Carpenter star shines brightly around the world.

For my trouble and discretion I will

receive eight million dollars for myself. Amazingly, all I have to do is send him my bank account information, so that he can wire it. It's an eminently reasonable request; if it takes me five minutes to do it, I will have earned one point six million dollars per minute. There are NBA players who don't earn that much.

Having said that, I'm thinking that maybe I'm not worthy of something like this. I'm debating this in my own mind, when I hear the doorbell. Laurie opens it and lets Hike in, and he comes into the den, carrying a filled cardboard box, which he puts down on the desk.

"Give me your bank account number," I say.

"What for?"

"Eight million dollars, that's what for. It's your lucky day."

"Is that the Ghana money?" he asks.

"How did you know?"

"I already sent them your information. You should get the wire any minute. Which is good, considering you're working for a client who hasn't paid you for six years."

He's referring to Joey, though of course I haven't done any work for him during those six years. There was little need to fight to keep someone out of prison when that

45

person was already in prison.

"Let's take a look at the file," I say, and proceed to take folders out of the box that Hike brought from the office. While I'm not being paid for this, Hike is, which is why he was so willing to pick up the file and bring it over. If I asked Hike to drive to Wyoming to pick up an acre of cowshit, he would be fine doing so, as long as he could bill by the hour, and he could get time and a half for washing off his shoes.

"Your schedule is a little off," Hike says.

"What do you mean?"

"It's not the end of the month."

Hike knows that my going through old files on cases I've lost is a common practice for me, as I'm always hoping I'll suddenly find something I'd previously missed. But I usually reserve the last week of every other month to do so, and the next time isn't for six weeks.

"I got some new information yesterday, from Nicky Fats," I say.

"Did you kill him after he gave it to you?"

"What does that mean? We did therapy with him."

"He's dead; I just heard it on the way over here. He died yesterday afternoon."

This is stunning news. "How?"

"They're not saying . . . but apparently he

was depressed, and they're hinting at suicide. Maybe you're not that good at the therapy stuff."

The timing of Nicky Fats's death is a direct violation of my coincidence theory, which is that coincidences don't exist. Of course, the theory might very well not apply in this case, since Nicky was very old, losing his mind, and not exactly a picture of health. There is also no real possibility that his rambling to me could have gotten him killed, since only Tara and I heard it. I only mentioned it to Pete, Vince, and Laurie, and that was apparently after Nicky was already dead. As far as I know, Tara hasn't barked it to a soul.

One thing is for sure: the death is untimely. It does not allow for further questioning of Nicky, should that be necessary. Of course, that in itself is a mixed blessing, since I had absolutely no desire to ever be in the fat man's presence again.

"So what did he say?" Hike asks.

"That Richard Solarno was into possibly illegal activities; he called him 'dirty.' Made me wonder if Richard might have been the target, rather than his wife, Karen."

Hike wasn't working with me back then, so he's unfamiliar with the case. I lay out the rough picture for him, that the prosecu-

47

tion's case was predicated on Joey killing Karen and her husband as an act of revenge. Joey and Karen had been having an affair, which Joey readily admitted to. She had broken it off, a fact which he also confirmed.

Richard was thought to be an innocent victim, first wronged by his wife, and then killed by her lover. He was essentially a fisherman, albeit a very successful one. He ran a shrimping company, which employed a fleet of more than ninety boats, stretching from New Jersey to Florida.

Probably being uncharacteristically kind, Hike doesn't ask the key question, which is how carefully did I check Richard Solarno out before trial. He doesn't have to; I've been torturing myself with that exact question since I left Nicky's house.

The answer is that I didn't do nearly enough. There were a combination of reasons for that. First of all, the police had conducted an investigation, and what I did do confirmed their view that there was nothing in Richard's past that would have made him a likely target.

Karen, on the other hand, was a different story. She was not exactly the faithful, doting wife, and she played around with a number of unsavory characters. Joey actually thought that she dumped him when she found out he was not in the family business; he ceased to represent the excitement and danger she naturally sought.

Our defense was to offer two possible theories for the crime. They were contradictory, except that each was designed to cultivate reasonable doubt.

One was that the killing was a random home invasion gone violent, and there had been a few similar, albeit less deadly, incidents in that area around that time. The second was that there were a number of Karen's ex-suitors both angry and violent enough to have done the deed, and that Joey was just one of the group. Our claim was that the prosecution quickly and unfairly picked Joey because of his family background.

Lastly, I was not Joey's original attorney, but they had a falling out, and I was called in just three weeks before trial. I wanted a continuance to give me more time to dig into the case, but Joey wouldn't hear of it. He was certain of his innocence, and confident in my ability to prove it, so he wanted out of jail as soon as possible.

Six years later he's in state prison, so his confidence doesn't seem to have been entirely warranted.

The point is that I have a lot of excuses

for not more thoroughly vetting the man that was Richard Solarno, but none of them feel acceptable at the moment. The fact that the file does not provide any fresh perspective is not surprising; I've been through it enough times that I could almost recite it by heart.

Most likely none of this will matter, and the ramblings of a soon-to-be-dead fat gangster will be shown to have no relevance in the real world.

But my sympathy for Joey having to sit in prison, plus my guilt at not keeping him out of there, adds up to one thing:

I'm going to find out what the hell Nicky Fats was talking about.

Janet Carlson could wake the dead, and is uniquely in a position to do so. Janet is the Passaic County coroner, and while I am not particularly knowledgeable about the history of that office, I can safely say she is the best-looking coroner in Passaic County history.

She's almost six feet tall, with jet-black hair and a body that is in Laurie's league, which is to say the major league.

She is also completely competent, a fact that often causes me aggravation. Just by the nature of the job and system, she is always a prosecution witness, so it becomes my job to make her look bad on the stand. Maybe someday I'll succeed at it.

It's possible she feels sorry for me, because she goes out of her way to be helpful whenever she can, at least out of court. Since I go out of my way to take advantage of helpful people whenever I can, the rela-

51

tionship works pretty well for me.

I'm in the lobby area telling the receptionist that I would like to talk to Janet when I
see her through a window into the main office area. Even better, she sees me, and
comes out into the lobby.

"Andy, you're not working again, are you?
I mean, have you taken on a client?"

"No."

She pretends to wipe her brow. "Whew,
that's a relief."

"Why?"

"I have three years from August in the
'when will Andy Carpenter get off his ass'
pool."

I laugh. "You've got a pretty good shot."

"Good to hear. So if you're not working,
this is a strange place for you to show up."

"Doesn't everybody show up someplace
like here eventually?" I ask.

"Now you're waxing philosophical? What's
up?"

"Has Nicky Fats come through yet?"

She looks puzzled for a moment, and then
says, "Is that Nicholas Desimone?"

"You never heard of Nicky Fats?"

"No, but after looking at him, the deriva-
tion of the name is fairly easy to understand.
I'm just getting to him now."

"Can I watch?"

52

"You mean listen?"

"Yes. Listen."

Janet knows the drill, since I've sat in on other autopsies with her before. I do so with my back turned to the body and table; I even walk into the room backward so as not to see the unfortunate ex-soul that's about to be cut up.

She shrugs. "Sure. I always like live company."

We go into the autopsy room. As we approach, I do a neat little pirouette and take the last ten or so steps backward, ignoring Janet's chuckling at my antics. As always, I'm struck by how cold it is in the room.

As Janet is getting ready, she asks why I'm interested in this particular autopsy.

"I saw him just a short while before he died. Just an hour or so, if the news reports are right."

"Was he a client?"

"No, I represented his nephew, Joey."

"The guy who shot those people?"

"Innocent as charged."

"Wasn't there a jury involved in there somewhere?" she asks, but doesn't wait for an answer. She starts talking into a recording microphone, describing what she is doing to the body, and what she is discovering.

I don't understand much of it, since there are a lot of medical terms. Also, since I can't see what she's looking at, and because she examines every part of the body, it's hard to know when what she is saying has any significance.

When she mentions "vertebral fracture" I perk up. "Broken back?" I ask.

"Broken neck; it was reported that he fell down in the bathroom. It's going to be the cause of death."

"So no chance of suicide?"

"Are you asking if he intentionally broke his own neck?"

"Withdraw the question. Could he have had help?"

"Let's see," she says, and then doesn't say anything for a few minutes. Finally, "It's not going to be definitive, Andy."

"What do you mean?"

"There are contusions on the left side of the neck, probably premortem. Slight ones on the right side as well, but much less pronounced. Possible that they were sustained in the fall, maybe if he fell against a sink or something."

"So it could have been a murder?"

"Possibly, but I'm not going to have enough to call it that. Unless you have something enlightening to add."

"He was an enforcer and hit man. Those kind of people make a lot of enemies."

"He lived a long life," she points out.

"True." I thank her and leave, walking straight out the door, since that leaves me with my back to Nicky Fats.

I'm not really sure what I wanted her to say, but what I got was the worst of all worlds. Had she said definitively that Nicky died of natural causes, I would have known that it had no connection to what he said to me, and I could have dropped it.

Had she said for sure that he was murdered, I would have been close to positive that there was something for me to find, and I could have plunged into it, for Joey's sake.

This was somewhere in the middle, enough to draw me in, and probably enough to waste my time.

"I heard it from a guard," Joey said. "He thought it was pretty funny."

"He thought what was funny?" I ask.

"The idea of Nicky falling out of the shower onto the floor. He said he must have looked like a beached whale." He shrugs. "That's what passes for humor around here."

Among the things I'd come back to the prison for was to tell Joey about Nicky's death, in case he hadn't heard. Obviously he had.

"I assume you didn't get to see him?" he asks.

"Actually, I did. The day he died."

"No kidding? That was fast. I'm glad you did. Was he coherent?"

"He went in and out. But he said a couple of things that I wanted to talk to you about."

I go on to tell him what Nicky said about Richard Solarno, and ask him if it makes any sense.

"Not much," he says. "I don't even think Nicky knew him. How would he?"

"I was hoping you could tell me that."

"I can't. They lived in different worlds. Unless Nicky was also sleeping with Karen."

Joey isn't serious when he says that; it just reflects his continued bitterness about the way Karen Solarno dumped him. It's an attitude that was damaging to him; witnesses testified about Joey's anger at Karen, and it contributed to the prosecution's theory on motive.

"Did you have any suspicions Richard might be into anything illegal?" I ask.

"Does domestic violence count?"

"He beat his wife?"

"According to Karen."

"Interesting, but it doesn't fit," I say.

"I wish I could say otherwise, but Nicky was probably just babbling," Joey says.

"Well, he did offer me some of his pasta when I saw him."

"So?"

"He was eating M&M's at the time."

Joey laughs. "You know, I should be trying to get you to think Nicky was sharp as a tack."

"Why?"

"Because if you dig into it, then maybe there's a one percent chance of you finding something. Which is one percent more of a chance than I've got now."

"You know damn well I'm going to dig into it," I say.

He smiles. "Yeah. You want me to get you some money for your time?"

"I should be paying you," I say.

"For what?"

"For getting me out of the therapy business."

I'm generally really nice to waiters and waitresses. I smile, ask them how they are, thank them whenever they serve me something, and tip really well.

I am Andy Carpenter, man of the people.

But there is one thing that some of them do that annoys me, and Laurie has just told me it's about to happen.

We're at the Bonfire, a restaurant on Market Street in Paterson. It's a nice place that I have some emotional ties to, in that it was a hangout on Friday and Saturday nights back in high school. It's where we would go after dates, or, in my case, after not having a date.

We've just sat down and are looking at the menus, though I pretty much know the selections by heart. Our waiter is taking the orders of the four people at the table next to us, and Laurie has been glancing over at them, so she knows that what's about to happen is going to bug me.

After she alerts me to it, she says, "In the meantime, tell me about Nicky Fats and Joey."

"Let's wait until we order. This could take awhile."

What Laurie had noticed is that the waiter is not writing anything down as people are ordering their food. He just nods and answers whatever questions they have. There is no way that waiters can remember everything, and I am always positive they are going to make mistakes. Sometimes they don't, but whenever it happens I am sure that they will.

This time, to drive me even more insane, the waiter doesn't put in the orders of the four people at the adjacent table. He just comes straight over to us, which means he's going to have to remember six people's worth of food.

What could possibly be the upside in not writing it down? He's going to have to tell it to the chef in a few minutes anyway. The chef will write it down, won't he? Or is he a memory expert also? Why not write it down, hand it to the chef, and be done with it?

He comes over to us and says, "My name is Danny. Welcome to the Bonfire. Are we ready to order?"

I say, "We sure are." What I don't say, but which I'm thinking, is "Danny boy, prepare to suffer."

Laurie orders first, a house salad and then the grilled salmon. She has a couple of additions and special requests, but nothing too complicated. Danny just repeats everything she says, smiling as he pretends to successfully commit it to memory.

"And for you, sir?"

"I'll start with the special salad. But I don't want the cheese, and maybe half as many croutons as normally would be served."

He's still nodding.

"I'd like kalamata olives instead of black ones, pitted, and let's add cherry tomatoes, shaved carrots, and red onions."

Still nodding.

"Is there oregano on the special salad?" I can see Laurie rolling her eyes, but I can't stop now.

He shrugs. "I'm not sure. I'll have to ask the chef."

I nod. "Please do. I'm violently allergic to oregano," I lie. "I can get oregano poisoning and go into spasm. You can substitute basil."

"Basil doesn't make him spasm," Laurie adds.

"Right, basil," I say. "No, on second thought make it thyme. In fact, the chef can throw in parsley, sage, rosemary, and thyme."

"What kind of dressing do you have?" I ask, and he reels off about ten of them. "See if the chef will mix the balsamic and lemon vinaigrettes. And I'll have that on the side."

I torture him even more on the main course, Mediterranean chicken, changing everything about it except the shape of the plate it comes on. Even with all that, I can't get him to cave and write things down.

When he leaves, Laurie says, "That was quite a performance. What are you going to do if he gets it wrong?"

"I'm going to be really annoyed."

"What if he gets it right?"

"I'll be even more annoyed. All I really wanted was onion soup and a hamburger."

She laughs. "You could use some serious mental therapy."

"Maybe I'll have Tara come visit me," I say. "Which brings me to Nicky Fats."

I tell her everything that has transpired. Laurie had worked on the original case with me; it was one of our first times working together, and preceded our romantic involvement.

She had left the police force just a few

months before working with me on the case, and definitely retained a pro-prosecution attitude. If someone was arrested, she felt it was probably for a good reason. I think deep down she still has that feeling, though it has lessened considerably. Especially since she herself was once wrongly arrested and subjected to a murder trial.

I'm sure she believed Joey to be guilty at the time, though I don't think she ever verbalized it. So I'm surprised when I finish my spiel and she says, "I'll help you look into it, Andy."

"You think there could be something to it?"

"I doubt it," she says. "But we really never dug into Solarno's life."

I nod. "I know. That's been bothering me."

"We had very little time," she says. "We had to make choices, and we made the logical ones. But that doesn't mean we were right. So we make up for it now. But Nicky's death doesn't figure to tie into this."

"Why do you say that?"

"Because you were alone with him, and he was dead before you told anyone what he said. It seems unlikely that with his shaky mind he called someone in and said, 'You'll never guess what I just told Andy Carpenter.' And even less likely that the person killed him for it."

"You're right," I say, "but it still bothers me."

"Because of the apparent coincidence."

I nod. "Yes, that. But one other thing. It's three o'clock in the afternoon, and Nicky is sitting there watching television. I doubt that he'd left that place in a month. He had crusted sauce on his shirt that looked like it was there since the Capone era."

"So?"

"So all of a sudden he decides to take a shower? Was he getting ready for a date? Where was he going, the senior prom?"

"I'm not sure the 'why would he take a shower' defense would work on appeal. We might need something more."

"That's why I chose to live with a crack investigator."

Richard Solarno's company wasn't Richard Solarno's company.

I didn't know that at the time of the trial, but it takes Laurie about four minutes to find it out now.

It was an easy mistake to make, since the company was called Solarno Shrimp Corporation. And according to Laurie, Solarno and his brother, Alex, had started the company almost twenty years ago, but sold it a year before the murder to a private equity company.

Since both companies were private, the terms of the sale were not disclosed, but Laurie uncovers some of the relevant information. Alex Solarno and Richard sold their company to Capital Equity, run by a man named Edward Young. The terms of the agreement called for Richard to stay on in a management capacity for three years, but he only made it through one before he took a bullet in the chest. Alex did not stay on, but left with his very hefty payout.

I vaguely remember an employee of Richard's testifying to his character in the penalty phase of Joey's trial, so I head to the transcript for some memory refreshment. His name was Larry Callahan, and he was a longtime employee of the company.

All witnesses fill out contact information, and Callahan's showed him having a home in Manhasset, Long Island. I call the listed number, and a woman answers.

"Is this Larry Callahan's residence?" I ask.

The woman's voice is hesitant. "Who's calling?"

"My name is Andy Carpenter. I'm an attorney."

That was probably a mistake; most people who seem to be talking tentatively generally don't suddenly open up when they find out the other party is a lawyer. "Why do you want Larry?" she asks.

I put on my nonchalant voice. "I just wanted to talk to him about someone he used to work with."

"Who?"

This is one protective lady. "Richard Solarno."

She takes about twenty seconds before responding, and that feels like a long time to maintain telephone silence. "Larry passed away," she finally says.

"Oh, I'm sorry. I didn't know. Did that happen recently?'

"No."

"Are you Mrs. Callahan?"

"I was."

The famed Carpenter charm does not seem to be having its usual effect. "Did you know Richard Solarno?"

"I met him. I've got to go now."

Click.

That didn't go that well, but I am undaunted, or at least only partially daunted. I call Sam Willis, my accountant, who also doubles as a member of my investigative team, during those infrequent occasions when I need a team.

"I'm working on it, Andy. They keep changing the rules on 501 c's."

Sam thinks I'm calling to ask for the income tax return he's working on for the Tara Foundation. It's a dog rescue organization that my former client Willie Miller and I founded and run, although he and his wife, Sondra, do a lot more of the "running" than I do. It's a nonprofit operation. In fact, it's about as "nonprofit" an operation as there could possibly be.

"It's not about that, Sam. I need some

67

help on a case."

I can just about see him light up through the phone. Sam is a top-notch accountant, and a computer-hacking genius, but that is not how he sees himself. He sees himself as Mannix.

I explain that I want a list of employees who worked for the Solarno Shrimp Corporation at the time of Richard's murder. He's disappointed in that; if he's going to be called into a case he would at least want a chance to shoot someone.

He promises to get me the information right away, and then asks, "You going out on the street?"

"I have to in order to get home. I haven't figured out how to beam myself there."

"You know what I mean," he says. "Because I've got some free time on my hands."

Sam wants to go out on "the street" to do hands-on investigating. "That won't be necessary," I say. "But if you have all that time, I also want to know how Larry Callahan died. He worked at Solarno's company. And tell me how I can get in touch with Alex Solarno, Richard's brother. And if you still have time after that, maybe you can do the tax return."

"Just call me if anything is going down."

"I will," I say. "I'm making a note to

myself. Call Sam if things go down."

"Wiseass," he snarls. "You think I can't handle myself? Because I'm the guy you want in the foxhole next to you."

"You would definitely be my first foxhole choice," I say. "Unless we include women, in which case I'd go with Laurie."

"Makes sense," he says.

Solarno's shrimping boats were spread out all over the East Coast, as well as the Gulf of Mexico. For that reason, not many of the employees lived in the New York / New Jersey area. One who does is Luther Karlsson, who was not an executive in the company but one of the shrimpers on a boat.

I'm interested in talking to him for two reasons. First of all, I have nobody else to talk to, certainly not within driving distance. Second, Sam told me that Karlsson had quit the company a few weeks before Solarno's murder. It may turn out to be irrelevant to my investigation, but it strikes me as interesting.

Karlsson lives in Belmar, which in a perfect world is about an hour from my house down the Garden State Parkway. Unfortunately, no one has ever confused New Jersey with a perfect world, and with traffic I'm allowing two hours to get there.

I called Karlsson first, and about all I discovered is that his Swedish accent is so thick I could only understand about every fourth word he said. I think he agreed to see me, but it's not a conversation I'm looking forward to, since the only Swedish I know is "Yaah, sssuuurre."

It turns out that Karlsson lives in what seems to be a boardinghouse, and the woman manager of the place directs me to a refreshment stand adjacent to the beach. I head over there, wishing that I had brought a heavier jacket with me, and wishing even more that I wasn't here at all.

There are small tables by the refreshment stand, and only one person sits there. He looks to be in his late sixties, maybe even older, but it's difficult to be sure because his face literally looks like leather. I've seen better-looking catcher's mitts.

He's sitting on a bench, sort of leaning over. It's hard to tell, but if he unfolded he'd probably be at least six foot four. He's the outdoor, powerful type, and I'm sure he could someday get off his deathbed to kick my ass.

"Mr. Karlsson?" I ask.

He nods. "Yup."

"My name's Andy Carpenter. I called you about your work with Solarno."

"Yup. You want some coffee?"

"Yes."

He nods. "Me too."

I buy us both coffees, and he surprises me by adding a lot of milk and two sugars; I would have bet my life he was the black coffee type. Seeing him add the milk and sugar would be like watching Jack Palance in *City Slickers* take out an iPad to watch *Steel Magnolias*.

Karlsson turns out to be much easier to understand in person, even with frozen ears. We start to chitchat about the area; I used to come down to Belmar and Asbury Park as a teenager, although the girls here were no more interested in me than the ones in Paterson.

He has lived here for forty-one years, ever since his arrival in this country from Sweden. I have to admit he looks perfectly at home here; his face was made for this weather, or more likely this weather created his face.

"Did you know Richard Solarno?" I ask.

He shakes his head. "Never met him. Don't know anything about him."

My next question should be, "Then what the hell am I doing here?" but I don't verbalize it.

"What about Larry Callahan?"

72

"Larry? Sure. Good man."

"Talk to him lately?" I ask. I don't want to be the one to tell him he died; as a general rule I refrain from saying bad things to people that frighten me.

"Nope. Not since I left."

"How come you left?"

"Everything changed. New people, new schedules. Shrimping took a backseat."

I'm not getting anywhere with him; the idea of trying to convince a judge that Solarno was a target because he wasn't doing a good shrimping job is a bit of a nonstarter.

"Do you know why they were making those changes?"

"Didn't know, didn't want to know. Just knew it was time to get out."

I'm floundering here, and starting to think that for me it's also "time to get out." "So the new people were not good shrimpers?"

"Couldn't be."

"Why not?"

"You ever try to shoot a shrimp?"

I can't help but laugh. "Not lately. I don't think that would work."

"So why would they need a boatload of guns?"

"You saw a boatload of guns?" I ask.

He nods. "I wasn't supposed to, but I did."

"Do you know where they were going? Or

who they were for?"

"Nah."

"Weren't you curious?"

He shakes his head. "None of my business."

"But you quit."

He nods. "Where I work is my business."

"Will you testify to this?" When he looks confused, I say, "In court. If it comes to that."

This elicits a shrug. "Why not? It's the truth."

It would be incorrect to describe Simon Ryerson as worried. Concerned and annoyed, yes, but not worried. Worried would imply that there was a chance the problem could become unmanageable, that it could spin out of control.

There was little chance of that.

It was a mistake for Iurato to let the lawyer visit with Nicky Fats. There was no telling what the old man might say, and what he did say wound up costing him his life, or at least what was left of it.

So the lawyer had picked up on it, and was chasing it down. That was his reputation, and he was making good on it. He was going to have to be watched now, to see whom he talked to and what he learned.

It would likely amount to nothing; there were too many layers to get through. It is always hard to find something when you have no idea what you're looking for, and the lawyer was completely in the dark.

But one never knows, not even when that one is Simon Ryerson. So Simon would have the situation monitored, and that would provide ample warning of possible danger.

The key to running a successful business was accumulating as much information as possible, analyzing that information intelligently and dispassionately, and then acting decisively. And his intelligence and decisiveness were the main reasons he was put into this position.

If more people had to die, then more people would die.

It was simply the cost of doing business.

The Solarno house has had a rough time of it.

Hosting a notorious pair of murders rarely does much for resale value, and this was no exception. It sits high up on a hill in an expensive Montclair neighborhood, and its seclusion has tended to add to the "creepiness" factor.

It gradually fell into disrepair, and was finally purchased from the bank a few years ago. The new owners planned a major renovation, but then the housing and financial crisis hit. They neither did the renovation nor moved in, and the bank has since foreclosed on their loan.

I, of course, laugh in the face of both danger and superstition, so I have no concern that the house could be haunted. Having said that, I invited Laurie to come with me to examine the murder scene. She's a terrific investigator, and she carries a gun, on the off chance that we have to shoot any ghosts.

Both Laurie and I have been in the house before, in preparation for the original trial, but neither of us is prepared for what we see. The formerly beautifully landscaped property is overrun by weeds, windows are broken, and the front porch seems to be rotting. I don't think real estate agents will be holding open houses anytime soon.

If an agent ever did get someone through the front door, that's as far as it would go. There are actually still faded bloodstains in the carpet where Richard lost his life. It looks like someone halfheartedly tried to wash it, with limited success.

The rest of the interior, at least from our vantage point in the front hall, looks as bad as the exterior. "I love what they've done with the place," I say. "Think we should make an offer?"

"Excuse me?"

"Never mind. Just some murder-scene humor."

We go upstairs, then walk down a long hallway to Karen Solarno's room. Once again, bloodstains from the violence are still on the floor.

"Hard to make the case that Richard was the target," Laurie says.

"Why?"

"Because he was killed right near the doorway downstairs. We have to assume that Richard opened the door, and got shot almost immediately. Probably didn't take more than a few seconds, though I suppose it's possible they talked briefly."

"Agreed." I know where she's going, but in situations like this I find it helpful to our thought process to let her get there without interrupting.

"So there would have been no reason to come up here and kill Karen. No reason to think she saw anything, and since her window didn't face the front, she wouldn't have seen him arrive."

"I don't agree," I say. "Or at least I see another alternative. I think the killer could have been covering all his bases. Assuming he had no respect for human life, and that seems a safe conclusion, then what's the downside to killing her? Even if there's a one percent chance that she saw him, or heard him, then why not remove that danger?"

"It would mean spending a longer time on the scene," she says.

"We're on a private, dead-end road at the top of a hill, so there's almost no chance some other witnesses were going to wander by. He kills Karen and he pretty much removes any chance of detection."

"It's cold-blooded."

I nod. "That's why I was so positive Joey was innocent. I just can't see him doing this, not the way it was done. It wasn't a crime of passion."

Laurie never bought into my belief in Joey, but she doesn't contradict me. "You could be right about him, Andy. And you could be right about the reasons the killer came upstairs and killed Karen Solarno."

I finish her thought. "But it's still tough to make the case that Richard was the target."

She nods. "Right. It's possible, but it's a stretch. The murder scene doesn't work in our favor."

"Didn't do much for the Solarnos either."

"And we still have the two-gun issue," she says.

She's referring to the fact that the two people were shot with different guns. The one that killed Richard was never found, but the one that killed Karen was left on the scene. Devastatingly, a partial fingerprint of Joey's was on it.

We leave the house and walk to the car. I turn and look back, and I realize something that's strange about it. "We need to find out why this place is in this condition."

"I would assume it's because there was no one living in it, no one to fix it up, and no one willing to buy it."

"But why would anyone have to buy it, at least at first? Wouldn't Richard have left it to someone? Someone would have owned it, right?"

She nods. "I would think so. We know he had a brother named Alex. They were partners, and sold to Edward Young's company a year before the murders."

I nod. "Richard stayed on to run it, but Alex left."

"Did they have a falling out?" she asks.

"Time to find out."

Every case is an uphill struggle, but this one more than most.

Defense attorneys always start with their legal back to the wall. A client would not have been charged with a crime had not the law enforcement system gathered enough evidence that the prosecutor is confident guilt can be proven beyond a reasonable doubt.

Prosecutors hate to lose; it makes them look bad. If they don't bring charges, they can't lose, so they only bring them when winning seems close to a foregone conclusion. Juries instinctively believe that it's far more likely than not that the prosecutor is right, which is why I feel our system carries a presumption of guilt.

But a situation like this one with Joey is far more difficult, because a jury has already spoken. He's been found guilty by his peers, and the system quite properly has a healthy respect for their decision.

In order to get Joey a new trial, we would have to ask a court to invalidate that verdict, something they are inherently loathe to do. In fact, the legal standard set is a very high bar. Not only do we have to come up with new evidence, but the justices have to believe that there is more likelihood than not that we would prevail in a new trial.

Those are the general rules. Complicating our situation somewhat is that we don't have any new evidence. At this point we really don't even have a theory. All we have are the ramblings of a senile, now-dead, fat guy. It might be hard to find a judge who would be impressed by that.

So it's clear I need to be aggressive about this. It's the only way I'm going to resolve the matter one way or the other. I have to shake the tree, though that is also complicated, as at this point I need a GPS to even find the forest.

I catch a break, because Laurie is heading into Manhattan today to have lunch with Cindy Spodek. Cindy is an FBI agent, ranked number two in the Boston office. We met on a case a number of years ago.

We've since become friends, or we at least have a relationship that fits neatly into my definition of friendship. It's one in which I can call on her for favors whenever I'm in need, and in which she can respond by granting those favors.

The truth is that I like her a lot, despite her position in law enforcement, and the fact that she likes to arrest the very people I'm sworn to defend. But she and Laurie have really hit it off, and whenever Cindy has occasion to come to New York, they have lunch.

They're eating at the Redeye Grill, on the Westside in Midtown. It's one of Laurie's favorites, because she loves their oysters. If death by starvation were imminent, I would not eat an oyster. I would prefer fried dirt.

Laurie tells me that their lunch is at noon, so I time my own trip into the city to let me arrive at the restaurant at one-fifteen. I tell the woman at the desk that I'm meeting someone already there, and I set out in search of Laurie and Cindy. It's a large restaurant so it takes a few minutes, but I finally find them, at a secluded table back near the bar area.

"Oh, my God," I say, feigning shock with all of my considerable feigning ability. "What are you two doing here? What are the odds against that?"

"You mean what are the odds of us having lunch at the restaurant I told you we were eating at?" Laurie asks.

"Did you say Redeye Grill? I thought you said the Thai Mill." Then, to Cindy, "It's a small Asian place in the village; if you go there try the shrimp rolls."

"What do you need, Andy?" Cindy asks.

I pull up a chair and sit down at their table. "Did I mention you're looking wonderful?"

"You always mention I'm looking wonderful when you need something," Cindy says. "Even when we're talking on the phone."

"No, then I say you're sounding wonderful."

Between the two of them, they seem to be conducting an eye-rolling contest. "Are you hungry, Andy?" Laurie asks.

"No thanks. I'll just chat for a minute and then get out of here before the check comes."

"I already told Cindy about the Joey Desimone situation."

This time I feign horror. "You did? Why? I had hoped this would be a social lunch."

"Land the plane, Andy," Cindy says. "What do you want?"

Time to stop feigning. "I want to know if the Bureau had any information that Richard Solarno was dirty."

"Dirty how?" she asks.

"I'm not sure, but I think it might be arms smuggling. One of his employees saw a boatload of guns where shrimp were supposed to be. And I also want to know, if he was doing it, where those arms likely would have gone."

Cindy doesn't respond, but instead looks at Laurie. After a few moments, she signals to the waiter and says, "The gentleman will take the check, please."

"Let's get one thing straight; I'm not going to say anything bad about my brother."

It's a strange way for Alex Solarno to start our conversation. All I had told him was that I wanted to talk to him about Richard; I certainly gave him no reason to think I was looking to hear bad things.

I had called Alex to ask him to see me, but he initially refused. He finally relented after I turned on the Carpenter charm, including endearing witticisms like "No problem; I'll just have you served with a subpoena and question you under oath for eight hours."

IIc had agreed to talk to me at his house in Closter. Taking into account the decline that housing prices in New Jersey have experienced along with the rest of the country, I'd estimate that his house is worth three million dollars. Throw in another couple of million for furnishing and art, and it's fair to say that Alex Solarno is not hurting financially.

"I didn't ask you to say anything bad about your brother."

"Then what do you want?"

"I want what I'm sure you want: to find out who murdered him."

"A jury settled that awhile ago," he says.

"That doesn't make them right."

"You got evidence that they were wrong?" he asks.

Why does everybody have to bring up that "evidence" thing? It's really annoying.

"Here's what I have," I say. "I have reason to believe that Richard was the target, that he was involved in arms smuggling, and he pissed off the wrong people. I'm hoping you can tell me who those people are." I'm taking a leap on this, especially the arms smuggling part, but it seems worth the risk.

"His bitch wife was the target."

"That's not quite the information I'm looking for."

"Then you came to the wrong guy."

I decide to try a different tack. "Why did you leave the company when you did?" Alex had stopped working there when the private equity sale was made, while Richard stayed on.

"I didn't want to work anymore." He mo-

88

tions with his hands, inviting me to take in the room and the house. "And I didn't have to."

"So that was it? You just suddenly decided to retire because you had money?" I can sympathize with that sentiment, since I pretty much made the same decision. But I refrain from mentioning that.

"Yeah."

"You didn't have a falling out or anything with your brother?"

"No way."

"You were close?"

"Yeah."

"Why didn't he leave anything to you in his will? The house went back to the bank."

"If he was here, we could ask him."

"So you have no knowledge of any enemies he might have had, anyone who might have had a reason to kill him?"

"No."

"No connection to the Desimone crime family?"

"No," he says, though he does not seem surprised by the question. Most people, when asked about a connection to an organized crime family, would have a stronger response.

It's been clear since I entered the house that I was not going to get anything out of him, and I haven't really been trying to for a while. Which, of course, does not make this a waste of time.

"Here's how this is going to work, Alex. I'm going to develop this information I have; my coming here today was simply to give you a chance to climb aboard the train. Based on your attitude, I've got a feeling that you're going to tie yourself to the tracks. It's a good way to get run over."

"Get out of my house," he says, a logical response to my threat. All I had really wanted to do was piss him off. Mission accomplished.

I leave, get into my car, and drive away. Once I'm out of sight of the house, I stop and call Sam Willis.

When Sam hears that it's me, he says, "I've got your information."

"Good, but right now I need you to do something." I give him Alex's name and phone number, and say, "I just left his house. I want to know if he makes any calls starting around five minutes ago, for the next couple of hours." Sam has demonstrated that he can break into every computer in existence; accessing phone records is a piece of cake.

"You got his cell number?"

"No."

"I'll get it and check that also. You want me to come down and stake out his house?"

"No, Sam, no need for a stakeout at this point. Don't buy any doughnuts yet."

"There's no substitute for boots on the ground, Andy."

Boots on the ground? Sam can make New Jersey sound like Afghanistan. "Sam, when you don't buy doughnuts, don't buy boots either."

Alex Solarno made the call as soon as Carpenter left.

He was unnerved; this was supposed to have been behind him years ago. But now it was back, and the danger to Alex was suddenly as real as it had ever been.

Alex hadn't called the number in years, but had kept it in his desk drawer for situations just like this. He hoped the number was still good, and didn't want to think about his next move if it wasn't. It was unlikely there was a listing in the yellow pages for "Mob Bosses."

A voice he didn't recognize answered the phone with a simple, "Yeah?"

"I need to speak to Carmine Desimone," Alex said.

"Yeah?"

"This is Alex Solarno. He gave me this number."

"Hold on."

Alex waited nervously for what seemed like half an hour but was really less than five minutes. Finally there was a click, and another voice came on the line.

"Hello."

Solarno didn't recognize the voice, though that didn't mean it wasn't Carmine, since he had only spoken to him once, a long time ago.

"Is this Carmine Desimone?"

"No."

"Who am I speaking with?"

"Tommy Iurato."

"I need to speak to Carmine."

"You talk to me, you're talking to Carmine."

Iurato's voice had an authority to it that intimidated Alex. "OK . . . yeah, sure. You know who I am?"

"I know who you are. And I know who just came to visit you."

This was stunning to Alex, and left him with two conflicting reactions. On the one hand, it literally sent a cold chill through him that he was obviously being watched by these people; there was no other way they could have known Carpenter was there.

On the other hand, it was strangely comforting for him to know that they were actively on top of the situation. They had every reason to keep a lid on things, and they had the means to do so. No lawyer poking around was going to bring them down, and if they were safe, then so was Alex.

"He knows what's going on. Not everything, but enough. And he'll find out the rest. He's smart."

"What did he say?" Iurato asked.

"That Richard was the target, and that he was dealing arms."

Iurato was surprised and a little concerned that Carpenter had already learned that the "illegal activities" Nicky Fats had told him about involved arms smuggling. "What else?"

"Nothing," Alex said. "He was asking me to fill in the blanks."

"And did you?"

"Of course not," Alex said, quickly and defensively. "Are you kidding? Come on, Carmine knows me. He'll tell you I can keep my mouth shut."

"Then continue to do so."

"Of course; I'm not the problem. Carpenter is."

"Keep it that way," Iurato said. "Call again if he contacts you."

It was clear that Iurato was ending the call, but Alex wasn't feeling secure about things yet. "So are you guys going to handle this?"

"We'll handle it."

"So I don't have anything to worry about?"

"That will be up to you."

Click.

Alex got off the phone thinking that if it really was up to him, then he had plenty to worry about.

Robby Divine has more money than I do, and I have a lot.

I have a total of about twenty-six million dollars at this point. It started as a little less, but Edna's cousin Freddie, who handles my investments, is on a hot streak.

But twenty-six million is nothing compared to what Robby Divine has. Some people with Robby's kind of money wouldn't bend over to pick up twenty-six million if they saw it laying in the street. But Robby would, because he doesn't just want a great deal of money, he wants all of it.

Robby is an investor, but I don't think he uses Cousin Freddie. He's not a lawyer who's an investor, or a corporate executive who's an investor; he's just an investor.

He's got a sweet deal going. I'm told that when Robby makes an investment, it's a large one and it attracts attention. He's considered so smart that people follow him in, buying stock in the same companies. This then causes the stock he had just bought to go up. As my grandmother used to say, "Money goes to money."

I met Robby at a charity dinner in Manhattan to benefit a large animal rescue foundation. We sat next to each other, mainly because he and I were the only two people being honored. We talked a lot, and found out that one of the things we have in common is a hatred for charity dinners.

Robby stood out that night, because he was the only one wearing sneakers and jeans. I learned later that he considered himself overdressed compared to his usual garb, and in fact it's the only time I haven't seen him wearing his Chicago Cubs cap. If he ever blows his money, it won't be on clothes.

We get together for dinner once every six months or so. We used to alternate picking the place, but then I took him to Charlie's once, and he was hooked. Tonight is our dinner, which is timely, since otherwise I would have called him anyway.

Robby isn't into sports, has no interest in it whatsoever, but is definitely into burgers and beer. Charlie's burgers are the best, and Robby has three of them. He's maybe a hundred fifty pounds, runs in the Boston and New York marathons, and downs burgers by the bucketful. If I ate three burgers, they'd have to wheel my fat ass out to the parking lot.

Vince and Pete are not allowed to join us at our dinners; it's always just the two of us. That of course drives them insane, so they sit at our normal table and stare daggers at us. I make faces back at them.

We're all very mature.

"So what do you know about Edward Young?" I ask.

"He's a Cardinals fan, which makes him a prick," Robby says, and since he's again wearing his Cubs cap, that needs no further explanation. "I keep telling him it doesn't matter where he grew up; he needs to recognize that the Cardinals are pure evil."

"That's not particularly helpful. What else do you know about him?"

"He's rich."

"Richer than you?"

"Watch your mouth."

I laugh. "Tell me what else you know about him."

"Well, he cheats at golf."

"So you know him personally?"

"Sure. Who do you think I hang around with, poor people? You're the only one."

"Can you get me in to see him? I've called twice, but can't get through."

"Depends. What's it about?"

"I'm investigating a murder of one of his employees. He bought the victim's company a few months before it happened."

"If the guy worked for Edward, chances are he committed suicide."

"Tough guy?"

"Controlling guy. He and I do things differently. When I come into a company, I'm placing a bet on the company and it's management. I can be annoying to them, but if they succeed, so do I. And I only buy into large companies."

"And Young?"

"He's much more hands-on. He'll buy a controlling interest in smaller companies: retailers, techs, airlines, whatever. He wants to make money, same as me, except he's positive the only way that can happen is if they do what he says. So he takes over, either up close or from a distance. He'll deny it, but it's true."

"Is he smart?"

"One of the smartest guys I ever met. What do you want from him?"

"Nothing specifically. I'll ask a bunch of questions, and see if he has any useful information for me. Chances are he won't,

99

but you never know."

"Call his office tomorrow morning after ten. He'll see you. He owes me one."

The waiter brings over the check and hands it to me. "My turn," Robby says. He takes the check out of my hand and looks at it. "Nine beers? We had two each."

I point to Vince and Pete at their table; Vince is waving to me. "That's because it's not our check; it's theirs. Unlike you, they think I'm rich."

"Good," Robby says. "I didn't want our check yet. I think I'll have another burger."

I've got a feeling that I'm on to something. I don't get these feelings a lot, mainly because I spend very little time trying to be on to anything. But when I get one, I pay attention to it, because it's usually right.

Except for the times when it's wrong.

I've come to realize that these feelings are based on three factors. One is experience; I've been doing this long enough to understand what's happening, and to be able to accurately assess the evidence, even if some of that assessment is instinctual.

A second factor is more aspirational. If I'm chasing something down, then I want it to be real and substantial, or I wouldn't be chasing it. So I have to fight off a natural desire to think that what I want to be real actually is real.

The third factor is arrogance. While I am investigating something because I think it's important, my ego tells me that it must be important, or I wouldn't be spending so much time on it. I'm looking for validation of my project, but psychologically giving it validation *simply because* it's my project.

Substantially complicating matters in the Joey Desimone case is that old maxim that it doesn't matter what the lawyer believes, only what he can prove. And right now, not only is there nothing I can prove, but there's nothing I can credibly allege.

Based on what Nicky Fats said about Solarno, and Luther Karlsson's having seen a boatload of guns, I believe that Richard Solarno was into some illegal activities, most notably arms trafficking. Unfortunately, not only do I not have enough evidence to present to a court, even having that evidence wouldn't make me successful.

It's one thing to demonstrate that Solarno was a bad guy, doing bad things. But even if I were able to do that, and right now I'm not close to doing so, it's a huge legal jump to then show that he was the target of the killer.

The list of things I don't know goes on forever, starting with who Solarno was dealing with, how he got the arms, who were the customers, why they might have turned against him, and why they would have gone on to kill Karen, with about a hundred etceteras thrown in.

So I need to keep digging, and to try and avoid frustration. I impose my own time frame on these things, and I feel an urgency that might not be real. Joey has been in prison for six years, and is scheduled to spend the rest of his life there. If this takes me six months, or a year, as bad as that might be for Joey, it's more than worth doing.

One of the problems is that what I'm looking into happened a long time ago, and there is little reason for the real bad guys to feel threatened. I have to change that; if I can get them to react to pressure, there's a much greater chance they'll make a mistake.

To that end, I stop in to see Vince Sanders. While Vince is the single most disagreeable and obnoxious human being on the planet, he's as good a friend as one can have. He's come through for me a number of times in the past, as I have for him. And that is how we define friendship.

Vince is editor of the *Bergen News*, one of New Jersey's larger newspapers. He has held that job for approximately four hundred years, and is a legend in both his field and his mind. But even in an age where newspapers have taken a huge step back in terms of media power, Vince is a force that pretty much no one wants to reckon with.

Much as I know Vince can be counted on, I cement the deal by bringing a bag of doughnuts with me. He comes out when the receptionist calls to tell him that I'm there, takes one look at the bag, and says, "Jelly?"

"Half jelly, half cream-filled."

He nods as if I gave the right answer, which I did. "You may enter," he says.

I walk through the door toward the back, where his office is, and he grabs the bag from my hand as I do so. He holds it up, as if weighing it, without opening it. "Dozen," he says. "You did good."

We go back to his office, which makes mine look neat. He sits at his desk and says, "What's up?" though it's a little hard to understand him, since his mouth is filled with a cream-filled doughnut.

"I've got a story for you," I say, and proceed to lay out the situation I'm in on Joey's case, starting with Nicky's hopefully lucid revelation. I had referred to it the other night at Charlie's, so Vince is not totally surprised.

When I finish, Vince doesn't say anything. Just sits there.

"Well?" I ask.

"That's it? You're finished?"

"I'm just starting, but that's where I am now."

"So what's the story?"

"Come on, Vince, a shrewd newspaper guy like yourself has to see the potential here. A dying mob boss inadvertently drops a bombshell that has reopened a huge, notorious murder case," I say. "And a courageous, dedicated lawyer is exposing a deadly conspiracy and finding the real killers."

"Here's what I see, as a shrewd newspaper guy," he says. "I see a desperate hack, feeling guilty that his client is stuck in prison, floundering around trying to use something a dying, senile fat guy said to get his client off the hook."

I nod. "That's an interesting angle."

He continues. "And I see that hack trying to take advantage of an innocent yet brilliant newspaperman, who has done nothing but be a good friend. He's trying to get that legendary newspaperman to run a bullshit story, probably on the front page, so that things in the case can get shaken up, possibly resulting in that lawyer being able to finally take his legal thumb out of his ass."

I nod again. "That sums it up pretty well, except you forgot about the doughnuts, and the beer that you haven't paid for in two years."

"Nicely played," he says. "Let me think about this, run it by a couple of our reporters."

"I'm telling you, Vince, the story is going to be solid."

"We've got a fairly high bar on what we need to go with a story. Trust me, Kobe Bryant couldn't jump and hit that bar from where you are."

"If you don't go with it, I'm going to take it elsewhere." It's an empty threat, if ever there was one.

He laughs. "I would suggest *Sixty Minutes*." Then he takes another doughnut out of the bag and bites into it. "You know how you keep from getting jelly all over you when you eat a jelly doughnut?"

"No, actually, I don't."

"You bite into where the hole is."

"Thanks for sharing that, Vince. Let me know what you decide."

"You'll be the first call I make."

"Wait until you hear about Larry Callahan." Sam is standing at my front door, just having arrived as I was about to take Tara for a walk. He must think it's important, because for Sam almost all communication is electronic, in one form or another. For him to have driven here this early in the morning from his house in Englewood means he thinks whatever he's learned about Larry Callahan is a big deal.

"You found out how he died?" I ask.

"I did."

"Tell me about it on the way."

"On the way where?"

"Eastside Park. It's time for Tara's walk." Tara is wagging her tail and generally acting excited, most likely annoyed at the unusual delay here at the door.

"Can that wait?" He holds up his briefcase. "I've got some things to show you. And it's thirty degrees out."

"You want Tara to wait for her walk once she has the leash on? Are you nuts?"

I tell Sam to leave the briefcase at the house, that he can show me whatever documents he has when we get back. We start on our walk, pausing only as Tara does to take in the aromas.

"What's she sniffing?" Sam asks.

"The world. Tell me how Larry Callahan died."

"Hit-and-run accident. About a block from his house," he says, then adds pointedly. "He was walking his dog."

"Was the dog killed as well?"

Sam frowns in frustration. "Who cares?"

"I do, and I'm sure the dog did."

"According to the newspaper article, the dog was fine."

The news is interesting but not earth-shaking. A hit-and-run death is obviously potentially sinister, though not necessarily intentional. "Night or day?" I ask, only because if it was night it would seem more likely that someone had not seen him, and that it was an accident. Sherlock Holmes, eat your heart out.

"Night."

"Did you see the police report?"

He looks at me as if insulted. "Of course. No witnesses, no leads, nothing."

108

I'm a little surprised that Sam felt it necessary to give me this news in person, but I guess he felt he was thereby putting his "boots on the ground." "OK, thanks," I say.

"There's more."

"Good."

"I also got a list of all the people who worked for Solarno in the six months before he died. There were a hundred and fourteen of them."

"Is that what the papers are in your briefcase?"

"Yes."

"Good . . . thanks."

"There's more," he says.

"Are you going to dribble it out, or come out with it?"

"Callahan was the captain, they called it the lead officer, of one of the shrimping boats. He had a crew of five with him, which was standard. I included all their names, but not their information . . . addresses, contacts, etcetera. I've given you that stuff for all the other employees, but not those five."

"Why?"

"Because the information about them is all bullshit. Those people do not exist, at least not as they are listed. Names, addresses, phone numbers, next of kin . . . all fake."

"And that's not true of all the other company employees?"

"All the others are legit. Only Callahan's crew was bogus."

I have no idea what all this means, but I know enough to think it's very significant.

"Where did you get the information?"

"You really want to know?"

Sam is protecting me because the hacking he does is for the most part illegal. Since he's doing it for me, I decline the protection. "I really want to know."

"The computers at a company called Capital Equity; they bought Solarno's company about a year before he died."

I nod. "It's owned by Edward Young."

"Right," Sam says. "It was company policy to have the employee information, but I don't think they've accessed it since. They might not even know they have it. It's an investment firm; it's not like they have a big HR department, or schedule alumni reunions."

"By the way, did you find out who Alex Solarno called after I left his house?"

He nods. "I've got the name and number, but I'm still checking it out. Won't be long now."

"Great work, Sam. You can take me through the information when we get back. I want Laurie to see it as well."

"Are we going to be getting back soon? My face is frozen."

"Afraid not, we haven't even stopped for our bagels yet." Tara and I always loop around to a bagel place on Broadway. We sit outside, in all but the absolute worst weather, and Tara graciously accepts petting from passersby as we munch.

"Any chance of getting the bagels to go?" Sam asks.

"Zero. But I'm buying."

He nods. "Then I'll have an onion bagel, with cream cheese. And a hot chocolate. A very hot chocolate."

"That's the spirit."

Robby Divine really came through. Within three hours of my calling Edward Young, I'm in his office at Capital Equity, on Fifty-first and Sixth. The offices themselves are so modern I think they must be updated every couple of weeks, and I have a hunch cost does not come up in discussions about furnishing and decorating the place. There are paintings on the wall that could feed Third World countries.

I'm brought into Young's office within five minutes of my arrival. Robby Divine's mode of dress apparently isn't standard issue among billionaires, because Young is wearing a suit and tie, though his jacket is draped over his chair.

His office is as modern as the rest of the place. The art on the wall is no doubt nouveau-something, except for the signed Bob Gibson Cardinals jersey, which is framed and proudly hung behind his desk.

I've done some research into Young, so I basically know where he's from, where he went to school, what companies he runs, and where they're located. Since the companies are privately owned, they don't have to file financial reports, so the actual amount of his holdings is unknown. But suffice it to say that his career has been a very impressive one, and has obviously paid off.

He's at least fifteen years Robby's senior, which probably puts him in his early fifties, and he has a relaxed air about him, smiling as he comes over to greet me. "Andy, Edward Young, nice to meet you."

"Thanks for seeing me."

He laughs. "I didn't have any choice. I lost to Robby last week at golf. We play for favors, and he called this one in."

That makes sense to me. Betting money wouldn't make it interesting, not for guys this wealthy. "But it snowed last week."

He smiles. "Not in Cabo."

"He says you cheat."

"He's right about that. But this time I lost by so much that cheating wouldn't have done any good. What can I do for you?"

"I'm investigating a case involving Solarno Shrimp Corporation."

"The murder? Didn't they put someone away for that years ago?"

I nod. "My client. But he's innocent."

"Aren't they all." It wasn't a question, but rather a cynical comment.

"Some aren't, but this one is. What made you buy the company?"

He frowns. "Temporary insanity. There's a fairly short list of bad business decisions I've made. That one would be near the top of the list had it been a more expensive purchase."

"How much did you pay?"

"Seventeen point five million."

"Your memory is precise," I say.

"Mistakes stay with me longer than successes. My advisers studied the company and said it was undervalued at the price, because the owner of the company was in need of cash."

"Did they say why?"

He shakes his head. "Not that I can recall."

"You only ran the company for eighteen months."

He smiles. "Is that a question?"

"Sorry, let me rephrase. How come you only ran the company for eighteen months?"

"A combination of factors. Once Solarno died, I had no one to run it. I could have found someone, but the company was not what I thought it was."

"Meaning?"

"Meaning it started bleeding cash."

"Was there anything about Solarno that concerned you?"

He frowns. "That's a broad question, Andy. When I take on a company, I hire good people to run it, I pay them very well, they give me their best advice, and I make the major decisions. If those decisions are consistently wrong, and they cost me money, I get rid of them."

"You make the decisions but get rid of them?" I ask.

He nods, and smiles. "It was their advice. Besides, who am I going to fire? Me? Anyway, buying the company was a mistake, and keeping Solarno on compounded it. I didn't realize the depth of the problem until he was gone, and by then it was fiscally responsible to shut down the operation."

"Do you keep records of all the employees?"

He shrugs. "Probably somewhere. Maybe in a warehouse, or on some computer."

"Do these names mean anything to you?" I take out the list of five names that Sam had given me, and read them aloud.

He shakes his head. "Afraid not. Who are they?"

"They all worked on one of Solarno's

boats. Run out of Portsmouth, New Hampshire."

"So?"

"So the guy they worked for was the victim of a hit-and-run about a month after you closed the company."

He frowns. "Sorry to hear that. What about the other five?"

"They all had fake identities, and can't be traced."

"Whoa," he says, obviously surprised. "I don't like the sound of that. Are you saying there were some kind of criminal activities going on? Maybe including a hit-and-run murder?"

I nod. "It's definitely a possibility. Maybe more than one murder."

He thinks about this for a few moments, shaking his head. "I said that buying that company was near the top of the list of bad decisions I've made. It is now the permanent champion."

I smile. "And we're just getting started."

He sighs, apparently resigned to his inadvertent involvement in this.

"So where is it going?"

"I think Solarno was smuggling arms into the country, and he was doing it through that ship. And he was doing it with hand-picked people, who didn't want to be identified, and melted away when they were done."

"So who killed Solarno, and maybe the hit-and-run guy? Those five people?"

"I don't know yet. But you can bet I'll find out."

"You ready for bed?" Laurie asks. It is a question I simply never get tired of hearing, and on the list of questions I root for every day, it ranks just above "What will you do with your lottery winnings?"

"I'll race you to the bedroom," I say.

"You think you're going to get lucky?"

"Hey, babe, there's no luck involved."

She smiles and takes my hand, leading me toward the stairs. "We don't need to race. We can take it slow."

I'm about to reply with some banter, but force myself to be quiet. The only way I can blow this is by saying something stupid, so I clench my teeth as hard as I can, to prevent my mouth from opening. Then I say, "Mmmm," because that's all I can manage.

We go upstairs, and as we approach the bed, the phone rings. "Don't get it," I say. "People shouldn't be calling at this hour."

"It's nine-thirty," she points out.

"East Coast time," I counter, seeking refuge in a non sequitur. "In France it's four o'clock in the morning."

Laurie doesn't seem moved by this logic, and she answers the phone with "Hello?"

"Get to the point," I say, but she's not listening.

Laurie engages in some more chitchat, then says, "Hold on, he's right here."

She hands me the phone, and it turns out to be Cindy. "I've got some information for you," she says.

"Can I call you back in the morning?" I ask.

"I need to make an appointment to do you a favor?"

"I'm a high-powered attorney," I say. "My calendar is booked solid."

"OK. How about a year from Thursday?"

"Actually, I just had a cancellation. So now works."

"Good," she says. "And just so we're clear, if you reveal where you got this information, your life will have a cancellation."

"You're a cold woman."

"It's part of my charm. Homeland Security was investigating Richard Solarno around the time that he was killed."

Laurie is undressed and under the covers already, so I want to move this along, but what Cindy is saying is crucial. They didn't cover this dilemma in law school.

"For arms dealing?"

"Yes."

"Why didn't they intervene at Joey's trial?"

"Come on, Andy. Trial intervening is not their specialty, you know that. And there was nothing to indicate that the murders were related to anything they were investigating."

"What specifically did they think he was doing?"

"Using at least one of his fishing boats to bring in mostly small arms, and possibly shoulder-fired missiles."

"Did they know where it was going?" I ask.

"Montana. And probably elsewhere."

"Militia?"

"Land of the free, home of the brave. Montana State Police could be your source on the other end. If you call my office in the morning, I'll give you a contact name there."

Laurie seems to be about to doze off, inducing a wave of panic in me. But I need to finish talking to Cindy.

"Can I use this?"

"Make an application through Freedom of Information. You'll get it. In the meantime, you can use it."

"This is great, Cindy. Thanks. Gotta go."

"Yeah, yeah, yeah. Let me talk to Laurie."

"*LAURIE?*" I scream it into the phone, hoping it will wake Laurie up from the beginnings of sleep. "Laurie took Tara for a walk."

"Andy," Cindy says, "you've got mental problems."

It didn't work; Laurie is asleep. "Mental problems are the least of it," I say, before hanging up.

Now my dilemma is how to wake Laurie up without making it look like I'm intentionally doing so. It's got to be handled with some subtlety.

I pretend to stub my toe on the foot of the bed, and I scream in pain. Torture victims have screamed less loudly than I do, and when that doesn't work, I do it again. She doesn't wake up, but neighbors up and down the street are probably calling 911.

I scream again, figuring if she hasn't woken up yet, then as far as she knows, it's the initial scream. Her eyes finally open, and she looks at me. "Why are you pretending to be in pain?" she asks.

"So you'll wake up."

"A gentle, loving nudge would have done the trick."

I nod. "I'll try that next time. I'm going to Montana."

"Tonight?"

"No."

"Then get into bed," she says, raising one side of the covers so I can do so.

"If you insist," I say.

I decide to call Edna in to work. I break the news to her over the phone.

"You've got a client?" she asks, the surprise evident in her voice.

"We've got a client" is how I correct her.

"Who?"

"Joey Desimone."

"Again?"

She agrees to come in this morning, not a major concession since she has to pick up her check anyway. But I'm going to need Edna to woman the phones and coordinate communication among the team members while I'm in Montana.

I've called a meeting of the team, such as it is, this morning. It includes Sam, Edna, Laurie, Hike, Willie Miller, and myself. As teams go, it's not exactly the '27 Yankees, but we get the job done.

Willie, my former client and partner in the Tara Foundation, our dog rescue operation, is almost as rich as I am, since we won a big civil case after he was wrongly imprisoned for seven years. So he and his wife, Sondra, work at the foundation full-time, while I just show up when I can. I feel guilty about it, but not as a result of anything they say or do. For them it's a labor of love. I feel the same way, except for the labor part.

Willie likes to be involved in our investigations whenever he can, I think primarily because he feels protective of me. As protectors go, he's pretty good at it, holding a black belt in karate and a fearlessness that's a perfect complement to my fearfulness.

Before the meeting starts, Sam comes over to me and tells me that the name of the person Alex Solarno called after I left his home was Richard Atkins. It was his cell phone.

"But he's a fake also, Andy. The name and address he gave the phone company aren't real. But I'm still working on it."

Rather than being upset by the information, I'm heartened. It confirms my belief that Solarno was worried about me, and that he has something to hide. It also reinforces my general belief that we're on the right track.

I start updating everyone on where we stand with the case when the door opens and Marcus Clark comes in. Rooms always become instantly quiet when Marcus enters; everything stops, including breathing.

Marcus is a talented investigator I sometimes use as a bodyguard when Marine battalions aren't available. He barely talks, never smiles to anyone other than Laurie, and is willing to inflict pain and death with no apparent conscience.

He's not a guy you'd hire to entertain at your son's bar mitzvah.

Suffice it to say I'm glad he's on our side, though I have no idea what he's doing here today.

I call a pause to the meeting, and ask to speak to Laurie in the other room. "What is Marcus doing here?" I ask.

"He's going to Montana with you," she says.

"No, he's not."

"Yes, he is."

This conversation is not heading toward a quick resolution, so I try to move it along. "Why?"

"Because you're going to confirm that weapons were sent there. Which means you might run into people who possess and are willing to use those weapons. Which means you need Marcus. Are you following my logic so far?"

"You don't think I can handle myself with dangerous people."

"If that is a statement, it's a correct one. If it's a question, then the answer is, no, I don't."

"That's because you haven't seen me angry," I say. "You haven't gotten on my bad side. You don't want to get on my bad side."

"I tremble at the mere thought of it," she says.

I'm not thrilled by the prospect of Marcus accompanying me to Montana. I've traveled with him before, and he makes me uncomfortable. It's not a big deal; I'm just constantly afraid that I will accidentally say something which will make him kill me. Marcus's bad side is something I may not quite be equipped to handle.

On the other hand, he likes me, which means he will stop other people from killing me. I do have a tendency to annoy people, and in this case the annoyed might have guns.

"OK, Marcus is in for the Montana trip. But don't you think we should call and warn the governor?"

In the desolation of Central Peru, the warehouse attracted absolutely no attention. This would have been true even if there was someone around to notice it, but this was not an area that had a lot of passersby. There was no one living within twenty miles of the place, and pretty much no reason for anyone to change that. You wouldn't want to be a real estate agent there.

On this day, like all other days at this time of year, it was hot and dry, the terrain browned by months without precipitation. That would change when the rainy season came, and the dust would turn to mud. When the changeover was taking effect, there might even be a day or two when the area seemed inhabitable.

The nearest town, Canalin, was more than three hours away to the east, with only dirt roads to connect to it. To the west, the closest town was almost nine hours away, but the roads were better.

The trucks came from the west that night.

Just as they came every night.

A crew of seven men lived inside the warehouse, never venturing outside. Because the windows were blackened, they never even saw the sunlight, not for the months they had been there. The only times they got to experience any fresh air at all were during the nights, when they opened the door for the incoming trucks.

Between the men on the trucks and those in the warehouse, there were at least fifteen people each night. Yet if a single word was ever spoken, it was unusual. Everybody knew their job, and no one wanted to call any attention to themselves.

This was the most important thing they would ever be involved in, and it would make each of them more money than they had seen in their lifetimes.

It was a difficult existence to endure, at least for those assigned to the warehouse. But there was a light at the end of the tunnel, and no one was complaining. They didn't know when the end day would be — that was a decision well out of their control. But the men sensed that it would be weeks, rather than months, because the warehouse was filling up.

Their sole focus was on doing their job, and doing it well, because that would mean great wealth.

The opposite meant death.

I leave at 6:30 A.M. to pick up Marcus. The early departure means I only get to do an abbreviated walk with Tara, though Laurie promises to take her on a longer one later.

Our flight isn't until ten forty-five, but Marcus says that he'll be at a diner in Oakland, which is north of Paterson off Route 208, putting it in the opposite direction from JFK Airport.

Marcus is standing in front of the diner, holding a small duffel bag, when I arrive. I'm not sure what he's doing there, although a place of residence is one of the many things I am in the dark about concerning Marcus. His cell phone is a 646 area code, which is Manhattan, so I always assumed that's where he lived. But maybe not.

"Unhh," he says, when he gets in the car, which is likely to sum up the quality of the conversation for the rest of the trip.

I offer a "good morning," but that either

isn't worthy of a response or "Unhh" is Marcus-ese for an early-morning greeting.

"Is your car here?" I ask.

"Nunh."

And we're on our way.

Route 208 is fairly empty at this time of the morning. It never gets very crowded, but the peak will be in an hour or so when people start their daily commuting trek into the city.

Marcus changes the station on the radio to classical music. I've driven with him before, so I'm not surprised by either his musical preference or his sense of entitlement regarding the radio. I have a tendency to indulge Marcus.

We're passing near Wyckoff when I detect Marcus sitting up slightly and seeming to grow more alert. He also seems to be looking at the passenger-side mirror.

"Something wrong?" I ask, but I don't get a response. There is no doubt he's staring at the mirror. I look in the rearview mirror, but nothing seems amiss.

"Marcus?"

Still nothing; it's as if I'm not here.

We're in the left-hand lane, going about seventy in a sixty-five-mile-per-hour zone. I notice a car approaching from behind on our right. It's probably going seventy-five or so, and is therefore steadily gaining on us. And Marcus hasn't taken his eyes off the mirror.

The trailing car is about two car lengths behind us, when I notice with horror that there is a gun in Marcus's left hand. *"Marcus! What the hell is going on?"*

No answer from Mr. Chitchat, but that is to be expected. What is not expected is that the car on the right has inched slightly ahead of us, and is slowly drifting toward our lane. The trunk of the other car is even with the front of our car.

My horror at the gun in Marcus's hand pales next to the realization that we are approaching a small tunnel, with large concrete stanchions on each side. If the car moves much closer to our lane, cutting us off, I will have no way to move to the left, because of the stanchions.

"Marcus, he's cutting us off!"

The other car can't be more than a few inches to our right, and I have no breathing room at all. If he so much as nudges us, we're going to crash head-on into the concrete.

The gun, which was in Marcus's left hand, resting on his lap, is suddenly in his right hand at the window, and is firing, I think twice. It looks like he is aiming low, at the

132

tires, but I can't tell if he hit anything, because my attention is drawn back to Marcus's left hand, which violently grabs the steering wheel and yanks it to the right.

We smash into the car on our right, and send it spinning away from us, toward the right shoulder of the road. Suddenly that shoulder is no longer there, as we have reached the stanchions, and the other car crashes into it in the largest, most fiery collision I have ever seen, in real life or the movies.

But we're not out of the woods yet, going into a spin of our own, through the length of the tunnel and out the other side. Marcus still has his hand on the wheel, and he is desperately trying to maintain control of the car. I have been reduced to a passenger in the driver's seat.

I have no idea how far we travel like this; it's hard for me to simultaneously estimate distance and prepare for death. But finally we start to slow down, and we wind up along the side of the road, scraping against a railing.

"Holy shit" is all I can manage, when we are stopped and all is quiet. My heart is beating so loudly that it seems like we're listening to a drum solo on the radio.

"Yunh," Marcus says.
You can say that again.

My first call when we come to a stop is to Pete Stanton. There are going to be a lot of uncomfortable questions asked when officers on the scene realize that Marcus fired at the other car, and I want Pete here to intervene. He knows us, and he knows we don't go around randomly taking potshots at other drivers.

He promises to get here right away. I'm feeling shaky, and my voice must reflect it, because he goes the entire call without insulting me.

My second call is to Laurie. When she hears about this, I want it to be from me, so she'll know that I'm OK. She gets upset, which makes me even more upset, but we manage to calm each other down.

"I think Marcus coming along might have been a good idea," I say, and she refrains from responding with an "I told you so." Instead she says, "I love you, Andy," which is definitely preferable.

My third call is to Vince Sanders. Vince hasn't run the story yet; he hasn't even agreed to run it at all. This makes that story a hell of a lot more interesting. Vince also says that he's on the way.

I don't bother calling 911, because I'm sure that other motorists and witnesses must have already done that. Something about a car crashing and exploding attracts attention.

I tell Marcus to let me do the talking when the police arrive, which is sort of comical on its face. It has to be the first time in his life that Marcus has been asked not to talk. He doesn't bother to answer me, a sure sign that he's down with the "not talking" approach.

We are not anywhere near the burning car, since after it crashed we went through the small tunnel and wound up much farther up the highway. I feel no need to drive back there; the arriving cops will eventually make their way to us. It will give Pete more time to get here, so that we can deal with him first.

I can see flashing lights through the tunnel as the cops reach the scene, and they start to close off the highway in both directions. Pete shows up maybe three minutes later, and comes straight to where I told him we'd be.

He takes one look at the car, which has been damaged from hitting a railing a few times. "Any injuries? You guys need medical treatment?"

Weirdly, I haven't even thought much about that. "Nothing hurts. Marcus?"

"Nunh."

"We're OK. Can we give you our statement?"

"Not yet. But you can tell me what happened."

I detail all that happened, and his eyebrows raise when I get to the part about Marcus shooting at the tires.

He turns to Marcus. "Did you hit the tires?"

Marcus just gives him a look which silently says, "I'm Marcus Clark; if I shot at the tires, I hit the damn tires."

"Did either of you recognize the driver?" Pete asks.

"I didn't see his face," I say, and Marcus just shrugs.

Pete asks a few more questions, and then says, "Let's get you out of here and down to the precinct, so you can sign your statement."

"You have jurisdiction?" I ask, since we're

not in Paterson right now.

He nods. "I told them it's part of a case we're already working on, which is technically true, if you count Solarno. They were happy to hand it over. So let's go."

"We've got a flight to catch."

Pete laughs. "No chance."

My cell phone rings; it's an annoyed Vince calling. "They won't let me through; Stanton has the road blocked off."

"He's here now," I say.

"Tell the son of a bitch to let me through. I've got a story to cover."

"Hold on," I say, and then turn to Pete. "Vince insists that you let him in so he can interview me."

"Tell that scumbag to kiss my ass."

I talk back into the phone. "Lieutenant Stanton says that he greatly respects journalism in general, and you in particular."

"I heard what he said; I'll deal with him at Charlie's," Vince says. "You and I need to talk as soon as you're done there."

"You forgot to ask if I was hurt in the crash."

"Were you hurt in the crash?"

"No, Marcus and I are fine. But thanks for caring."

"Of course I care. If you're hurt it makes for a better story."

Marcus and I are just finishing signing our statements when Pete comes back into the room.

"Can we get out of here?" I ask.

"Yeah. But I just came in to tell you that you lucked out," he says.

"Yeah, I'm feeling real lucky about now. What happened?"

"They ID'd the guy you charcoal broiled."

"Who is he?" I ask.

"Oh, now you want to stay here and talk?"

"I just have this thing where for some reason I always want to know who's trying to kill me. Call it a quirk."

Pete puts a piece of paper on the table in front of Marcus and me. It's a mug shot, and identifies the person in the photo as Tony Mancini. "You recognize him?" he asks.

Marcus shakes his head, and I say, "No. Tell me about him."

139

"He's a mob guy out of Philadelphia, suspected of at least a dozen murders, probably guilty of twice that. He's been arrested three times, which is why we have the mug shot, but it never stuck."

"So a mob hit man tried to kill me . . . us? Why exactly am I lucky?"

"Because if the guy was a schoolteacher, or a priest, or something, nobody would believe your story. And you'd be looking for a good lawyer."

"I am a good lawyer," I say.

"I think if your life were on the line, you'd want to get someone better than you."

We get up to leave, but I stop and ask Pete, "These other murders that he was suspected of, how did he kill those people?"

"Usually a bullet in the back of the head," he says.

"So this time it was supposed to look like an accident."

Pete nods. "Any idea why that would be?

"So it wouldn't appear I was being silenced and prevented from pursuing Joey Desimone's appeal."

"Why would the mob want to stop you from getting Carmine Desimone's son out of jail?"

"I don't know," I say. "If Nicky Fats were

still around, and not drooling, I could ask him."

When we leave, I call Edna and ask her to reschedule our flights for tomorrow. She mutters something about how long the airline will keep her on hold, and that she'll have to use the speaker phone because her arm hurts when she holds the handset too long, but she agrees to take care of it.

Edna always rises to the occasion in a crisis, no matter how long she has to stay on hold.

Marcus tells me to pick him up at the Coach House Diner on Route 4 in the morning. I don't know what this thing is with him and diners, and I have no intention of asking.

I decide to stop at the prison before going home, but my car was towed away. I'll rent one later, but for now I have Hike pick me up and take me out to see Joey. If Hike's going to be working on the case with me, he should meet our client, and vice versa.

Once we get in the car, Hike puts the prison address into the GPS, even though I tell him I know the way. He is very much into technology, but in typical Hike fashion, doesn't quite always appreciate what it has to offer.

We are driving on the highway, when

things slow down and we find ourselves stuck in traffic. Hike is infuriated by this turn of events, blaming the GPS lady for our misfortune. "Do you believe this?" he asks. "She's supposed to warn us when there's traffic, and give us a different route."

"Traffic ahead," the GPS voice says.

"Thanks a lot," snarls Hike. "Now you tell me."

"Hike, let's look at the situation," I say. "You're sitting in a car in New Jersey, and a fake woman is talking to you from a satellite. She knows where you are, and she's giving you directions. She'll also tell you where you can eat, get gas, go shopping, whatever you want. Can you not see the bright side of that?"

"I can't see anything with this truck in front of us."

Fortunately, the traffic breaks up; a cop had pulled someone over on the side of the road, apparently neglecting to inform the satellite GPS lady.

Joey is brought into the visiting room fairly quickly, and I introduce him to Hike. "How ya doin'?" Joey asks, a phrase he uses instead of "hello."

Hike treats it as a sincere question. "Not so good," he says. "I made the mistake of getting a flu shot; it's been making me nauseous. I gag myself to sleep every night."

"Oh," Joey says, and then turns to me. "What's up?"

Unfortunately, Hike still seems to think he has the floor. "Make sure they don't give you any vaccines in here," he says. "I read in an article that they use prisoners like guinea pigs, testing all this weird stuff on them. And watch what you eat. Make sure it's wrapped."

"Thanks, Hike. Excellent advice," I say.

He nods. "Just check out miseryisevery where.com; that's where you'll find the real story about stuff like this."

"Moving right along," I say, and then I update Jocy on what is going on. I like to keep the clients as informed as possible, but it's often a delicate balance. The trick is to make sure they are realistic about our prospects for success, and someone who spends twenty-three hours a day in a cell has positive or negative expectations that are often very hard to manage.

He is surprised by how much has taken place, but a little skeptical that an attempt was made on my life because of his case. "Why would anyone care if I got out?" he asks.

"I don't think it has anything to do with you," I say. "I think it's about somebody not wanting the whole thing reopened and looked at."

"Who?"

"I don't know yet," I say, and then add, "You're not going to like this, but it could well be someone in your family."

He shakes his head. "Not possible."

"Joey, Nicky Fats knew about this; that's how it all started. And the guy that went after me; he was a mob guy for hire."

"I'm going to talk to my father," he says.

"I don't think that's a good idea. At least not right now."

"You think he could be involved in this? He's been upset about my being in here since day one, Andy. He once told me it's the only thing in his life he couldn't fix, and that he'd give up everything to be able to."

When I don't say anything, he continues, "Andy, he's my damn father."

"My father took off when I was four," Hike says, and in the moment it seems understandable.

"And Nicky was your uncle, Joey. Just lay low on this for the time being. At least until we learn more."

He reluctantly agrees, and we leave. Hike drops me off at home, where Laurie and Tara are waiting.

Seeing them is incredibly comforting, but

also shakes me up some. What happened today was as scary as anything I've ever been through, and it's having a delayed effect on me.

Laurie cooks dinner, and we take Tara for a walk together. Laurie brings her gun with her, something she rarely does. She's obviously concerned about my safety.

Join the club.

We don't talk much about the case, and when we get home we head upstairs and make love. I've got to get up early and leave for the airport, but at this moment I never want to get out of this bed.

Sam Willis finally got his boots on the ground. That's how he viewed it, even though he was wearing sneakers, and he was sitting in his car the entire time.

Sam had run into a brick wall chasing down the real name of the owner of the phone Alex Solarno had called after Andy left him. As with the five mysterious employees assigned to the boat with Larry Callahan, the identity and the address, as listed in the phone company records, were fake.

But because it was a cell phone, Sam had another option. Many people don't realize that embedded in every cell phone is a GPS device. Through their computer tracking, the phone company can identify where a phone is at all times, providing it is turned on.

Sam, because of his ability to access the phone company's computers, could do the same. So, with his laptop turned toward him on the passenger seat, he set out to find the phone, and thereby find the owner.

The tracking system didn't show a physical address, but Sam realized where he was heading long before he got there. It was the Elizabeth house where Andy took Tara to meet with Nicky Fats, and where Nicky Fats died shortly thereafter.

Which is to say, it was Carmine Desimone's house.

Of course, that didn't mean it was Carmine Desimone's phone. The house was large enough that there must have been plenty of other people in it, "family" members, and Sam figured that as long as he was there, he might as well see if he could learn more.

So he stopped at a Dunkin Donuts, because that would make it an official stakeout, and he waited two blocks from the house. That way he wouldn't be seen or suspected, but he was close enough that if the cell phone moved, he could follow it.

It was four hours and six doughnuts before it moved, and the computer showed it coming straight toward and past Sam. Sam figured out which car it was in, and pulled out behind it. He stayed at a safe, respectful distance, since there was literally no way he could lose track of it.

The car was driven to a coffee shop by a man Sam did not recognize, but who could not have been Carmine Desimone. He was at least thirty years younger than Sam knew Carmine to be, and besides, there was no way a Mafia don would be driving himself to a coffee shop. Not even if Fredo was with him.

Sam parked across the street and waited. The tricky part had been reached; just following the man gained him nothing. He needed a photograph.

Sam put his own phone to his ear, with the camera lens within it facing the front of the coffee shop. The man came out in less than five minutes, not carrying anything, so Sam had no idea why he had gone in there.

But that didn't matter. What mattered was that Sam get the picture. Since he couldn't properly aim it, he pressed the button repeatedly, at slightly different angles, hoping that at least one of them would capture the man's face.

The man got back in the car, heading in the general direction of the house he had come out of. But Sam had no need to follow him. He made a mental note of the license plate, and drove back to Paterson.

As stakeouts go, Sam figured, that was a

damn successful one. There would never be a good substitute for boots on the ground.

On our second try, Marcus and I make it to the airport without anyone dying. There's a line at the check-in desk, which looks like July 4 at Disneyland, but fortunately Edna decided I was rich enough to book us first class, so we are able to circumvent the peasants.

The agent asks if we've been in possession of our bags since we left the house, which is when Marcus mentions that he's carrying a handgun. He shows them a document that is called "full carry," which I guess means that the government has decreed him to be one of the good guys.

Suffice it to say this doesn't speed up the process any. We are sent through a special security area, in which they take the gun, confirm that it is unloaded, and confiscate both the gun and the separate ammunition. They then inform us that all of it will be held in the pilot's cabin until we land. It's a process that I didn't know existed, but one which Marcus seems quite familiar with.

As I've previously learned is his tendency, Marcus falls asleep the moment the plane starts to taxi, and wakes up when it pulls into the gate. This happens at our first stop in Minneapolis, and again in Missoula.

By the time we land, collect our bags and armaments, and rent a car, it's almost three-thirty in the afternoon. We're supposed to meet the state cop that Cindy put us on to at four-thirty, and I call to confirm that he's still available to see us. He is.

Lieutenant Chris McKenney of the Montana State Police makes me glad that I brought Marcus instead of Laurie. He's probably six three, two hundred pounds, and looks like Robert Redford looked when he still looked like Robert Redford.

He's also pleasant and gracious in a small-town America kind of way, and combines a seriousness of purpose with an apparently genuine desire to help.

He's the anti-Vince.

McKenney says, with no apparent attitude, that the local FBI Bureau chief called McKenney's captain, asking that they be forthcoming with us. Good old Cindy Spodek comes through again.

I tell him what we're interested in, though

151

I had communicated that by e-mail before we came. He had gone through the case history and updated himself on the particulars.

"I had just been on the force for three years at the time," he says, "when I got this case."

"I understand arrests were made?"

He nods. "Three of them. Lester Harmon, his brother S. J., and Chuckie Simmons. Lester was, and probably still is, the leader of the group. S. J. is his right-hand guy, and Chuckie is one of the flunkies."

"Were they convicted?"

He nods. "All three. Chuckie went away for six months, S. J. for three years, but he got out in two, and Lester is still in. He's serving ten to twenty, because he tried to use one of the rifles on an ATF agent."

"And the militia unit they're in? Lester ran that?"

"Yes."

"Is it still active?"

He nods. "Yes, not as big as it used to be, but still dangerous. They probably have about forty-five recruits, maybe half of whom are serious, the rest hangers-on. They train pretty much every week."

"What are they training for?" I ask.

"Primarily resistance. They're sure the United Nations is coming to take over."

"So where did Solarno fit in?"

"He supplied them with arms, mostly rifles. We didn't uncover the connection until he was dead. Lester was not a big fan of his, and wasn't shy about mentioning it."

"Why?"

"According to Lester, Solarno didn't deliver what he promised. They got rifles when they were probably expecting something much bigger. Lester had apparently threatened him, but our people had no reason to think he had carried through on it."

"So that's why you never told the authorities in New Jersey?"

He looks surprised. "Oh, we told them. I called and sent a letter to" — he looks at a document in the folder — "Dylan Campbell. He was in the prosecutor's office."

I nod. "He prosecuted the case." This is major news; this would constitute exculpatory evidence for Joey, and Dylan had an obligation to turn it over in discovery. The fact that he didn't is a major plus for us in going after a new trial.

"Can I get a copy of that letter?" I ask, but McKenney doesn't answer right away. He's staring at Marcus, probably wondering if he can talk at all. When I get his attention, he agrees and calls in an assistant to make a copy for me.

"Where is this guy S. J.?" I ask.

"He lives about twenty-five miles out of town," McKenney says. "A place called Millbank. Take the highway east. That is, if you really want to talk to him."

"Would he have information about So-larno?"

McKenney shrugs. "Probably. But you might not get a friendly reception."

"It's worth a try. Any idea where he might be?

"Well, if you get there after eight, try the bar. There's only one of them, so you can't miss it. S. J. will be the fat guy with the beard, but that won't narrow it down for you much."

"Thanks."

"Be careful. Is Marcus going with you?"

For the first time, Marcus speaks, and it is worth waiting for. "Yuh," he says.

McKenney looks at Marcus, and then back at me. "Good."

Marcus is hungry.

Since he had slept on the plane, he didn't get to enjoy the first-class food, as I did. And since Marcus insists that his stomach always be full, we eat at a Missoula restaurant before heading out to find S. J.

Missoula is a college town, home to the Montana Grizzlies, and it seems simultaneously quaint and sophisticated. It's also cold, but at the moment doesn't feel any colder than New Jersey.

The restaurant is terrific, though I expect they're going to have to close for a couple of days to restock after we leave. Marcus eats three entrees and four side dishes, and would probably eat the table if I didn't rush us out. I want to find S. J. before he's too drunk to give us decent information.

We don't hit any traffic on the drive out to Millbank. My guess is that no one ever hits traffic on the way to Millbank, because there's no real reason for anyone to ever go to Millbank.

The town is basically one street, with small, run-down rural roads emanating from it. Pickup trucks outnumber cars probably three to one, and our rented Saab is the only foreign car to be found.

Easy to find is Red's Bar, since as McKenney had mentioned it's the only one in town. From outside it seems to be hopping, and the sounds of the music spread down the street.

The interior of Red's is larger than I expected, and has three separate centers of activity. One is the bar, which has six stools, all occupied, and another five people standing between the chairs. The other two main attractions are a pair of pool tables, near the back. Both are being played on, with numerous spectators watching.

Surprising, at least to me, is the fact that there are no televisions. Vince and Pete wouldn't come in here on a bet.

In the old Westerns, if two people as out of place as Marcus and I strolled into a room like this, things would get really quiet, and everyone would stare at us. That doesn't happen here; if anyone has even noticed us, it isn't apparent to me.

Everybody in the joint looks large and

intimidating. I don't think there's a person here who couldn't kick my ass, and I'm definitely including the women. Plus, they're probably all carrying guns, courtesy of Richard Solarno.

If I wasn't with Marcus, I'd be back in Missoula, ordering room service and watching ESPN in the hotel room, with the door locked.

But I'm here, and my primary goal is to get this over with as soon as possible, so that I will no longer be here. So my mouth takes matters into its own hands, and before I even realize it, I'm hollering, "S. J.!"

Pretty much everybody in the bar looks in my direction, sizes up both Marcus and myself, and then looks toward the bar. They're all looking at a very large guy with a beard, and I'm as sure that this is S. J. as I would be if he were wearing his name tattooed on his forehead. Actually, his forehead seems to be the only place on his body that isn't tattooed. He is surrounded by other large people, in varying degrees of fatness.

I walk over to where S. J. is sitting, casting a quick glance to the side to make sure that Marcus is with me. I'm not at all comfortable with these surroundings, and I don't recall seeing this situation on the bar exam.

"Hi, S. J.?" I say, just to break the ice.

"Who the fuck are you?" is his pleasant rejoinder.

"Touché," I say, since I can't help saying stuff like that.

"What?"

"My name is Andy Carpenter." I throw in, "I'm a lawyer," just to scare him. "This is my co-counsel, Marcus Clark."

S. J. barely glances at Marcus, as he says, "You hear that? He's a lawyer." Then, "What do you want, lawyer?"

"I want to talk to you about Richard Solarno."

S. J. sits up straight, or at least as straight as he can. It's as if I shoved a hot poker up his ass; the Solarno name definitely struck a chord. "What about Solarno?"

"Can we talk somewhere in private?"

S. J. makes eye contact with the bartender, who nods a silent assent. "In the back," says S. J., and he hoists himself off the stool and makes his way around the bar toward a room in the back. Marcus and I follow him into what must pass as the bar manager's office. It's got a desk, a couch, and a small table with a TV on it. A small metal garbage can sits on the front corner of the desk, and S. J. plants his fat ass on the opposite corner.

I wait until Marcus follows me into the office, and then close the door behind us.

"What the hell are you doing with So-larno?" S. J. asks.

"I'm not doing anything with him. He's dead. I'm trying to find out who killed him."

"You think I did it?"

"Did you?"

"I would have, if somebody didn't beat me to it. We put the word out on him, I'll tell you that. The son of a bitch ripped us off."

"Would you be willing to testify that there were people other than yourself that wanted to do harm to Richard Solarno?"

S. J. points to Marcus. "He talk? Or do you do all the talking, lawyer?"

I decide to ignore that salvo. "Would you testify to that, S. J.? You'd get a free trip to New York out of it."

Just then, the door behind us opens, and three of S. J.'s large friends walk in. Each of them, like S. J., is at least six foot tall and probably two hundred seventy pounds of rolled skin. They must all have the same personal trainer.

But the arrival of these newcomers is not a positive development, and I look at Marcus to make sure he's alert to what's going on. He has no expression at all; if his eyes weren't open I'd think he were asleep.

"The shithead lawyer and his mute friend

159

want to take me to New York, see the big city," S. J. says, pronouncing "mute" as "moot." Two of the newcomers respond by chuckling at the thought of it, but the third doesn't respond. The third one instead watches Marcus, which probably makes him the smartest of the group. Of course, being the smartest of this group does not qualify one as a Rhodes Scholar candidate.

Nobody seems concerned enough to watch the shithead lawyer.

"Have you seen our city yet, lawyer? Maybe we should show you the 'little city.' "

The four of them are generally in a three-quarters circle around us, but somehow it feels as if Marcus has them surrounded. They seem to think otherwise.

I'm not going to get anything out of S. J.; it was clearly foolish to come here at all. My goal is now reduced to simply getting out of this town in good health, but to do so I'm going to have to rely on Dr. Marcus.

The guy who was eyeing Marcus says, "We don't need this, S. J."

"He's right, S. J.," I say. It's all I can do to get the words out.

S. J. does not seem pleased to have anyone questioning his authority. He ignores me and talks directly to the bright guy, the one who is preaching restraint. "I'll decide what we need, and I say we need to show these two assholes the town."

S. J. and his two friends start to move toward us, and what happens next takes place so quickly that I wish I had filmed it so I could replay it in stop-action. Even though he wasn't bending over, Marcus seems to uncoil. He grabs the top of the metal wastebasket that is sitting on the desk, and swings it in a circular, counterclockwise motion. It first hits S. J., and then his two friends, in their faces.

It's as if they're a synchronized team, as all three reach for their already bleeding faces, one after the other, in perfect rhythm, like fat, wounded Rockettes. Marcus then addresses them individually, one at a time. He hits one in the stomach, a short, stunning punch that leaves the man moaning and retching.

Before he even hits the floor, Marcus has clubbed the next one in the side of the head, and he topples like a stone on top of his retching comrade. S. J. barely has time to panic, before Marcus lifts him off his feet and throws him against the wall. He bounces off, and his face has the misfortune to ricochet into Marcus's fist. He's going to be unconscious for a really long time.

Marcus now turns toward the brightest of

the three, who has so far done the same as me, which is absolutely nothing but watch the carnage. The bright one holds up his hands, palms out, as if to say this is not his fight, and he means us no harm.

I look at the pile of humans on the floor, two unconscious and the other moaning and retching, and I say, "You guys had enough?" My voice is shaking a little, but I don't think the three of them notice.

In any event, they don't respond, so I tell Marcus in a slightly firmer voice, "Our work here is done."

We're back at the hotel in less than an hour, and waiting for us in the lobby is Lieutenant McKenney. "We received a report that two guys beat up S. J. and two of his buddies. The two assailants apparently looked very much like you two."

"To be honest, you throw a dart in that town and you'll hit guys who look like us," I say. "We're a dime a dozen. How are S. J. and his friends?"

They're in the hospital. S. J.'s got a broken jaw."

I shake my head sadly. "Boy, that really puts things in perspective, doesn't it? One minute you're fat and happy, sucking down Thunderbird, and the next you're taking oatmeal through a straw."

"You probably shouldn't go back to Mill-bank," he says, smiling.

"So I should withdraw the offer on the trailer?"

"I think that's wise."

Marcus sleeps the entire way back, so we don't chitchat the morning away. I called Laurie from the hotel last night, and told her roughly what had happened. I made myself sound slightly more heroic in the telling than it actually happened in real life, and when I finished she said, "Was Marcus there?"

"He was," I said. "But he pretty much let me handle things. I think he might have been intimidated by the surroundings."

I use the time on the plane to plan my strategy. I've developed some real evidence that Solarno was peddling arms, but that alone won't get me to the new trial. He could have been an arms peddler who got murdered by his wife's jilted lover.

The real bombshell is that the Montana State Police notified Dylan Campbell about threats on Solarno's life, and Dylan didn't disclose it. That was exculpatory evidence, and we were entitled to it.

The best thing about it is the fact that it is hard to assess what the value of the information would have been at trial. The fact is that not only would we have been able to use it in our defense case, but more important, we would have been able to investigate and develop it further.

What that means is that the trial judge is somewhat in the dark; he can't honestly dismiss the evidence as not substantial enough, because he can't know what other evidence it would have led us to.

I don't know whether Dylan deliberately withheld the document. He had powerful evidence against Joey, and I would think he would have felt that his case could have survived the Montana information. I also think he would not have wanted to risk the wrath of the court if the information got out, which he is about to feel now.

Fortunately, intent is not the determining factor here. Justice demanded that we get the information, and the reason we didn't is of secondary importance.

I think we now have a real chance to prevail and get our new trial, and I'm going to get Hike started on preparing a brief. He is outstanding at it, far better than I am.

But should we get the new trial, we're

then going to have to come up with a way to win it, and we're a huge leap from that. For one thing, I don't have a real suspect to point to; I don't believe for a second that S. J. and his chubby gang of idiots traveled cross-country in secret and pulled it off.

I have to consider the possibility that if Richard Solarno double-crossed his Montana customers, then he might have done the same thing to people more competent, and more deadly. But I have no idea who those people might be, or if they exist.

The incontrovertible truth is that somebody killed the Solarnos, and I'm no closer to figuring out who than I was six years ago.

The most puzzling aspect of this is the role of the Desimone crime family. One of their own is in prison, their flesh and blood, yet it seems that members of the family knew the truth about what happened. Certainly Nicky Fats did; the essential accuracy of his ramblings has been confirmed. And Alex Solarno called the Desimone house after I scared him.

Why would Joey's own family be conspiring against him?

Most of my knowledge of how organized crime families operate I got from Michael and Sonny Corleone, though I have had some rather frightening dealings with Dominic Petrone, the rather courtly and deadly head of the dominant family in North Jersey.

I am vaguely familiar with the concept of *omertà*, which is the code of silence that members of Mafia families are sworn to uphold. There are no limits on this; for instance, "person A" cannot tell the police that "person B" committed a crime, even if "person A" is himself being wrongly accused of that same crime.

Violation of *omertà* is said to be punishable by death, which seems a tad harsh for the crime of "tattling," but the code has lasted for centuries. It is said to be loosening in recent years, as prosecutions of Mafia figures have risen dramatically.

Faced with the prospects of years in prison, loyalty is proving to be a fading concept, and the more *omertà* is broken, the more breakable it becomes.

I suppose it is possible that someone else in the Desimone inner circle killed the Solarnos, and *omertà* has stopped them from turning that person in. The net result is that Joey has suffered for it, but perhaps the code dictates it. That would at least explain how Nicky Fats knew about it, but leaves countless questions unanswered.

I go straight to the office from the airport, and Hike meets me there. He's already started preparing the petition, and for Hike, he seems excited about the prospects.

"Are you going to give Dylan a heads-up?" Hike asks.

It's an interesting question, and one I've been thinking about. There is no legal reason for me to alert the prosecutor, Dylan Campbell, that we're going to be seeking a new trial. Once we file the motion, the court would obviously inform his office so they can contest it.

This is a charged situation, since much of our case is based on misconduct by Dylan in not notifying us about the warning from the Montana State Police. Disclosure of this will be embarrassing to him at the very least, and career-damaging at the worst.

I can't stand Dylan, which sets him apart from most prosecutors I deal with. Unlike many defense attorneys, I have no inbred bias against them; my father headed up the county prosecutor's office back in the day. But I find Dylan to be arrogant and obnoxious, in addition to smart and relentless. I've beaten him the last few times we've faced each other, and I'm sure it drives him crazy.

Resurrection of the Desimone case in this manner will infuriate him, which is what I'm counting on. Dylan makes mistakes when angry, when he lets things get personal, and mistakes are what I'm hoping for.

"What do you think?" I ask Hike.

"I think he's going to be really pissed either way, but much more pissed if you blindside him."

"That's what I think also," I say, "so blindsiding is the way to go."

He nods. "Works for me."

"Vince really came through," Laurie says, handing me the paper.

I'm still in bed, but she has gotten up to retrieve it from the lawn, where it's left each morning. Tara finds "paper fetching" to be way, way beneath her.

I could easily read the paper online every morning, as I do everything else, but I'm afraid if I cut off delivery of the physical paper, Vince will find out and cut off part of my body.

The story is on the front page, which is actually giving it more credit than it deserves. The attempt to kill Marcus and me jazzed it up a lot, but there is no proof that it was related to the Desimone case at all. Our attempt to reopen that case is in itself news, but the overall story is still somewhat short on substance. I hadn't provided Vince with that much to work with.

That's about to change.

I call Vince to thank him for running the story, and he says, "I can't believe I put that drivel on the front page. You know what my problem is? I'm too nice."

"That's always been your problem, Vince. But this time it's going to pay off."

"I like the concept of paying off."

I give him the follow-up to the story, which includes the Montana information, and the fact that we're filing a petition with the court today. He can run the story in the online edition the moment we file, and follow it up as soon as possible in print.

"If you time it right," I say, "Dylan will find out about it from you."

I actually think I can hear Vince salivating through the phone. "He's going to go bat-shit," Vince says. "This is beautiful."

I get up, shower, and go downstairs to take Tara on our walk. I stop in the kitchen to have some coffee, only to see Marcus standing next to the refrigerator. The door is open, and Marcus is in the process of emptying it.

Marcus can eat like no one I've ever seen. I almost expect him to lift the open refrigerator, lean his head back, and pour the contents down his throat.

I wave feebly and do an about-face, heading back up the steps. Tara stays down there with Marcus, maybe hoping for him to drop some scraps.

Laurie has just gotten on the treadmill, which is a device I completely do not understand. I don't like walking anywhere, and in a million years would not walk nowhere.

This particular treadmill has a video screen that shows fake mountains, I guess under the very misguided assumption that mountain walking is an appealing concept. It isn't; in fact, it's one of the reasons they invented tunnels. I never really envied the Von Trapp family much.

Laurie is constantly telling me how much better exercise makes her feel, but I've never been a fan of gasping and sweating.

"You saw Marcus," she says, while walking furiously.

"I did."

"I hired him as your bodyguard. I knew you wouldn't do it on your own, Andy. But people are trying to kill you. People who do that kind of thing professionally."

I know she expects me to argue about this; Marcus has protected me in the past, and each time I've resisted his hiring. But he does it silently and unobtrusively; I never know he's there until I need him, or until I walk into the kitchen.

"OK," I say, no doubt shocking her, and I head back down the steps. I put on Tara's leash and take her for a walk; there's no trace of Marcus the entire time. I can't even hear the sound of chewing. But the truth is that I feel confident and a hell of a lot safer knowing he's there.

After the walk, I shower and head to the office, where Hike is waiting for me with the finished petition. I make a few edits on it, but they don't improve it much. He did a terrific job, but it probably won't carry the day on its own. We'll have to do that in the hearing that will be called to decide the matter.

One factor that works against us is the judge who will preside, Judge Henry Henderson. He handled the original trial, and he has unfortunately not retired since, demonstrating that prayer, at least when lawyers do it, has its limitations.

Judge Henderson is commonly referred to by those who practice before him as "Hatchet," a nickname he did not get by being warm and fuzzy. Legend has it that he got the name after various lawyers left his courtroom with fewer testicles than they had entered with.

Over the years, my charm has been even less effective on judges than it has been on women, but Hatchet Henderson has been the most resistant of all.

He's generally impartial, torturing both the prosecution and defense equally. But in the original trial, I felt that he sided with the prosecution more than he should have, and his comments at the sentencing seemed to confirm that. I doubt he will be terribly sympathetic to Joey's getting another shot, but the system doesn't allow for me to go judge shopping. It's going to be Hatchet all the way.

The actual filing is a formality, done with the clerk, and Hike heads down to the courthouse to do it. I call Vince to give him a heads-up that it will be filed in twenty minutes, and he almost seems appreciative. And human.

There are reporters assigned to the courthouse from various local outlets, and they will pick up on it when it's filed. But they'll have to digest it, and follow up, while Vince will have all his journalistic ducks in a row.

It's a half hour later that Vince calls and says, "I just spoke to Dylan."

"You did?"

"Of course. I had to give him a chance to comment before we went to press."

"And?"

"I should have taped the call; you would

174

have loved it. He went absolutely nuts; there's nothing he said that I can print."

"Did he deny it?"

"Does 'It's bullshit, it's bullshit, it's bullshit' constitute a denial? Then he mentioned something about 'nailing Carpenter to the wall for this.' It was the most fun I've had in a really long time."

"Glad I was able to brighten your day," I say.

"He should be calling you any minute."

"No, not a chance. He might call me, but first he'll be digging out the file and figuring out what happened, and how culpable he is. He'll want to know exactly where he stands right away. I know I would."

"When will you get this in court?"

"We asked for an immediate hearing, due to the gravity of the miscarriage of justice. If I know Hatchet, he'll be crazed about the possibility that Dylan screwed up the trial by violating the discovery rules. He'll want to get to the bottom of this as soon as possible."

"Let me know."

"I will. But Vince, you know this can't be contained anymore, right?" I'm telling him that it's no longer a story his newspaper can dominate, that other news organizations will be all over it.

"I hear you, but we were the first ones in. We got to have all the fun."

At twelve thousand feet, Simon Ryerson couldn't feel the poverty. Not that he was looking for it. In fact, his attention wasn't really on the poor villages at all, which were tucked into the basins below the focus of Simon's attention.

He was staring at the Montaro River and the massive, aptly named Montaro Dam that kept it under control. It was a significant structure, probably the most impressive Simon had seen since his South American travels began.

"How long did it take to build?" Simon asked.

The pilot, Victor Lescano, shrugged. "There is no easy answer to that. It has been here in some form for centuries, but as the need became greater, more work was done. More work is always being done."

"How long will it take to come down?"

Lescano smiled, though there was no

humor in it. "Not centuries. Minutes." He pointed down toward the villages. "They will have very little time, and nowhere to go."

"Do not warn them."

This time Lescano did not smile. "Do not tell me my job," he said. "We are committed to this, once we get the money."

"You will have it. When will the explosives be planted?"

"They are in place already," Lescano said.

Ryerson was surprised and pleased to hear this. "Show me the airfield."

Lescano nodded and turned the helicopter toward the east. Within thirty-five minutes they were at the airfield, with a runway surprisingly large and clearly adequate.

"Excellent," said Ryerson. "Now all we need is the cargo."

"That is being taken care of."

"I've heard that before, but the matter is growing more urgent now."

This surprised Lescano; it was the first time Ryerson had ever indicated that things weren't going perfectly smoothly. "You are having difficulty?"

"Nothing unexpected, and nothing that can't be easily handled. But we prefer to move quickly. Which brings us back to the cargo."

"Nothing like this has ever been done before," Lescano said. "It cannot be accomplished overnight."

"The money you will be making is equally unprecedented."

Lescano didn't respond to that. There was no need to; they both knew the enormous amount of money that was on the line here.

"Have matters been cleared with your man at the Transportation Department?" Ryerson asked.

"Yes."

"Good. I like a civilized country in which money carries the day."

Lescano pointed to the villages, receding as they flew away. "Those people have no money."

Ryerson nodded. "And they will not carry the day."

"I have no idea who that is," I say, when Sam shows me the picture. "But I do know you shouldn't have taken it."

"It was easy," Sam says. "No problem."

"Finding the location was enough," I say, though I'm actually happy Sam did much more than that. I just don't want to encourage him too much, because I don't want him taking risks in the future.

"I figured if someone took the phone outside the house, then it's probably not Carmine's. We just need to find out who this guy is."

"Sam, this is a big help. Thanks."

He waves me off. "No sweat. Glad to do it."

I call Pete Stanton to confirm he'll be at the precinct this morning. He says that he will.

"I need your help," I say. "I'll be there in fifteen minutes."

"That'll barely give me time to get my hair done," he says, and hangs up.

"Let's go," I say to Sam.

"You want me to go with you?" he asks, his pleasure at being asked obvious.

"Absolutely."

When we get to the precinct, we're quickly brought back to Pete's office. When he sees us he says, "Well, if it isn't the Hardy boys."

"If you would catch an occasional criminal, we wouldn't have to," I say, and then put the picture that Sam had taken on his desk.

"Who's that?" Pete asks.

"That's what we were hoping you could tell us."

"I don't have the slightest idea. Give me a hint."

"He hangs out at Carmine Desimone's house."

"And how would you two know that?"

"We ran a stakeout," I say. "Staked the whole thing right out. You should try it sometime."

Pete starts to say something, but then just shakes his head in disgust. "Wait here," he says, and then walks out of the office, leaving Sam and me sitting there.

"He's got an attitude, huh?" Sam asks.

I shake my head. "He was just showing

off for you."

It's about five minutes before Pete comes back, still holding the picture, but with a cop he introduces as Carl Griffith. "Carl knows him."

"Who is he?"

Pete jumps in before Carl can answer. "First tell me you won't be going near him. I don't want to have to start running a tab at Charlie's."

"If I talk to him, it will be on a witness stand. Or Marcus will be with me."

That's good enough for Pete; he knows Marcus's talents very well. He turns to Sam, who says, "Don't look at me; I'm just an accountant."

Pete nods the OK to Carl, who says, "His name is Tommy Iurato. He is a seriously dangerous individual."

"He works for Carmine Desimone?" I ask.

Carl nods. "A member of the family going on eight years. From the new school."

"What does that mean?"

"You know that phrase, 'Honor among thieves'?"

I nod. "What about it?"

"The new school doesn't teach that."

"Is it possible he's operating independently of Carmine?"

Carl shakes his head. "I would strongly

doubt it. Iurato's not a leader; he's a follower. He wouldn't hesitate to kill you, but it wouldn't be his idea."

"Could he be taking orders from someone else, besides Carmine?" I ask.

Pete jumps in. "Like who?"

I shrug. "I don't know. But I believe Nicky Fats was murdered in that house. Is there any chance Carmine ordered it done?"

"No way," says Carl.

"Then maybe someone else did."

Carl seems adamant about this. "It is inconceivable that Carmine would tolerate it."

"Maybe Carmine had no choice."

Carl shakes his head. "Carmine got to be Carmine by making sure he always has choices."

Sam and I leave Pete's office and head back to mine. On the way, I say, "I need you to do something, but you have to promise me that you won't leave your office to do it."

"Come on, Andy, don't put it that way. Tell me what you're talking about."

"Not until you promise; these are dangerous people."

"Fine," Sam says, no doubt lying through his teeth. "I promise."

"You've got Iurato's phone number, the

one that Alex called."

"Right."

"Can you find out who Iurato calls? And who calls him?"

"Of course."

"From your office?"

"Fine. From my office. You happy?"

"Thrilled."

I had an affair with Rita Gordon.

I say it that way because it sounds really adult, and it fits the technical definition of affair, which includes the words "an event or series of events." What we had was an "event," though certainly not a series. There is also nothing in the definition that says the "event" has to last more than forty-five minutes, and ours didn't.

It was back when Laurie had moved to Wisconsin, and I thought we were over for good. Rita was in retrospect probably doing me a favor, sort of welcoming me back to the dating world.

It was a wild forty-five minutes.

Since then we have reverted back to our previous type of relationship, which consists of friendly, usually sexual banter. Rita is the court clerk, so I'm able to occasionally combine the banter with information gathering, and this is one of those times.

"How did Hatchet react to the petition?"
I ask. I'm in her office, so I can't claim that
I just coincidentally ran into her. Therefore
I come right to the point.

She laughs. "You know I can't tell you
that," she says.

"Then no more sexual favors for you."

"How will I live?"

"It will be an empty existence; you'll
spend all your time yearning. Come on,
what did he say?"

"Haven't you seen the ruling yet?"

"Did he issue it?"

She nods. "This morning. We faxed it to
your office."

"I wasn't there, and Edna probably didn't
check it. The fax machine is almost twenty
feet from her chair. Have you got a copy?"

She opens a file, takes out a document,
and hands it to me to read. It's only one
page, addressed to Dylan and me, ordering
that we appear to have a preliminary discussion of the matter tomorrow morning.

"Good old Hatchet," I say. I'm pleased by
the result, but a little taken aback by the
timing. It's even faster than I expected,
though I'll certainly be prepared to make
my arguments.

I thank Rita and leave. I call Edna in the
office and ask if I received a fax, and she

says, "I think I heard the machine, but I haven't gotten over there yet."

She tells me that Willie Miller was in looking for me, so I head for the building in Haledon that houses the Tara Foundation, the rescue group that I run with Willie and his wife, Sondra.

Willie has led a rather interesting life. He spent seven years in prison for a murder he didn't commit, and I successfully represented him in a retrial. A follow-up civil suit netted him ten million dollars.

Not too long ago, while helping me on a case, he thwarted a major terrorist attack on a natural gas plant near Boston and established himself as a national hero. He even ghostwrote a successful book about the event, and at some point he intends to read it.

Yet Willie and Sondra spend their days at our foundation building, taking care of the dogs we've rescued, and making sure they get adopted into good homes.

Sondra is at the desk in the reception area when I arrive, and she tells me that Willie is in the back playing with the dogs. "He's worried about you," she says. "He wants to help."

I head into the back, and, sure enough, Willie's throwing tennis balls across the large play area, and the dogs are having a great time running and fetching. It looks like a great way to spend the day; instead of law school, maybe I should have gone to fetch school.

When he sees me, he comes over and gives me a fist bump. Fist-bumping is not a strength of mine; I simply cannot do it in a way that looks cool, and doesn't hurt. Besides, the greeting world is moving too fast for me; I've only recently semi-mastered high-fiving, and now all of a sudden fists are the way to go.

"Tell me about these guys that are after you," he says, obviously having heard about the incident on the highway.

I explain that I really don't know who sent the killer, but that I assume it has something to do with my investigation in the Desimone case.

"They're trying to scare you off?" he asks.

"I wish. I think they're trying to kill me off."

"I want to help," he says. "I'll watch out for you."

"Marcus is on the case."

I can see the relief on Willie's face. He's a black belt in karate, an immensely dangerous individual when crossed, but he knows that compared to Marcus he's a Cub Scout.

"Good," he says. "Laurie force you into it?"

"It was her idea, but forcing wasn't necessary."

"So as long as your ass is covered, how else can I help?"

"There's really nothing for you to do right now. If that changes I'll let you know. But with the case going on, I'm going to be here even less than usual."

"No problem. Me and Sondra got it under control."

"Thanks, Willie. I'm sorry about this." I'm constantly feeling guilty that I don't contribute enough time, but Willie truly seems to have no problem with it.

"You just let me know what I can do, you hear? Tell Marcus the same thing."

"I will."

"I don't want your ass getting shot up."

"I don't either."

"You going to get Joey out?"

"I hope so."

"Being inside is really bad," he says, remembering. "Being inside for something you didn't do is the worst."

"You could have come to me and told me what you were doing," Dylan says. We're standing near the defense table in the Passaic County Courthouse, waiting for the hearing to begin.

I nodded. "And you could have turned over the documents in discovery like you were obligated to."

"That's all bullshit."

Out of the corner of my eye, I see the bailiff stand, meaning he's about to announce Hatchet's arrival.

"You're about to have your chance to convince Hatchet of that."

We head to our respective chairs, and the bailiff introduces the Honorable Judge Henry Henderson. He comes in looking like Pissed Off Judge Henry Henderson, a scowl on his face. Of course, Hatchet looking annoyed is not exactly a news event; if he smiled it would be reason to alert the media.

Vince's story, which was picked up by other media outlets, has generated some interest. The gallery is about half full, and it seems like most of them are reporters. If anything, that has a tendency to make Hatchet more cantankerous, but that's OK with me, because for a change I don't expect to be the one on the receiving end.

"Counsel for Joseph Desimone has filed a brief with this court seeking a retrial for the double murder conviction of Mr. Desimone. You have read the document, Mr. Campbell?"

"Yes, Your Honor."

Hatchet turns to me. "As I'm sure you are aware, most of the items you cite would not have gotten you through the door today."

"I believe much of our new evidence is compelling, Your Honor, especially when supported by our witnesses."

"What a surprise," he says, drily. "Moving right along, this hearing will focus on the defense's contention that exculpatory evidence was unlawfully withheld in discovery."

He turns to Dylan, picking up the folder on his desk, which I assume contains the brief. "Included in this, as I am sure you have noted, is a letter from Lieutenant Chris McKenney of the Montana State Police. Said document is addressed to you, Mr.

Campbell, and I'm paraphrasing accurately here, informs you that members of a Montana militia group had vowed to murder Mr. Solarno.

"Coincidentally, it is the same Mr. Solarno whom Mr. Desimone stands convicted of murdering. It also states that Lieutenant McKenney followed up the letter with a phone call, and spoke to you directly, during which time he repeated the same information."

He puts the folder down and leans forward slightly, peering ominously at Dylan. "You have a satisfactory response to this?"

Dylan stands. "I do, Your Honor. First, I would remind the court that these events transpired more than six years ago, and I have had many cases since, quite a few of which have been before Your Honor. I —"

Hatchet interrupts. "Try and finish your speech before it becomes seven years since these events. And if you'll recall, I didn't ask if you had a response. I specified a 'satisfactory' response."

Dylan nods. "Yes, Your Honor. But since my memory of these events is obviously not perfect, I've called all the files from the warehouse, and gone over them methodically. I can find no evidence that this letter was ever received by my office, and I certainly have no independent recollection of it."

"You would acknowledge that withholding such a letter, had you received and been aware of it, would have been a serious violation of the laws of evidence?" Hatchet asks.

"Certainly, Your Honor. Had that been the case, I would be so stating it today."

"Are you disputing that the letter was sent?" Hatchet asks.

"I have no reason to doubt the veracity of the officer; I simply have no recollection or independent evidence of ever having read the letter or spoken to him."

Hatchet turns to me. "Mr. Carpenter?"

Hike hands me two pieces of paper. "May I approach, Your Honor?"

He allows it, and I walk forward and hand him one of the pages. The other I hand to Dylan on the way back. "Your Honor, this is a copy of Lieutenant McKenney's contemporaneous notes, taken during and just after his conversation with Mr. Campbell. You'll note that he writes that Mr. Campbell expressed his appreciation for the information contained in the letter."

"That document was not in the filing, Your Honor," Dylan says, a stricken look on his face.

"Oops," I say. Then, "I didn't think it was

necessary to include it, Your Honor. I had assumed Mr. Campbell would belatedly acknowledge the communication."

"And you wanted to, I believe the phrase is, sandbag him," Hatchet points out.

"Any wounds the prosecution is suffering here are self-inflicted," I say.

"Mr. Campbell?"

"I'm sorry, Your Honor, but I still have no independent recollection of any of this."

I move in for the kill. "Your Honor, since the prosecutor is not even attempting to affirmatively refute this evidence, merely saying he doesn't remember, I think our position should be accepted as the truth of the matter. Certainly it is highly unlikely that a Montana State Police officer would forge a document, as well as his notes, regarding a crime here in New Jersey that he has no other connection to."

I continue. "I would also point out that a good deal of evidence is not included in our petition."

"Why is that?"

"Because had we been aware of the exculpatory evidence from Montana, we would have had time to investigate and develop it, likely leading to even more compelling evidence. Mr. Campbell's violation of the rules of discovery prevented that."

"Your Honor —" Dylan begins, clearly angry, but Hatchet cuts him off.

"Mr. Campbell, unless you have something substantive to add beyond pleading a faulty memory and filing system, I suggest we leave it right where it is."

It stops Dylan in his tracks; I'm not even sure Marcus can protect me from what he's thinking.

"I'll be issuing my ruling shortly. I trust no one is in suspense as to what that ruling will be. This hearing is adjourned."

It's dark when I leave my office, a sure sign that I'm working on a case. Actually, the fact that I'm in my office at all is a sure sign as well. But working past dark is not exactly my M.O.

My parking spot is in an uncovered lot at the end of the block, and I'm halfway there when a large black sedan pulls up alongside me. The rear door opens, simultaneous with my heart hitting the sidewalk. There can't be any doubt that I'm about to die; not even Marcus will have time to intervene.

But the person in the backseat, calling me by name, is Willie Miller. "Andy, get in the car," he says.

It's dark in the car, and I can't see who is with him. Certainly he's not alone, because he's in the back and obviously not driving. So I hesitate; I trust Willie, but he could have a gun trained on him, or something.

"Come on, Andy. It's OK."

I look quickly around for Marcus, but I don't see him. I've got two choices; I can trust Willie and get in, or I can turn and run like a coward.

Cowardly running is by far my first choice, but I force myself to do otherwise. I don't think there is anything anyone could do to get Willie to force me into a trap.

Once I'm in the car, I see that Willie is alone in the backseat. However, the front seat is occupied by two people, who are each so wide that at first I think it's three of them. The driver doesn't turn around, simply pulls back onto the road and drives off.

The person in the passenger seat turns to face me, and I recognize him as Joseph Russo. Russo and I have never met, but I've seen his picture in the paper quite a few times, though never on the sports page, and absolutely never in the comics.

Russo is number two to Dominic Petrone, which is to say he is a powerful figure among people who regard law enforcement as the bad guys. Petrone is in his mid-sixties, a courtly type who seems more like a CEO than a don. Russo is much younger, but is a throwback to the older, more violent school. He is also said to be Petrone's choice to succeed him.

A lot of people would want to get on Russo's good side, if he had one. But I am aware that he and Willie have a relationship of sorts, and Russo considers himself indebted to Willie, with good reason.

When Willie was in prison, just a few months before the retrial, Russo was there as well. It was the one conviction on Russo's record, and he was only gone for a year.

One day three men decided to make a name for themselves, or perhaps they were being paid for their actions, but they cornered Russo in the exercise yard. They had makeshift weapons, which would have been more than enough to do the intended job of killing Russo.

The plan was a good one, but the execution of it left something to be desired. They neglected to notice that Willie was there, observing what was happening. He had never met Russo, but had an instinct that in any three-to-one fight, he belonged on the side of the one.

Russo wound up with minor injuries, while Willie put the three assailants in the hospital. Willie heard that they met with even more decisive justice from Petrone's people shortly thereafter, but that didn't interest him much either way.

For all of his faults, like the fact that he

murders people and commits other criminal acts, Russo recognizes a debt, and he has been helpful to Willie in the past. I'm not sure why the three of us are together now, but I'm about to find out.

Willie breaks the ice. "Andy . . . Joseph Russo. Joe . . . Andy Carpenter."

He makes no motion to shake hands, so I don't either. Instead I just say, "Hey." That's how we tough guys talk.

He doesn't return the "hey," a slight I'm willing to overlook. Instead he says, "You're asking questions about Carmine Desimone?"

Technically, I haven't been asking questions about Carmine, except to our investigative team. Willie, as a member of that team, has clearly gone to Russo to get the answers.

I nod. "Yes, I'm trying to find out whether he had Nicky Fats killed, and why he doesn't seem to be helping Joey, and why he sent someone to kill me." I don't know if that last part is true, but I talk as if it is.

"I don't know about any of that," Russo says.

"Great," I say. "That clears that up."

"Willie's a friend of mine," Russo says. "So he says you're OK, I say you're OK."

"I'm definitely OK."

"Until I learn otherwise" is Russo's quali-
fier.

"You won't; I'm completely OK." All I
want to do is get out of this car; there will
be time to strangle Willie later.

"So what I say stays with you, and me,
and Willie."

He doesn't seem to consider the driver a
human worth including in our little secrets,
but I don't mention this. "Fine. Sure."

"Carmine came to us," Russo says. "A few
months ago."

"Us? Meaning you and Dominic?"

His voice gets about four hundred degrees
colder. "Leave Mr. Petrone out of this."

Russo is obviously fiercely protective of
his boss, Dominic Petrone, to the point of
not even discussing him with outsiders like
me. My guess is that Dominic doesn't know
Russo is talking to me. "OK . . . sure. Won't
mention him again. What did Carmine
want?"

"Some of our people."

"Your people? What did he want your
people for?

Russo looks at Willie with raised eyebrows,
as if asking Willie why he wanted him to
talk to this idiot, meaning me. "He wanted
them to do what they do," he says.

I nod. "Makes sense. What did you say?"

"We said 'no fucking way.' "

I notice that Willie, who's been silent, is nodding in agreement at everything both Russo and I say. "Joseph, why would Carmine need your people? Doesn't he have people of his own?"

"So, you finally asked the right question. He don't trust his people. Without trust, you ain't got shit."

Words to live by.

"Do you know why he doesn't trust them?"

"No."

"Do you know if Nicky Fats was murdered?"

"No."

"Is there anything else you can tell me?"

He thinks for a moment, then says, "Yeah. Carmine was scared."

Hatchet issues the ruling at 9:00 A.M., less than twenty-four hours after the hearing. I think he would have issued it earlier, but it probably took awhile to get it scathing enough for his satisfaction.

It calls for a new trial at the earliest possible date, and excoriates Dylan for the violation of his discovery obligations. It stops just short of accusing him of knowingly withholding the evidence, because he could not be certain of that.

But he minimizes the difference between intentional and unintentional, describing them as almost equally egregious, since if it were unintentional, it would speak to "extreme incompetence."

I head down to the prison to meet with Joey, and while I'm waiting to be brought in to see him, I try and figure out how this conversation can go well.

Unfortunately, it can't. I am certainly

delivering great news. To be telling him the opposite, that we didn't get the new trial, would be devastating. But in the process, I'm going to be doing that which I always try to avoid . . . building false hope.

The truth is that if we had the information we have now, back at the time of the first trial, we still would have lost. We need much more, and have very little time to get it. Making matters even tougher is the fact that back then we were investigating fresh occurrences; now we are rehashing trails that have been cold for six years.

Joey takes one look at me and says, "We got it. I can see it in your face."

I nod. "We got it."

He doesn't say anything for at least a minute. He seems to be trying to control his emotions and process this information, and that can't be easy to do. If hopelessness is the bottom of the human condition, then it's impossible to overstate how elevating its removal can be.

He wants to hear every detail about the hearing, and literally asks if he can get a copy of the transcript. I promise to get him one, and then launch into my ten-minute speech about how he shouldn't get too hopeful, and how precarious his situation remains.

It doesn't seem to take; nothing I say can diminish the joy he is feeling. I think the only way I can bring him down would be to have Hike deliver the transcript. After a one-on-one chat with Hike, Joey will want to plead guilty, and then hang himself in his cell.

I bring up the rather weird goings-on in the Desimone family, though I do so carefully. I certainly don't want to reveal anything that Joseph Russo told me. He made it clear that it was in confidence, and there are few promises I'm more inclined to keep than those I make to a mob boss.

But it certainly seems likely that it was the Desimones who hired the man who tried to kill Marcus and me. I've pissed plenty of other people off, but none very recently.

Joey surprises me by blurting out, "I called my father. I'm sorry, I know you told me not to."

"That's OK, Joey. He's your father. What did he say?"

"That you were a smart guy, and that I should listen to you. He also said that Nicky's death was an accident. And he told me to be careful in here."

This last statement makes me angry, not at Joey or Carmine, but at myself. Maybe my mind is atrophying from not working often enough, but one fact completely slipped by me.

If someone's goal was to eliminate me, it wouldn't have been anything personal. It would have been to stop me from pursuing the case, and from trying to get Joey out of jail. I've been thinking that the bad guys therefore want Joey in jail, but that's not it at all; they just want me to stop trying to get him out, because of what I might uncover in the process.

Which means that Joey is in as much danger as I am, maybe more.

"I want to get you protected in here. You need to go into solitary," I say.

"I've been protecting myself for a long time."

"Nobody had reason to kill you before. Except for your personality."

He laughs. "Thanks."

"I'm serious about protecting you, Joey. If there's no you, there's no case, there's no investigation."

"You'd keep at it," he says.

I nod. "I probably would, but they wouldn't have any way of knowing that."

He thinks about it for a few moments, then, "No. I want to stay where I am. If someone takes a run at me, I'll handle it. And I'll find out who sent them."

I want to say, "It might be your father that sends them," but I don't. And I have no luck talking him into taking the protection that solitary would offer.

As I'm about to leave, he says, "Andy, there's no way I can thank you for this."

"We haven't done anything yet."

"You've given me a reason to get up tomorrow."

We have one major advantage heading into this trial. We called very few witnesses last time, because we had very few to call. But Dylan had plenty, as he successfully made his case. Those witnesses are all now on the record, and must stick to their story. Knowing what they're going to say makes it easier for me to challenge them.

Also, the roles are at least somewhat reversed here. Usually the prosecution is on offense most of the time, since they are the one doing the charging. The defense is aptly named, since it must fend off and refute those charges. But while Dylan will still present and make his case, he must now primarily worry about what we will throw at him.

I hope and expect that he will spend time and energy demonstrating that the Montana militiamen, who made the threats, had nothing to do with the killing. That would be a waste of time and energy, because I am going to spend very little time making the case for their guilt.

I don't think there's any chance that one of those dopes made it to New Jersey and murdered the Solarnos. The significance I attach to them is not as suspects, but as customers of Solarno's illegal armaments.

I want to demonstrate, both through logic and actual evidence, that Solarno wasn't limiting his dealings to that one group, but that he was also selling to other, even more dangerous people. If he cheated the Montana group, then he might very likely have cheated other customers as well.

Cheating victims with rifles make good suspects.

Our case has to focus on that which we have recently learned about Solarno. We need to understand exactly what he was doing and who he was doing it with. And we have to turn the people that are trying to stop us into unwitting helpers.

Solarno went relatively uninvestigated and unmentioned last time, and that's going to change dramatically in the retrial. For all the hand-wringing that often takes place about defense lawyers attempting to put "the victim on trial," that is what is going to happen here, or we'll have no chance.

I tell Laurie that Solarno is to be her prime focus; we need to re-create his life. We need to know whom he called and whom he met with. If he shared his wife's penchant for infidelity, we must know whom he saw and how often he saw her.

If we can get the jury to believe that he was the target, then we're close to home free, since the prosecution has gone on record as saying Joey's motive was to kill Karen Solarno.

I call Edward Young, who surprisingly takes my call on the first try. Maybe Robby Divine beat him in golf again. In any event, I tell him that I'm going to need all of the business records of Solarno Shrimp Corporation, with particular focus on the six months preceding the murder.

"I assume we've got it somewhere," he says. "I'll put someone on it."

"Thanks. I'm going to subpoena it through the court, simply as a formality, but if you can get someone started on it sooner, that would be a help."

"No problem."

"What about phone records? Would you have records of calls Solarno might have made or received from his office?"

He thinks for a moment, and then says, "I wouldn't think so; doesn't seem like we'd

209

have any reason to keep that."

"Probably not," I say. It's not a big deal to me; I can subpoena it from the phone company, or have Sam steal it from their computer. I'll probably do both.

"Is that it?" he asks.

"Almost. I'm going to be putting your name on our witness list."

He hesitates, and when he speaks, I can tell by the sound of his voice that he's not enthusiastic about the prospect. "Why? I have nothing to say about your case."

"I know, but I might need you to set the stage for Solarno's company. And I probably won't call you, but I have to put your name on the list in case I need to."

"I do a lot of traveling," Edward says.

"You'd get plenty of notice."

"I think I'm finished playing golf with Robby."

When I get off the phone, I call Hike and tell him to add Edward Young to the witness list. I doubt that I'll call him, but the more names I have on the list, the more preparatory work Dylan has to do.

Besides, it makes me feel like I actually have a witness list, which would be just a few steps away from actually having a case.

Tommy Iurato was annoyed by the decision.

Not so much because he disagreed with the strategy; strategy was not his thing, and he was not privy to all the factors that were called into play.

When the word came down not to continue to go after Carpenter, Iurato argued the point. He didn't make a full-blown argument — that wasn't his style. What he did was point out that the hit would be successful if again ordered, that the screw-up on the highway would not be repeated.

Carpenter had Marcus Clark protecting him, and while Iurato was well aware of Clark's reputation and ability, he was still just one person. Iurato was prepared to send in enough manpower that the job would get done.

Iurato was worried about Carpenter. Not from any particular knowledge about what the lawyer was doing, or what he might have

211

already learned. His worry stemmed from the fact that he had been told to hit him once, the hit that failed on the highway.

The fact that the hit had been ordered then must have meant that he was a danger to the operation. Carpenter was a prominent figure, and his death would have attracted attention and investigation. If that was a risk worth taking, then Carpenter must have been a significant concern. The fact that Iurato was now being instructed not to remove that danger was troubling to him.

The operation itself meant everything to Iurato. He had no use for the conventions of the traditional Mafia families. The very idea of "the family" was ludicrous to him.

He had his own family, and they remained separate and apart from his work. And that's what this operation was . . . work. No different than if he worked for IBM or General Motors. He did his job, and he was paid for it.

Actually, the pay was the one difference. Maybe the presidents of those companies received pay like Iurato was about to receive, but he doubted it. It was going to be more money than he could use in ten lifetimes, and no one was going to stand in the way. Not Carpenter, not Marcus Clark, not Joey Desimone . . . nobody.

Old-timers used to tell Iurato about being "in the life," which was how they described the criminal enterprises, the "families," in which they worked. They never considered leaving that life, and probably would not have been allowed to if they tried.

The day they made their bones was the best day of their lives, and it dictated how they would spend the rest of their years. Their loyalty was a given, almost never to be questioned.

But not Tommy Iurato. He was going to walk away, and he dared anyone to try and stop him. He would retire just like any other businessman, only he would be younger and wealthier than any of them when he did it.

And the idea of lifetime loyalty struck Iurato as outdated and ridiculous. Didn't employees in other industries move from company to company? Why wasn't their commitment and loyalty dictated to be forever? They went where the money was, or where the conditions were more to their liking.

And when they wanted to, for whatever reason, they left.

And Iurato would leave. He wouldn't wind up like Carmine, or that pathetic Nicky Fats. The old-timers could take "the life" and shove it.

But Iurato was told no, Carpenter was not to be hit, and neither was Joey Desimone, at least for now. So it worried him, but at that point there was nothing he could do.

If and when that changed, he'd be ready to act.

When it came to going to work, Edward Young was old-fashioned. Which is to say, when he was not traveling, he got up every morning and went to an office.

He clearly didn't have to. Edward insisted on state-of-the-art communications within his companies, and he certainly had that. He was in touch in any number of ways, all the time, and the truth is he could easily conduct at least the investment side of his business, and most of the rest of it, from anywhere.

The companies he controlled and invested in were all over the world, so except for occasional visits to keep them on their toes, in person contact was not required, and not desired by Edward. And Edward Young had reached a position in which, if he didn't desire something, it didn't happen.

So his routine when he was not traveling was fairly rigid. He would wake up at his

Alpine, New Jersey, home at 6:00 A.M., exercise in his gym for an hour, shower, have a small breakfast, and leave for the office. His driver, Roger Lavin, was told to have the car out front at seven forty-five, so that he could be at his desk in midtown Manhattan by nine, thirty minutes before the market opened.

It was also early enough that he could conduct business with associates in Europe before they left for the day. Asia was a different story, and the timing often forced him to deal with issues there from home.

The limo was itself an office, with high-speed wireless computer and phone connections, and wireless combination printer, fax, copier, and scanner. Edward was a techie of sorts, and had been very exacting in his demands when the car was set up. It was a stretch limo, but one full set of seats had been removed, creating what felt like a spacious office.

There is probably not a person who lives in North Jersey, and commutes by car over the George Washington Bridge each day, who doesn't have a preferred route to avoid the traffic.

For Edward, that meant avoiding the Palisades Interstate Parkway at all costs, and wending his way down city streets into Fort

Lee, then circling and coming in the back way to the lower level of the bridge. It didn't circumvent all the traffic, but cut the traveling time by at least twenty minutes.

Twenty minutes of Edward Young's time was worth a lot of money.

On this particular morning, like every morning, Edward was not just sitting back, enjoying the scenery. He was always on the computer, or the phone, or reading the *Wall Street Journal*, but he was never looking around. Lavin had been driving Edward for eighteen years, and he certainly knew enough not to bother him, unless it was a matter of great importance.

So he was reading the *Journal* when the phone rang. It was one of his financial people, calling to say that a meeting had been scheduled for nine thirty. It concerned a company Edward was considering taking a large position in, and the purpose of the meeting was to make a presentation concerning the company and whether or not it would be a wise investment.

Because of the timing, Edward looked up to see where they were, and how much progress they were making. It was for that reason that he saw the car pull up next to them on the left, and saw the tinted window on the passenger side come down. Which is how he was able to see the gun.

Edward's reaction was instant; he dove down to the floor just as the barrage of bullets hit the car. The firing was indiscriminate, blowing out windows front and back.

He yelled, "Roger!," but didn't know whether his driver had been hit or not. It was certainly possible that the driver didn't hear him above the din, or that he hadn't heard the response.

It wasn't until he felt the limo crash into something, which turned out to be a parked car, that he believed his driver had been hurt. And it wasn't for six minutes, after the police had arrived on the scene, that he knew Roger Lavin was dead.

My cell phone rings when I'm walking Tara. We're having the first snowfall of the year, an inch or so, and Tara just loves it. She rolls around on her back, in what certainly seems like dog ecstasy. Then she picks up a small, fallen tree branch and holds it in her mouth as if it's a treasure. Which it is.

I feel a little guilty going so slowly, since I know Marcus must be watching us somewhere from Marcus-land, and being both cold and bored out of his mind. I don't see him, but I know, and hope, he is there.

I don't usually bring my cell phone on my walks with Tara, but I do when I'm in the middle of a case. She's pretty understanding about the interruptions; she knows that my work brings in money, and she knows how her biscuits are buttered, or something like that.

I see on the caller ID that it's Hike, which makes me not want to answer it. In fact, it makes me want to put the phone on the snowy ground and stomp on it. This is not a moment that calls out for Hike. No moment has ever existed that called out for Hike.

"Hello?"

"You may not be a good-luck charm, boss."

"What does that mean?" I ask.

"An attempt was made on Edward Young's life this morning. His chauffeur was killed."

This is stunning news. "Was Edward hurt?"

"Doesn't seem like it. But the news is pretty sketchy."

I question Hike, but there aren't many details, other than where the shooting took place, and that the assailants escaped the scene.

I was initially willing to accept the idea that Nicky Fats's death right after talking to me was a coincidence, but there's no chance of that here. Soon after I talked to Edward Young, and almost immediately after I put him on the witness list, someone tried to gun him down.

Nicky Fats spent his life with dangerous people, many of whom could reasonably be thought to be his enemy. Edward Young is a respected businessman, an investor and financier. He no doubt deals with killers, but their weapons of choice would be their checkbooks, or their lawyers.

Tara is fine with our cutting our walk short, in return for some biscuits. I tell Hike I'll meet him at the office, so we can plan a strategy for dealing with this new turn of events.

It would seem to make the most sense that the attempt to silence Edward was to prevent him from speaking to me. There are, however, two problems with that.

First of all, he had already spoken to me, twice. How would the killers know that he had not yet told me the information they were afraid he would reveal?

Second, he has given me no indication that he knows anything that could be of value to my case. Why would the killers think otherwise? Is it possible that he has key information, but is somehow unaware of its significance?

I put in a call to Edward, but get no further than one of his assistants. Reaching him is now going to be tough; he's a smart guy, and if he has a well-developed self-preservation instinct, then he must know I am the kiss of death.

In addition to the tragedy of the chauffeur getting killed, the attempt on Edward's life highlights and continues a frustrating pattern for our case. Events are happening, large and small, which convince me that we are on the right track, but which will not be admissible in court.

Large things like the efforts to kill both Edward and me, and less significant things like Alex Solarno calling Tommy Iurato after I left his house, all represent conclusive evidence to me that someone is trying to stop our investigation. Someone is afraid of what we will find, which makes me all the more anxious to find it.

But all of those things are legally unrelated to Joey's case. The attack today represents the clearest example of that; there is simply no way we can demonstrate relevance to Hatchet's satisfaction, which means the jury will not hear it.

But either Edward has information which can bridge that gap and make it relevant and admissible, or someone thinks he does. He went on the witness list, and they tried to kill him. I simply must find out what he knows, or what the killers think he knows.

My only real link to any of this is Tommy Iurato, so I call Sam to find out if he's traced the phone records. He answers on the first ring, as happens every single time I call him.

"I was just going to call you," Sam says, opening the conversation.

"You have Iurato's phone records?"

"I sure do, and you're going to find them very interesting."

"Can you bring them over right away?" I ask.

"No."

"Why not?"

"Because you made me promise I wouldn't leave my office."

I laugh. "You are released from your promise on a temporary basis."

"I'll be right over."

He made four calls in the last three months, and received six. Two of the received calls were from Alex Solarno, one just after you left, and the other the next day."

"That's it? How could he only make four calls? I make more than that in a month ordering Chinese food."

"That's it, Andy. I rechecked it twice."

"He's either the least sociable mob hit man I've ever met, or he's got another phone. You know who the calls were with?"

He nods. "Except for the Alex Solarno calls, every one that was made or received was from or to the same number. And it's not even listed in a fake name."

"Who was it?

"Simon Ryerson."

"The name sounds familiar," I say.

"Maybe you represented him. He spent two and a half years in jail. Got out about four years ago."

"What was he in for?"

"Fraud. But high-class stuff; this guy didn't go around passing bum checks in bodegas."

Sam goes on to tell me that Ryerson was a Harvard Business School graduate who had gotten something of a reputation turning around troubled companies. They were mostly small, relatively new companies that were in danger of going under. Ryerson came in with sound but aggressive business techniques and stabilized them. He was well paid for his efforts.

Sam gives me a list of the companies Ryerson worked for, and then says, "But then he got greedy, and turned one of the companies into his own private ATM. Hasn't really been heard from since, though now he heads up SR Finance. 'SR' is Simon Ryerson; pretty clever name, huh?"

"Where is his office?"

"Englewood. He lives in Englewood Cliffs."

Englewood Cliffs is a very upscale town near the George Washington Bridge. If Ryerson is living there, it's likely he has managed to tuck some real money away.

"Thanks, Sam. You did great on this."

"So what's my next assignment, boss?"

"Dig into Ryerson's life. Credit card

receipts, traveling, whatever. I want to know as much about him as I can, with a particular focus on the past year."

"You want me to keep an eye on him?"

My knee-jerk reaction is to say no, but I've got to do something to move the case along. "It's not a bad idea . . . if you can do it from a distance, with no contact whatsoever. And I'd prefer you didn't shoot him either."

"Great. Willie and I can do it together . . . trade off when we need to. Willie told me he wants to help."

This is feeling like a huge mistake. "Will you tell Willie the ground rules?"

He nods. "Yup. No contact, keep a distance, no shooting."

"OK. And any problems you call me. Any danger, call Marcus first, then me."

"Will do."

When Sam leaves, I call Laurie and tell her about Ryerson, tasking her to find out whatever she can about him as well.

It's hard to figure what connection Ryerson might have to the Desimone crime family. When it comes to illegalities, what Ryerson has done in the past and what the Desimones do on a daily basis represent apples and oranges.

Perhaps Ryerson is using his business and

financial acumen to launder money for them. He could be getting a percentage of the action for doing so.

I hope that's not the case, because if it is then it has nothing to do with the Solarno murders, and is therefore of no value to me. Just because Alex Solarno was in contact with Iurato, and Iurato has been in occasional contact with Ryerson, there is no link yet established to connect Ryerson with Solarno.

I need to find out if that link exists, and I need to do so quickly, as the trial is bearing down on us.

I make a quick trip to the prison to see if Joey has heard of Ryerson, but I'm not surprised that he hasn't. Joey has been cut off for more than six years, and Ryerson hasn't been out of prison very long. There is little likelihood that their paths crossed, and Joey confirms that they hadn't.

Joey has a thousand questions for me about the upcoming trial and the state of our defense. I don't sugarcoat it; we are simply not making enough progress at this point, and don't have much time to turn things around.

"We'll get there," Joey says. "Look how far we've gotten already."

"There's a winner and a loser in this

game, Joey. They don't give partial credit. Unless we get all the way there, then we've gotten nowhere."

When Gino Bruni came into the room, Carmine Desimone closed the door. He had already determined that Tommy Iurato was out of the compound. Carmine had no doubt that the interior of the place was bugged for audio, though Carmine was sure he had disabled the only video camera. In any event, he didn't want to take a chance on being overheard.

So he turned up the music to a very high volume, so high that it was annoying to his ears, which represented the first time in his life that he didn't enjoy listening to Frankie Valli. But it was necessary, and Gino understood that.

So they talked into each other's ears, and even from a few inches away it was hard to hear. It was also humiliating to Carmine; he was not used to having to behave in this manner.

But that would soon be changing.

Everything would soon be changing.

"It's all set," said Bruni. "I spoke to Tommy."

"You told him exactly what we talked about?"

Bruni nodded. "Yes. He's to bring Ryerson to the meeting. Just the two of them, and just you and I. I said that you had a proposition for them, which would be good for all concerned."

"What did the prick say?"

"That they're always happy to talk."

"And you've got the people we need?"

"Three guys from Detroit. They're as good as they come. They'll be there that morning to set it up."

"Tommy is smart," Carmine said. "He'll bring extra muscle, just in case."

"We'll be ready for them."

"We'd better be."

They went over the details for the next ten minutes; Carmine wanted to make sure that everything was nailed down, that every possible eventuality was accounted for.

"This is going to put you back on top, Carmine. You're going to be bigger than ever. We're going to take back the family."

"You did good, Gino. We pull this off, and you're right there with me. And when I die, you will take control."

"You'll be here a long time, Carmine. I've learned a great deal from you, and I'll learn much more in the future."

Carmine smiled. "The first thing you'll learn is what happens to people who betray the family. There are many of those, and they will all suffer for it. Every one of them."

"They deserve their fate."

"We will get revenge for Nicky," Carmine said.

Gino promised to get back to Carmine when the final details were set, and when they had confirmation that Ryerson was coming. Carmine was sure that he would; Ryerson was the type to feel invulnerable and completely in charge.

It was a feeling Carmine had had himself for many years, and would soon have again.

As a former FBI agent, Jerry McCaskill has always known that crime doesn't pay. What he learned from his years in the Bureau is that stopping crime pays even less.

As law enforcement personnel go, FBI agents are paid quite well. But compared to people at the top of other professions, they are substantially undercompensated. So with three kids barreling toward college age, Jerry left the FBI to head up security at a start-up tech firm.

Financially, at least, he's never looked back. He got a bunch of stock when the company had its IPO, and he has a terrific salary, a large staff, and a bunch of perks. He's given a great deal of autonomy to make the security rules, and a healthy budget to implement and enforce them.

The company's offices are in Fort Lee, literally within walking distance of the George Washington Bridge, though I can't imagine why anyone would be interested in walking to the George Washington Bridge. Cindy Spodek had suggested that I talk to McCaskill about Carmine Desimone's criminal enterprise, since he had been in the Central New Jersey bureau's organized crime division.

Techno-systems Inc. occupies the top three floors of a building so modern it looks like it must have been finished this morning. Yet compared to the interior of their offices, the rest of the building seems like a prewar colonial. Techno clearly wants to convey the impression that they are on the cutting edge, and for all I know, they may be. I wouldn't recognize the cutting edge if I sliced my finger on it.

Jerry McCaskill comes out of the reception area to greet me with a big smile on his face, a firm handshake, and a sincere sounding "Nice to meet you, Andy." If a working FBI agent ever displayed this demeanor, they would send him for behavior modification treatments, with electroshock therapy the fallback position.

Once we're settled in his office, I thank him for seeing me. "I'm doing it for Cindy," he says. "She was a big help to me in the Bureau, and actually gave me a recommendation for this job."

"Good old Cindy."

"She's terrific, smart, and a great judge of people," he enthuses.

"Yes, she is." I'm agreeing quickly, in the hope of moving this along. The trial will start before he stops praising Cindy.

"She says you're a pain in the ass."

"She's not the sharpest tool in the law enforcement shed," I say.

He laughs. "I hear you're taking another shot at letting Joey Desimone walk?"

"This time he will."

"I didn't follow the first trial; I was out of town on an assignment. But I understand the jury didn't have to deliberate too long."

I certainly don't want to rehash my past failures, so I say, "Let's not talk about Joey. Let's talk about Carmine."

He nods. "OK. What about him?"

"I think he had Nicky Fats killed."

"Then you're not such a sharp tool yourself. There's no way."

"That's what everybody says."

"Everybody's right."

I tell him how this all started, about the comment Nicky Fats made to me, as it turned out just a few hours or so before he died. "He didn't decide at three o'clock in the afternoon to take a shower. Somebody killed him, and they killed him in Carmine's house."

"I doubt it," he says. "But let's assume for a moment that's true. Maybe it had nothing to do with what he said to you. Was there anyone else around?"

"No. And I would think you might be right, if it had ended there." I go on to tell him about the attempted hit on me on the highway, and the murder yesterday of Edward Young's driver. "It simply isn't possible that this is coincidental."

He thinks for a moment, and then nods. "OK, again let's assume you're right. Nicky Fats got killed, and the same people are coming after you, trying to stop your investigation. Even if that's all true, what are you doing here?"

Part of the truthful answer to that is I have nowhere else to go, and I want to at least fool myself with the illusion that I'm doing something productive. But I don't think I'll mention that.

"I've done some research on arrests and convictions of organized crime families, from Chicago to New York," I say.

"And?"

"And the Desimone family has been getting off easily. Any idea why that would be?" I'm taking a risk of angering him with that question, since for quite a while he was one of the main people who was in a position to arrest them.

But if he's angry, he's hiding it well. "Two reasons, which are in some way connected. First of all, there are manpower priorities within the Bureau, and our resources were not aimed at them in any targeted way. Second, they have been comparatively inactive for a while, which is likely why they were not targeted."

"Inactive?"

He nods. "Not totally, but they stayed in what you could call their low-key comfort zone. Prostitution, gambling, minor drug stuff . . . very little violence, or big-time drug involvement."

"Was that unusual for them?"

"Historically, yes. But their business model has had to change because they're not as insulated as they once were. The commitment by their people is not what it was. Less loyalty, less sense of honor, as law enforcement has made their lives more difficult."

"Which came first, the law enforcement success, or the lack of loyalty?"

He thinks about it for a moment. "Probably the success, but they sort of went hand in hand."

"And why were you guys suddenly able to pressure them?"

"A lot of reasons, but mostly attitude. When the system decides that enough is enough, it can be really powerful. And then the surveillance methods improved, to the point where we heard everything the bad guys said."

"What can you tell me about Tommy Iurato?" I ask.

"Typical of the new breed; loyalty is to himself. But very, very dangerous."

"Dangerous enough to kill Nicky Fats?"

"Dangerous enough to kill anyone, without a moment's hesitation."

"Like the Solarnos?"

He hesitates a moment. "The jury said your client killed the Solarnos."

"I don't believe he did."

He smiles. "Said the lawyer to the cop. The evidence was pretty convincing."

Arguing Joey's guilt or innocence is not why I'm here, so I ask, "Ever hear of Simon Ryerson?"

"No."

"He may not be a player in the case, but I need to find out if he is, and what his business is with the Desimones. Any idea how I can do that?"

He shrugs. "Ask him?"

Luis Zavala knew and accepted his limitations. He had already risen higher than the overwhelming majority of his countrymen by achieving the position of minister of the interior. While he used to dream of someday advancing even further, perhaps even to the presidency, he eventually came to understand that his current position was as high as he was going.

The forty-nine-year-old Zavala's limitations were political, and in no way related to his competence. He simply could not inspire the way the elected leaders could; he was neither eloquent nor charismatic. But he had done an excellent job since joining the government, a truth that was conceded to by officials both inside and outside his party.

So he was respected and relatively well off; his salary did not provide luxuries, but it certainly provided a higher standard of living than most Peruvians enjoyed. Zavala lived with his wife and two children in an upscale Lima neighborhood. He was far removed from the impoverished areas where many of the citizens lived, but tried to be sensitive to their needs.

As Peruvian government departments go, the Interior Ministry was a model of efficiency. They had proven themselves in recent emergencies, such as a terrible storm that devastated three communities. Eleven people died, but if not for Zavala's insistence on a high level of emergency preparedness, the toll would likely have been much higher.

On this particular day Zavala could relax at home and enjoy the life he had built for himself and his family. They were celebrating a holiday called Día de Todos los Santos, known in English as All Saints Day. His wife was also off from work, and schools were closed, so the Zavalas were experiencing a rare and welcome day of togetherness.

The doorbell rang and Luis answered it. It was a young woman who explained that her car was failing to start, and she wondered if she could use the Zavalas's phone to call for help.

Since Luis was mechanically inclined, he offered to take a look at it, and she gratefully accepted the offer. He followed her to the car, which sat with the hood open. When he walked alongside it, three men suddenly appeared behind him, one holding a gun, and shoved him into the backseat.

The woman then calmly closed the hood, got into the driver's seat, and drove off. By the time she did so, Luis Zavala was blindfolded and gagged on the floor of the car.

Kidnappings in Peru, like elsewhere in Latin America, have increased in frequency. They are always of prominent people, since those are the ones likely to fetch significant ransoms. It is a thriving industry.

It took twenty minutes for Luis's wife to notice that he was gone, and even then she assumed he had gone to the store or something without telling her. It wasn't until three hours later, after checking with various friends, that she called police.

There were no leads, and all they could do was wait for the expected ransom demand. The police said that in situations like this the ransom demand usually came within forty-eight hours.

That did not happen in this case, for a couple of reasons. First, the kidnappers were not after money, at least not after ransom money. Their economic goals were much higher. Second, ransom was not demanded for Luis Zavala's return, since he was never going to be returned.

Two and a half hours after Luis was kidnapped, he was executed with a gunshot in the back of his head.

The killing shocked the country, and the president gave the obligatory speech of outrage, vowing a return to law and order. Zavala's deputy minister, Omar Cruz, assumed the vacated position, promising to be true to Luis's legacy.

He was lying.

Asking Simon Ryerson anything is proving very difficult. I've called his office eleven times, and the first ten times an assistant told me that he wasn't in. Each time they've asked what the call is in reference to, and I've responded that it's a personal, legal matter.

On the last call I elevated the stakes a bit, and left word that if I didn't speak to him, I would have to issue a subpoena. It was an empty threat, since I don't possess the power to do so. Hatchet would make me prove relevance before I could compel him to testify, even in a deposition, and Ryerson is apparently savvy enough to know that, since he's still avoiding me.

Between Laurie and Sam, we have gotten some information on Ryerson. He's wealthy, having taken in almost seven million dollars in the past year. We haven't discovered the source of that wealth though; since it's been awhile since Ryerson has held down anything approaching a real job.

Unemployment hasn't stopped him from accumulating frequent flier mileage. He hasn't traveled that much domestically, flying to California once and St. Louis four times.

But interestingly, he has traveled to South America seven times in the past year. Colombia twice, Venezuela once, Ecuador once, and Peru three times. In each case he flew first class, and returned two days later. Certainly, his contact with Tommy Iurato, coupled with his South American trips, makes me suspect some involvement with drugs, but it's obviously not something I can come close to proving.

Ryerson's refusal to talk to me is in a strange way sort of encouraging. I'm fairly well known, and he could easily have me checked out. Because I've been so persistent, I would think that he would talk to me, at least to find out what I'm calling about. If he didn't talk to me personally, he could have an associate or a lawyer learn what the issue is about.

The fact that he doesn't do those things means he probably knows what it's about, and doesn't want to deal with it. And if he doesn't want to deal with it, that could be because it's problematic for him.

These are the kind of rationalizations that keep me going.

But Laurie is going to have to assume command of the Simon Ryerson portion of the investigation, because I'm heading into trial mode. I've given her the OK to spend money on finding resources in South America that might assist us in learning why Ryerson has been going there, and whether it has anything whatsoever to do with Joey Desimone's trial.

I'm going to be totally preoccupied with the trial. That's always the case, but I'm feeling even more obsessed with this one than most. In repeatedly going over the transcript of the first trial, I've been very disturbed at my performance.

I'm a better lawyer now, but I should have done better then.

And now I have a second chance.

"There is no law against adultery" is how Dylan begins his opening statement. "Nor should there be. We don't have to like those kind of actions, and we can be disappointed when we see them, but we should not legislate against them. It's just my opinion, but I don't think that's the role of government.

"Karen Solarno committed adultery; she was married to Richard Solarno, when she had an extramarital affair with this man, Joseph Desimone. That is an uncontested fact." He points to Joey, just in case the jury had any doubt whom he meant.

"In fact, you'll hear that Karen Solarno was prone to this sort of thing; that Joseph Desimone was certainly not the first man with whom she cheated on her husband.

"But he was the last.

"Karen ended the affair; she told him she didn't want to see him anymore, and that she wanted to try and repair her damaged marriage. That happens in things of this nature, and the rejected party can get hurt. But generally they get over it, and move on.

"But not Joseph Desimone. He didn't get over it. The evidence will show that he was furious, and expressed that anger publicly. And he tried to get her back; the evidence will show that as well.

"But nothing worked, so this defendant decided that he was going to get his revenge, both on Karen Solarno and on her husband. So he went to their house, and he killed them.

"That, ladies and gentlemen, is Joseph Desimone."

Dylan goes on to list some of the evidence he is going to present at trial. He takes too long to do it, which is characteristic of Dylan, but he also does it effectively. It's quite similar to his opening at the first trial, no doubt under the theory that if it ain't broke, don't fix it.

It's always difficult to assess the impact of anything on a jury, and one should never take significant action based on that kind of assessment. So I can't be sure if Dylan is succeeding in getting his points across, but it certainly seems like he is.

As always, I have the option of giving my

opening statement now, or waiting until we begin the defense case. And as always, I choose to speak now. It's important now, and will be throughout the prosecution's case, that I let the jury know that there is another side to this story.

"Forty-eight hours after the brutal murder of the Solarno family, the police settled on Joey Desimone as the prime suspect. In fact, the evidence will show that he was their only serious suspect. Forty-eight hours after that he was arrested in his New York apartment.

"This may surprise you, but I think there was good reason to have him on the list of suspects. You'll hear those reasons during the trial, and you'll think it was correct that the police considered him when trying to decide who committed this crime.

"But he should not have been the only suspect, and the police and the district attorney should not have rushed to judgment.

"Evidence will be presented to prove that a police lieutenant in another state wrote to the authorities here, telling them that people in his state had threatened Richard Solarno because he cheated them in a business deal. Don't you think that was something that would have attracted some suspicion? Called for some investigation? And it was a substantial threat; these people said they were going to kill him.

"And I should add that it wasn't exactly the chess club that was angry at Richard Solarno for moving his bishop to queen four, or something like that. And it wasn't a cooking club, irritated that he stole their soufflé recipe. No, this was a militia group. An armed militia group. The leader of that group is currently in jail for trying to kill a federal agent.

"And who armed them? Well, it turns out that it was Richard Solarno, who trafficked in illegal weapons. And how did he cheat them? The arms he gave them were not quite as deadly and powerful as they said he promised.

"Do you suppose law enforcement here might have checked into this? Well, they didn't."

I've milked this pretty well, and I can almost see the steam coming out of Dylan's ears. Time to move on.

"There was a quiz show that used to be on television when I was a kid called *The Match Game*. Part of the game was the contestants having to finish a phrase by guessing the most popular answer. So if we were playing and I said 'oil,' you might say 'oil well,' or 'oil and gas,' or something like that.

"If I said, 'trial by,' you might say 'trial by fire,' or 'trial by jury.' But what is happening here, what best describes the entire investigation, what you are a part of, is something that I call, 'trial by family.'

"Joey Desimone stands before you today because he is the son of Carmine Desimone, who I know most, if not all, of you are familiar with. But Joey has never been a part of what is said to be the family business, and there will be no evidence to show that he has.

"Joey Desimone has led an exemplary life, no matter who his father is, and that is a fact. But his last name made him an easy target, and once you have an easy target, why bother to look for a hard one?

"Mr. Campbell is right about one thing, and that is that Joey had an affair with Richard Solarno's wife. It's not something he is proud of, but it does not make him a murderer.

"Nothing could make Joey Desimone a murderer."

"She was afraid of him. She said he might kill her."

Dylan's first witness, Lisa Holland, is reprising her testimony from the first trial, albeit a bit earlier. I think Dylan moved her up in the order because she is testifying to a threat Joey allegedly made, which could counter my opening statement about the threat from Montana.

Holland was a neighbor and friend of Karen Solarno, and represented herself in the first trial as an intimate confidante.

"When did she say that?" Dylan asks.

"We were having coffee at her house; she asked me to come over because she wanted to talk."

"What was the status of her relationship with Mr. Desimone at that point?"

"They were having an affair, but she had just told him it was over."

"How did he respond to that, according

250

to her?"

These questions would ordinarily be disallowed as hearsay, since Holland wasn't actually there to see Joey's reaction, but because Karen Solarno is deceased, Holland's answers are admissible.

"She said he became furious, and said that no one rejects a Desimone. He said that he would have her or no one would."

"So she feared for her life?" Dylan asks.

"Definitely."

"Why was she breaking it off with him?"

"She wanted to make it work with Richard. She said she still loved Richard, but that she had treated him badly. She wanted to make it right, and she wanted them to have a child."

"Did she say that to Mr. Desimone?"

Holland nods. "Yes. She said that made it worse. That Joey said he would put Richard in the ground. Those were his words. And she was afraid he could do it, because of his family."

Dylan turns the witness over to me, and I start with a pleasant "good afternoon," and she responds in kind.

"It's nice to see you again," I say, "it's been a while. Do you remember that we've spoken before?"

"Yes."

"Actually, I was questioning you, and you were under oath, as you are now. Isn't that right?"

"Yes."

"And you were answering truthfully then, as required by law, just as you're doing now. Isn't that right?"

"Yes."

I hand her a page from the transcript of the last trial, and ask her to read it. She does so; it's a series of questions as to whether she intended to try and profit from the trial or her experience. She absolutely denied any such intention. "I only want justice for Karen," she had finally concluded.

"Did you profit from it?" I ask.

"I did not."

"Did you attempt to?"

She hesitates for a moment, afraid of where I might be going, and says, "No."

"Never tried to sell your story?"

"No."

I introduce into evidence a document that Laurie had uncovered in the investigation, and I ask Holland if she recognizes it. "Yes."

"Is it a proposal for a book?"

"Yes."

"Can you read the title, please?"

She doesn't want to do so, but can't seem to figure a way out. "Deadly Affair: The Karen Solarno Story."

"And what words come right after that?"

"By Lisa Holland."

"Which, coincidentally, is your name."

Dylan objects to my sarcasm, and Hatchet sustains. Before I can ask another question, Holland says, "My husband did that."

"Did what?"

"Tried to sell it as a book," she says.

"Without your knowledge?"

"That's correct."

"If it sold, were you going to write it without your knowledge?"

"I wasn't going to write it."

I read from the proposal. " 'The story that shook America, as told by the best friend she confided in.' " I put the proposal down. "That wasn't you? This is a different best friend we're talking about?"

"It's referring to me," she says. "But my husband prepared that proposal. I told him I didn't want to be involved."

"Because you swore under oath that you wouldn't do so?"

"That's correct."

"But he went ahead anyway? Without your involvement?"

"Yes."

"Are you still married to this guy?"

Hatchet sustains another Dylan objection,

so I move on to even more fertile ground. "OK, so forgetting whether or not you told the truth the last time you testified, this time you're telling the truth, right?"

"Absolutely."

"And everything you've said today is equally true? All your statements have had the same level of truthfulness?"

I can see in her face that she's scared of where I might be going, and she has good reason to be. "Yes."

"Does the name Nancy Ellman mean anything to you?"

She hesitates, as the import of what I just said sinks in. "Not that I can recall."

"Maybe I can refresh your memory. She's a senior editor at Prescott Publishing. They publish mostly nonfiction, current events kind of books. Actually much like the proposal that your husband wrote, without your knowledge."

"I can't recall."

"Well, that memory refresher obviously didn't do the trick, so let's try another." I hand three copies of a letter to Hatchet, Dylan, and Holland, and say, "Here's a letter from you to Ms. Ellman, thanking her for meeting with you and considering the book proposal."

She doesn't say anything, so I continue

with, "I sure hope that worked, because I only have a couple of memory refreshers left."

Finally, she says, "I did it as a favor to my husband. He asked me to."

"Did he ask you to lie about it today?"

I torture her a little more, and then let her off the stand. This was a case where the passage of time worked to my advantage. During the first trial, I suspected she was lying when she said she wouldn't try to sell her story, but I couldn't demonstrate it. Now I could, so I was able to nail her with it.

The rest of the witnesses won't be so easy.

Carmine Desimone always loved *The God-father*.

Unlike many of his colleagues, who thought it painted them in a negative light, he didn't think so at all. He thought Vito, Sonny, and Michael Corleone were heroic figures. He liked *Godfather II* a little less, and walked out of *Godfather III* after twenty minutes, but the original, in his mind, was a classic.

He identified more with Michael than with Vito, probably because he was born in the United States, and he also "inherited" the mantle of family leader from his father. But it wasn't that it seemed autobiographical, because there were many differences.

Like Michael, Carmine had to deal with changing times, in ways that his father never did. It had become a new and very different world, much more so than Michael ever faced, and it had proved very difficult for

Carmine to deal with.

Carmine had lately been thinking of his father often. He felt that his father would have been very disappointed in him, and how he had presided over the disintegration of the family business, of the family itself.

And he thought of Nicky. He had never bought Iurato's explanation of what happened; it was laughable on its face. He had no idea why Nicky was killed, or what possible threat the old man had presented. And even though he was just a shell of the old Nicky, he would be avenged.

He would be avenged that night. Because that night Carmine felt most like Michael Corleone, the night he went to the restaurant and shot Sollozzo and the police captain.

Gino Bruni picked him up at seven that evening for the fifteen-minute drive to Spumoni's restaurant in downtown Elizabeth. It was a favorite of Carmine's from the old days, though no business was ever discussed there. Law enforcement was all over the place, and it was probably the only restaurant in the New York metropolitan area with more "bugs" than cockroaches.

But that was then, and as Carmine and his colleagues stopped going there, the appeal to the cops faded as well. Now it was just a struggling restaurant with great food and a private room in the back. A private room reserved that night for Carmine Desimone, party of four.

Carmine and Gino arrived at seven twenty, ten minutes before the scheduled dinner. As Gino shut off the car, Carmine said, "Your people are here?"

"Yes. One is posing as a waiter, one as a busboy, and one is having dinner at a small table near the kitchen. He's with his wife."

"Good. I want to be warned if they come in with extra people. I don't want this to be a trap."

"It's a trap, but we're setting it," said Gino. "Why would they be trapping you? You called the meeting."

They went inside, and were greeted by the owner and led into the back room. Gino had earlier told Carmine that the owner had been paid more for that night than the restaurant would earn in a year, and he could be counted on to be quiet.

At exactly seven thirty, Gino looked out the window and saw a dark sedan pull up. Iurato and Ryerson got out of the backseat, and started walking toward the restaurant entrance. He said, "They're here."

"Alone?" asked Carmine.

"There's a driver with them, but he stayed

in the car."

"Good."

When Ryerson and Iurato came in, Ryerson immediately went over to Carmine, even before he took off his coat. "Hello, Carmine, you're looking well," he said, extending his hand.

Carmine did not shake his hand, simply saying, "What are you drinking?"

"Gin and tonic."

Carmine did not ask the same of Iurato, but merely signaled to Gino, who mixed the drink at the bar, and handed it to Ryerson. "So, you wanted to see me?" Ryerson asked.

"I want you out," Carmine said.

"I thought you had something new to tell me."

"I'm prepared to buy you out."

Ryerson laughed at the thought of it. "I represent money that can buy and sell you, Carmine. In fact, I've already bought you, or at least your company." He never referred to Carmine's operation as a family, always as a company. Ryerson then pointed toward Gino. "With the apparent exception of Mr. Bruni, here."

"One way or the other, you're out, Ryerson. So name a price."

"You disappoint me, Carmine. I knew you were old, and basically a piece of shit, but I thought you were brighter than this."

Carmine looked over at Gino, who walked over to the door and knocked on it. Moments later it opened, and two men walked in, carrying handguns. The other door to the room opened as well, revealing a third armed man.

"You should have named a price," Carmine said, then turned to Gino and said, "Kill them." He then indicated Iurato. "Take your time with him."

But nobody moved or said anything. Not Gino, nor Ryerson, nor Iurato, nor the three gunmen. "Do it now," Carmine said, and when everyone remained still, the truth of the matter dawned on him.

"You son of a bitch," he said to Gino. "Where is your loyalty?"

Ryerson laughed. "You're living in the dark ages, Carmine. He's an employee; employees go where the money is. That's the way the world works. A guy works for IBM, and Apple offers him twice as much money, you think he's going to stay at IBM because he's loyal?

"This was the company you built, but I run it now. You could have stayed on as chairman emeritus." He paused and chuckled at the thought. "And now you're about to be very emeritus."

Just before he walked out the door, Ryerson said to Iurato, "The most important thing is to make sure he is never found."

I hate cross-examining Pete Stanton.

I've probably had to do it seven or eight times, and I think I've more than held my own, but I hate the process. We're always adversaries, and it's my job to make him look bad. I obviously don't like it, because he's my friend.

I do it though, and friendship has to take a backseat, because of what his job is. His job is to put my clients in prison, very often for the rest of their lives.

Dylan takes Pete through pretty much the same testimony he gave during the first trial. It's basically a scene setter, describing Pete's arrival at the Solarno house, and the actions he took while there. Most of the specific evidentiary factors that led to Joey's being arrested will be told through other witnesses, so in that sense, there's nothing for me to attack.

He does bring up the fact that Joey's

fingerprints were on the scene, and more importantly on the gun, which was found on the scene. It's the gun that killed Karen Solarno, and which belonged to her. The weapon that killed Richard has never been found. In any event, the print evidence is certainly an area I can't let go unchallenged when I start my cross-examination.

Pete also reads from a statement Joey made to police before I was brought into the case. There is no way Joey's previous attorney should have allowed him to be interviewed; it's virtually legal malpractice to have done so.

In the interview, Joey had said that he did not own a gun, and couldn't remember the last time he had fired one. It's a statement that came back to haunt him, and will do so again.

"Lieutenant Stanton, what was your rank when the murder took place?" is how I start.

"I was a detective."

"How many promotions have you had since then?"

"Two."

"Congratulations." I asked these questions to further demonstrate to the jury how long ago the crime took place, and to tell them that I consider Pete a good officer. This is because I'll have very little to criticize about the actions he took; I'll be going after the actions he didn't take.

He doesn't thank me for my congratulatory remark, but I won't hold a grudge. "You said you found Mr. Desimone's prints in the house and on the gun that killed Karen Solarno. You ran them against a database?"

"Yes."

"Since not everyone's prints are in those databases, how was it that Mr. Desimone's happened to be there?"

"From his time in the Marines."

"So he had never committed a prior crime?"

"Not that we know of."

"Is your knowledge in this area somewhat incomplete?"

"Somewhat."

"Had he ever been charged with a crime?"

"No."

"That you're sure of?"

"Yes."

"Ever been arrested?"

"No."

"Sure?"

"Yes." Pete is getting annoyed, but he's too experienced a witness to show it to the jury.

"You said you found Mr. Desimone's

fingerprints in the house."

"Yes."

"Where in the house, specifically?"

"In the front foyer, the den, the living room, the kitchen, two bathrooms, and the bedroom."

"Wow . . . that's a lot of places. You've testified that the murder of Richard Solarno took place at the front door, and that of Karen Solarno in her bedroom. Is that right?"

"Yes."

"So is your theory of the case that he murdered the Solarnos, and then ran around the house touching as many things as he could?"

"No."

"Your report says that his fingerprints were on the microwave in the kitchen. Does your theory include his making some popcorn between murders?"

Dylan objects, and Hatchet sustains, admonishing me to be less argumentative. Good luck with that, Hatchet.

"His prints were also found on the gun, is that correct?" I ask, knowing that it is.

"Yes."

"Who owned the gun?"

"It was registered to Karen Solarno."

"And this is the same Karen Solarno that

was having a relationship with Mr. Desimone?"

He nods. "Yes."

"How long had she owned it?"

"Two months."

"Let me offer a hypothetical," I say. "Suppose she had shown Mr. Desimone the gun and he held it. Or suppose as a Marine marksman, she had asked him to take her out and teach her how to shoot it. Could his fingerprints have gotten on the gun that way?"

"There is no evidence that happened."

I fake surprise. "There is no evidence that she ever handed him the gun to show it to him? Never said, 'Look what I just got?' or even asked him to help her buy it?"

"No."

"I see. I hadn't realized your investigation was that complete. Why don't you show me a list of things she handed to him during their relationship, and if the gun's not on it, we'll know you're right."

Dylan objects and I withdraw the question. I've gotten other explanations in front of the jury, but the fingerprints on the gun is still the elephant in the already crowded room.

I point out to Pete that his report says that Joey and Karen Solarno were having an af-

266

fair, which had lasted months. "Isn't that a more logical explanation for how his prints got in the house? Or do you find that most people conducting extramarital affairs wear gloves?"

Dylan asks that we approach the bench, which gives Hatchet another chance to admonish me, and warn me to "be very careful." He also tells me to move on, which I'm happy to do.

I tell Hatchet that I now plan to question Pete about the Montana connection, and other information Laurie developed about Solarno's arms dealing, and which I turned over to Dylan in discovery. I was willing to do so because I wanted the police to then check it out and confirm it for the jury.

Dylan objects, saying that in cross I can only ask Pete questions relating to what Dylan asked on direct. "I never asked about the arms dealing," Dylan says.

"You asked about his investigation; this is all part of that," I say, and Hatchet has no choice but to allow it.

When I resume with Pete, I ask him to describe what he knows about Solarno's arms dealing, including both the Montana group and other activities that Laurie discovered. He lays it out in some detail, making no effort to conceal. This is partly because he's an honest guy, but mostly because he knows that I know all of it, and will nail him if he covers anything up.

When he's finished, I say, "When did you learn all of this?"

"Within the past month."

"Six years after the murders? Six years after Mr. Desimone was arrested?"

"Yes."

"So you were not aware that the Montana State Police informed the District Attorney's Office six years ago about threats on Richard Solarno's life?"

"I was not."

"Had you known that, would you have investigated it?"

"Yes. But I investigated it now, and there is no evidence that that group was involved in this case."

"Lieutenant, is it true that the best evidence in a murder case is usually developed in the first seventy-two hours?"

"That is often the case."

"Because trails can run cold?"

"Sometimes."

"In six years they can get frozen, can't they?"

Dylan objects, but I've made my point. I even think I've done so without making Pete

look bad, but he'll probably have a different
view of that.

Carmine Desimone had put pressure on Ryerson.

Not unbearable pressure. Not game-changing pressure. Not even enough to make him change the plan, at least not so far.

But he felt the pressure. It was his plan; he had recommended it, argued for it, and it was approved. Now it was up to him to execute it.

Technically, he could do so at any time. But to really do it right called for patience, which meant waiting for an event that was beyond anyone's control. It was up to Mother Nature.

Ryerson smiled to himself; there's never a natural disaster around when you really need one.

Carmine was stupid, so stupid that Ryerson had no idea how he had achieved his position in life. If there was one thing he should have learned by now, it's that there was no one in the organization that he could trust to have his back.

But instead he trusted Bruni, and had in the process put himself into a position where he simply had to be killed. Not that he wouldn't have been killed anyway, but Ryerson would have hoped it could have been done at a time of his choosing, in keeping with the plan.

Carmine, for all his stupidity, remained crucial to the operation. Whether alive or dead, he had a role to fill, and he would fill it perfectly.

He would be the person they would blame.

So all Ryerson could do was to be ready for all eventualities. He would have to make another trip to Peru, and would do so right away. He had been told that everything was ready, but wanted to make extra sure by seeing for himself.

There would be only one chance to get this right.

I wasn't looking forward to Raymond Fisher's testimony.

Now retired, Fisher was the director of the New Jersey State Forensics Laboratory at the time of the Solarno murders, and his words were a significant factor in Joey's eventual conviction.

Fisher is a defense attorney's nightmare. He comes off as sincere, even kindly, and with an apparent total knowledge of his field. This is because in real life he is sincere, kindly, and has a total knowledge of his field.

Jurors have no doubt that he is saying what he believes to be the truth, and recognize him as a person uniquely qualified to know that truth.

I barely laid a glove on Fisher during the first trial, and unless there is some divine intervention in the form of a list of new questions for me to ask him, I'm not going to do any better this time.

For once, Dylan takes the "less is more" approach to his witness, asking him questions concisely and directly, drawing out the meat of the matter but not weakening it through repetition. I suspect he does this because he's anxious to see me strike out again in my attempt to challenge Fisher, and he's even more anxious for the jury to see it.

Moving quickly through the forensic evidence that is basic to the murder, but has nothing to do with who committed it, Dylan gets to the heart of Fisher's testimony. It's a ski jacket, and Dylan asks Fisher if it is the one that was taken from Joey's apartment during a lawful search of the premises.

"Yes, it is," says Fisher.

"Did you conduct any tests on it?"

Fisher nods. "We did. We tested for blood and gunpowder residue."

"And what did you find?"

"No blood, but definite traces of gunpowder. The pattern clearly indicates that someone wearing this jacket fired a weapon."

"Is it possible to determine what kind of gun it was?"

"Not from examining the jacket, no."

"What about when it was fired?"

Fisher thinks for a moment, as if the question is new and intriguing, which it certainly isn't. "Hard to say. It would depend on how much the jacket was worn in the interim, in what weather, etcetera. But I would certainly say it was fired sometime within a week of the examination."

Dylan turns him over to me, no doubt with pleasure. My first question is, "Dr. Fisher, did you conduct the tests on the jacket yourself?"

"No, members of my —"

I cut him off, asking Hatchet to instruct the witness to answer "yes or no" questions with yes or no. Hatchet obligingly tells him not to volunteer information, to answer only the questions asked.

I repeat the question, and Fisher says, "No, I didn't conduct the tests myself."

"Were you in the room, or looking over the shoulder, of the person conducting the test while he or she was doing so?"

"No."

"Did you see the jacket when it was in the lab?"

"I did not."

"Were you in Mr. Desimone's apartment when it was taken?"

"I was not."

"Yet you identified it when Mr. Campbell asked if it was the same one."

"I have full confidence in my colleagues."

"If they were here, maybe the jury could have made that judgment for themselves."

Dylan barely has time to finish his objection before Hatchet sustains it and warns me to be careful.

"So, basically, Dr. Fisher, you're just here to report on someone else's work?"

"I suppose that's correct."

"But as you said, you have full confidence in that other person."

"I do."

"What is his or her name?"

Happily, Fisher has to look at the report, and I pounce. "You have to look at the report to find out who you have full confidence in?"

"I had an excellent staff. This work was done by Stephen Jordan."

"Tell us a little about Mr. Jordan."

"Well, he was a senior director."

"It says that on the report?" I ask, knowing that it does.

"Yes."

"Tell us more, please. Help us get to know him."

Dylan objects, but Hatchet lets me continue until I establish completely that Dr.

Fisher wouldn't know Stephen Jordan from Michael Jordan.

"How is it that this jacket came to be tested?" I ask.

"I couldn't say," he answers. "We just test what they give us."

"How many items of clothing were tested?"

He looks at the report again before answering. "Seven."

"From the entire apartment, they took only seven pieces? Do you know why?"

"I don't. No."

"Would Stephen Jordan know why?"

Once again Dylan successfully objects.

"Does the gun residue, in these trace amounts, leave a stain or something that the eye can see?"

"No, it would not."

"Most people have more than seven pieces of clothing in their apartment, wouldn't you say?" I ask.

"Generally yes, but I couldn't speak for Mr. Desimone."

I nod. "Because you weren't there."

"Yes."

"So they took very few items, as if they knew what they would find and where they would find it?"

Dylan objects again and I drop the question and excuse the witness. I've made some debating points, but at the end of the day the jury will believe the tests, and they probably should.

The troubling thing for me is that not only can't I give the jury a theory about the jacket that they'll find credible, I can't even come up with one for myself.

Joey told me, as he told the police, that he did not own a gun, and certainly none was found in his apartment. He also told me, and I believe him, that he had last fired two years previously, on a hunting trip. Records showed that he didn't even own that jacket then.

If it's a frame, it's a subtle one, since there was certainly a decent chance that they wouldn't have taken the jacket for testing. Had they not done so, maybe whoever might have framed Joey would have opted for a more direct approach.

I didn't know the answer then, and I don't now. It's one of the reasons Joey has been living in a cage for six years.

Sam knew Ryerson would be leaving the house, soon, even though he had been there all day. Sam had been in his car outside Ryerson's house for three and a half hours, since 5:00 P.M., when he had taken over from Willie.

Ordinarily, they would have stopped their stakeout by now, since Ryerson had not shown an inclination to go out at night. But Sam knew from his computer searches that six hours ago Ryerson had booked a first-class ticket to Lima, Peru, on American Airlines, which was leaving at eleven twenty that night.

Not that Sam expected the ride to the airport to be an eventful one, and he was aware that once he got to the airport, that would be it. There was no way he could follow Ryerson to Peru even if he wanted to; he didn't have his passport with him, and it was long expired anyway. But he figured he'd wait around, perhaps to see if Ryerson was traveling alone.

At eight forty-five, a car pulled up and the driver went in. The man was large but not fat; Sam thought he could have been an outside linebacker, or tight end. Sam drove up a little closer to the house, possibly closer than he should have, but he wanted to get the license plate number, which he did.

With his ever-present computer on the passenger seat, Sam started to run the license plate through the state database. He actually did it by having penetrated the police computer systems in Fair Lawn, and then pretended to be the Fair Lawn Police, accessing the state information. Like so much of what Sam did online, it was completely illegal, and he was completely unconcerned about it.

Before he could finish the search for the license-plate information, the visitor and Ryerson came out of his house and got in the car. Sam noticed that Ryerson carried a very small case, not even as big as a small suitcase. He was not surprised, since Ryerson was booked to fly back the next evening.

As they were leaving the house and walking toward the car, the driver seemed to look in Sam's direction, and for a moment Sam thought he had been spotted. But the man quickly looked away, and they got in the car and drove off. Ryerson got in the passenger seat rather than the back, which seemed to mean that the man was not a chauffeur.

Sam let them get out of sight for a short while, just in case the man had noticed him. He knew where they were going, so he knew he'd be able to catch up. He was at this point basically following to see if the man was also on the flight or not. Then he could cross-check the names on the passenger list, and possibly identify him.

As Sam drove, he broke driving as well as hacking laws by looking over occasionally and operating his computer, so that he could learn whose car he was following. They were nearing JFK when he finally learned that the plate belonged to Nicholas Costa, with a current address of 545 Riverside Avenue, in Hoboken.

Costa dropped off Ryerson at American Airlines and headed back toward the city. He didn't head toward North Jersey, but instead went south, which led Sam to believe that he could be headed home to Hoboken.

Sam decided to follow, but first called Andy at home. Laurie answered, but said that Andy was out and couldn't be reached;

he was interviewing a potential witness, which he had to do at night, because he was in court all day during trial.

"Does the name Nicholas Costa mean anything to you?" Sam asked.

"No, I don't think so. Why?"

Sam explained all that had happened, and that he hadn't had a chance yet to search online for information about Costa. "I'm going to follow him, maybe watch him for a while. If you want to check him out as well, he lives at 545 Riverside Avenue, in Hoboken. I think that's where he's headed now."

"I'm not sure that's a good idea, Sam. He could be a dangerous guy."

Sam laughed. "You sound like Andy. I'll be fine; I'm not going to even let him see me."

"Sam, we don't know anything about this man. I'll make some calls, but just keep your distance."

"I will, and I'll check him out online."

Sam followed him to the Hoboken address, which was a rather nondescript house in a middle-class neighborhood. He was clearly not in the same economic class as Ryerson.

Sam parked up the block and turned the lights off in his car. He expected that Costa was in for the night, but decided to hang around for a while anyway, just to see if anyone else came by. It also gave him time to work on his computer and search for information about Costa.

And information is what he found, in ample supply. Costa had spent ten years in prison for manslaughter, and was reputed to be an associate of the Desimone crime family. He would be happy to be able to report to Andy that Ryerson and the Desimones were definitely connected.

Sam had just turned off his computer, when the driver's side door opened and he was grabbed by the neck and pulled out of the car. He fell to the ground, and rolled over on his back.

Before he could react, a large shoe, attached to a very large man, was pressing down on his neck. The pressure was enough to make him very uncomfortable and gag, but not enough to cut off his breathing entirely.

"Who the hell are you?" the man asked.

Sam tried to answer, but the pressure on his neck became greater and greater, and breathing became impossible.

And then everything went dark.

Edward Young is scared, and I can't say I blame him. He plays in a rough financial world, but at the end of the day it's just real-life monopoly. Somebody shooting at him in his car, somebody killing his driver, that's "Untouchables" territory. And it has scared the hell out of him.

He's decided he needs to be protected, a logical decision. But when you have his kind of money, you cover all your protection bases. So I am sitting in his house in Alpine, and so far I have encountered two bodyguards and two attorneys.

The attorneys are sitting in the den with us as we talk. It's a remarkable room, with two walls of bookshelves and a fireplace so large it could be a studio apartment. I don't recognize the artwork on the walls, because I do not recognize artwork, but my guess is that the people that painted them are famous, European, and have been dead for five hundred years.

The meeting is at Edward's request, just as I have a feeling that everything done in Edward's life is at his request. Everything except getting shot at.

I start off by apologizing for what he's been through, and I express my condolences for his driver. He nods and says, "He's got two kids, an eight-year-old and a ten-year-old."

I say that it's horrible, because in fact it is horrible, and wait for him to continue. He called the meeting, so it's his agenda.

"I believe this happened because I was put on your witness list, and the people that did this had the connections to find that out. They think I have something to say that could prove helpful to you, and damaging to them."

"Do you?"

He nods. "I do, but I won't say it in court, and I do not want you to call me to the stand."

"Just to be clear," I say, "you're telling me that you have the information, but if I call you then you will deny it?" As I say this, I glance at the two silent attorneys. While I'm sure they're well paid, attorneys at any price level would know that Edward is saying he will perjure himself, something they are

284

legally obligated to not sit idly by and watch their client do.

"That is exactly what I'm saying." He says it with full confidence that he can get away with it, and he probably can. "But I am willing to make an arrangement that could work for both of us."

"What might that be?" I ask, knowing there is very little chance I'm going to like it.

"I was only partially truthful when I told you that I closed up Solarno's company because it was bleeding money. Had that been the case, I would have found someone to buy it, for whatever I could get. I found out that the reason it was bleeding money was that Solarno was conducting illegal activities, in conjunction with certain members of organized crime. When he died, that connection was severed, and the business could not stand on its own.

"Since I had no desire to reinstate that connection, and since the business could not survive without it, I shut it down."

"This would be powerful information to get before a jury," I say. "And once you say it, then the facts would be out there, and no one would have any reason to quiet you."

He frowns. "I'm not going to say anything; I already told you that. But Solarno did not know he was going to die so suddenly, and did not have the time nor the inclination to cover his tracks. So there are documents that support what I'm saying. I am prepared to turn these over to you, providing you do not reveal where you got them. You can call the investigator I hired; he will testify for you at trial."

My guess is that the bad guys will know where I got the documents, but I don't feel the need to point this out. "Who are the people Solarno was dealing with?" I ask.

"Members of the Desimone family. I'm not sure who or on what level."

"Do you know of any reason why they would have wanted to kill him, since doing so ended their business relationship?"

He shakes his head. "I do not. Perhaps he was defrauding them. Solarno was not the smartest man I'd ever met."

I'm sure I'm going to be pressured to make a decision on the spot, though I certainly have the right to delay if it's to my benefit. It seems to be a fairly easy call; I can either put on a witness who will say he has no information, or I can have documents that provide me with the crucial information.

Even though I'm going to be leaving here a hell of a lot better off than when I arrived,

I'm still annoyed. For all my desire not to actually work, I still maintain a healthy respect for the justice system. Edward is flaunting it by saying he will lie under oath, and it bugs me.

"Subject to the documents clearly providing the information you say they will provide, I'm willing to go along with the arrangement."

He stands up. "Good." Then he turns to the lawyers. "Please give Mr. Carpenter what he requires."

For Sam Willis, fear had become humiliation and returned to fear. He was tied to a chair; he certainly assumed it was in the house to which he followed Nicholas Costa. He had told them everything they wanted to know, in the hope that they would let him go, and spare his life.

Now that hope was gone. Costa and the man that Costa was calling Bruni were discussing what to do with Sam's body. Not what to do with him, or even whether or not to kill him. They were discussing what to do with his body.

Every time he tried to say something, tried to intervene in a way that might convince them he should remain alive, Costa simply said, "Shut up." When he didn't obey, Costa simply picked up the knife, the knife they threatened to do horrible things with, the knife that had gotten him to talk.

They also had a gun, at least one, and it

sat on a table about four feet from him. It might as well have been a mile; the straps that bound him to the chair were applied by experts, and had no give in them whatsoever.

He thought of yelling; after all, they were in a neighborhood, and there were houses not far away. But he couldn't envision it playing out in a positive way; the likelihood was that they would simply kill him right away. There was no way that a neighbor, hearing screams, could react in such a timely and aggressive way that it could save his life.

So all Sam could do was wait for an opportunity that would likely never come. Maybe if they took him somewhere else to kill him, he could fight for his life when they unstrapped him. If he got the chance he would take pieces of them with him, because mingled with the fear was a strong feeling of rage.

Finally, Bruni stood up. "Let's go," he said to Costa. He said it in a weary way, like they might as well end Sam's life now, to at least get it over with.

Costa walked over to Sam, but before he undid the straps, he bound Sam's hands together. The wire Costa used cut into Sam's wrists, but the pain was barely noticeable up against the realization that Sam was not going to get a chance to fight for his freedom.

Costa picked up the gun from the table and held it to Sam's back as they walked toward the door, Bruni in the lead. Sam felt as if his legs could barely support him, yet in the moment he came to a decision.

When he got outside, he was going to scream, and he was going to pull away and run. They weren't holding the knife to him, but rather the gun. The hope Sam was grasping to was that it did not have a silencer on it, and they would be fearful of killing him on the street, because they might be seen and heard.

It was less than a one in a million chance, and Sam knew it. But he was not going to be docile as they took him off to die.

Bruni reached for the door handle, and Sam saw the world explode. Actually, he quickly realized, it wasn't the world that exploded, it was the door. And it didn't explode; it came into the room, full force, as if blown off its hinges.

The rest happened so quickly that Sam only pieced it together later, replaying it in his mind. Costa moved the gun from Sam's back out and into the clear, so that he could fire at whatever had come through that door.

Before he could do so, Marcus Clark fired a bullet into his forehead, a bullet that whizzed by no more than three inches from Sam's own face. Sam felt moisture land on his shoulder, and he realized with horror and glee that it was Costa's blood.

Bruni had been knocked down by the door, and Sam saw him scramble to his feet and reach into his own pocket, perhaps for the knife, or a gun of his own.

Marcus was on him in an instant, hitting him across the face with the club that was attached to his shoulder. Bruni seemed to be lifted in the air, and landed with a thud, groggy but not completely unconscious.

Marcus looked at Sam for the first time and said, "Good?" Sam started to respond, and then realized to his horror that if he tried to say anything, he was going to break down and cry.

A minute ago he was sure he was going to die, and now the most important thing in the world was somehow managing not to cry. So he nodded that yes, he was good.

There was nothing to be done for Costa; taking a bullet straight on in the forehead was not the kind of injury that calls for CPR. Bruni was recovering his bearings, and making an effort to get up.

Marcus grabbed him by the collar, lifting

the very large man as if he was a rag doll. He put him in a chair, the same chair that Sam was trapped in. But Sam was bound with straps and wires; Bruni was confined by Marcus.

Marcus looked at Sam again. "You drive?"

Sam didn't know if he meant to ask whether Sam was OK to drive, or whether he had driven to the house, but the answer was the same. "Yes."

Marcus nodded; that was the answer he wanted. "Andy's."

"What about them?" Sam asked, meaning the live Bruni and dead Costa. "I can help you."

"Andy's," Marcus said. "Now."

Laurie comes out to meet me when I pull into the driveway. On second thought, since she has her car keys in her hand, I think it's a coincidence that I came home as she is leaving.

"Come on," she says, starting for the car.

"Where are we going?"

"I'll tell you on the way."

We get to the car, which is parked in the driveway, but Laurie turns when she sees Sam's car pull up. "Never mind," she says.

Sam parks on the street and gets out of his car. From a distance he appears to be staggering slightly, or at least having some difficulty walking.

Laurie walks out to the street to talk to him. She gets up close to him, but from where I am, I can't hear what they're saying. Then she puts her arms around him and hugs him to her, and he seems to rest his head on her shoulder.

I've got a hunch that something has transpired while I've been out.

Laurie and Sam walk toward me and the house, side by side, her arm around him. I don't think they're going to fit through the door this way, but I assume they'll figure it out. I go in ahead of them, leaving the door open and dreading what I'm going to hear when they arrive.

Once inside, Laurie brings Sam a beer, since we don't keep hard liquor in the house. He looks like he's going to need an entire brewery's worth to make him feel better.

He proceeds to tell us an amazing story about following Ryerson to the airport, getting kidnapped and nearly killed, saved only by Marcus showing up on the scene. His lower lip quivers when he talks, and he pauses occasionally as he remembers how he felt during his time in that house.

At one point he says, "I don't know how Marcus knew to come there."

"I called him and asked him to go there," says Laurie. "Just to make sure everything was OK."

"I thought Marcus was guarding me," I point out, petulantly.

"You were in a meeting. Marcus was just supposed to check things out, and make sure Sam went home. He'd have been back before your meeting was over."

"So Marcus was still there when you left?" I ask.

Sam nods. "Costa was dead, and Marcus told me to leave. I left him alone with the one Costa called Bruni."

"So much for Bruni."

"You think Marcus killed him?"

"I know how he operates. He'll question Bruni, and find out whatever Bruni knows."

"What if Bruni won't talk?"

"He'll talk; that's a given. When Marcus asks questions, everybody talks. Then he'll give Bruni a chance to take him on, even up, no weapons. If Bruni wants to, he's a dead man. If not, Marcus will let him go. How big is Bruni?"

"At least two forty."

"A tough guy?"

"Very."

"Then it's eulogy time."

Laurie goes off to get Sam another beer, and Sam seems to have been waiting for her to leave. He says to me, softly, "Andy, I told them all about the case, and what we knew."

"Don't worry about it, Sam. Anyone would have done the same, and it doesn't even harm us any. It's fine."

"I was so scared; I never thought I could

be that scared."

"I would have pissed in my pants."

"I don't even feel bad that Costa is dead, or that Marcus might have killed Bruni."

"Sam, these guys were planning to kill you. And I'm going to take a wild guess that it wasn't the first time either of them had killed someone. They are shit stuck to your shoe; don't think about them for another minute."

"I'm not the guy you want in the foxhole with you."

"Sam, we already had this conversation. Laurie is my first choice, particularly if there are private rooms in the foxhole. And a sunken tub would be nice. Marcus is now my second choice. After that, you."

He smiles; the first time he's done that since he got here. "Marcus was unbelievable. You should have seen him."

"I've seen him in action before. Actually, he and I are alike in a lot of ways."

"How?"

"Well, we both want to keep me alive. And Laurie likes both of us. That's pretty much it."

"When do you think we'll hear from him?" Sam asks.

"I don't know, but I hope it's soon. I need to know what Bruni told him."

The fact that today is Saturday is a positive. Actually, at this point anything that results in court not being in session is a huge plus. We're getting pretty much nowhere in court, and doing better in our investigation, out in the real world.

Unfortunately, court is where the jury is.

But the main reason I'm glad I'm not stuck at trial today is I can be here if and when Marcus shows up. I'm not worried about him — that would be a little silly — but I'm anxious to hear what happened after Sam left, and what Marcus learned.

Hike comes over to help me go through the documents that Edward Young provided. There's quite a bit there to support his contention that Solarno was an arms dealer, in cahoots with organized crime. And while there's no smoking gun regarding the Desimone family, there is certainly a great deal of evidence pointing in that direction.

I believe I'll be able to get the documents admitted, even though they don't bear directly on the murders. The Montana situation works heavily in my favor; it's already been established that Solarno was dealing arms and that they threatened him, and these documents relate rather directly to that.

Hike approves of my agreement to let Edward Young off the testimony hook, since we wouldn't have gotten anything from him anyway. Having the documents is clearly preferable to having a silent witness.

Hike leaves, and I call Sam Willis to make sure he's OK. He says that he is, but he isn't. He's going to take a while to recover from this.

I can identify with Sam very well, because I have been through a somewhat similar experience, actually more than once. There have been times where I thought I was going to be killed.

I was frightened out of my mind, much like Sam was. But the main difference between us is how we viewed ourselves. I knew then and know now that I'm a physical coward, so I was not crushed when I reacted that way. I expected nothing more from myself, so I was able to take it in stride.

Sam saw himself as a warrior, disguised as

298

an accountant. He considered himself a tough guy, and relished the chance to get some "street action." The fact that he got some and failed to live up to his own expectations is devastating to him.

He's also very anxious to hear from Marcus, and asks that I let him know when Marcus shows up. He obviously wants to learn what happened, but he also wants to come over and thank Marcus, something he didn't get to do last night.

Marcus shows up just before noon. If he's had a stressful time, you'd never know it from his expression. If he had an expression, which he doesn't.

Thus begins the most excruciating interrogation I've ever been a part of, at least since the last time I had to question Marcus. He throws around words like they were Winnebagos, and the words he does mutter, I can't understand. I keep looking to the bottom of the screen for subtitles.

As per usual, Laurie seems capable of chitchatting away with him, so I let her do the bulk of the talking, and for that matter, the bulk of the listening. She can download me on what I missed later.

We don't spend much time dwelling on what happened while Sam was still there, since we already know about that. What seems to have happened afterward is pretty much what I expected.

Marcus was successful in persuading Bruni to tell what he knew, and it's fairly stunning. Ryerson has effectively taken control of the Desimone crime family, though Marcus did not ask how that took place.

According to Bruni, Carmine Desimone is dead. Bruni claims to have done the killing himself just a week ago. The body was dropped off a boat into the ocean, weighted down with rocks, and will never be found.

Ryerson is in the process of pulling off an enormous crime, though Bruni did not know what it was, and Marcus believed his denial. He pleaded that he was a minor player in the operation, another claim that Marcus seems to have found credible.

According to Marcus, and as I predicted, after the questioning was over, Marcus offered to let Bruni have a fair shot at him, no weapons and no restrictions. Bruni took him up on the offer. I suspect there were at least two reasons for that, one of which was stupidity. The other was probably a fear that once Marcus revealed what Bruni told him, his bosses would not look too kindly on his weakness and betrayal.

I ask Marcus very carefully, "Is Bruni going to be a problem in the future?"

Marcus's response is a shrug and a simple "Nunh."

This is where I stop the questioning, and Laurie nods her agreement. The less we know about Bruni's fate the better. I don't want to actually hear whether Bruni is dead, how he died, or where the bodies are.

It's lucky I cut class so often in law school, especially the day they went over a lawyer's legal obligations. I know of two people that died last night, and I should be telling the authorities about it.

There are a number of reasons for why I'm not doing so, and right at the top of the list is my near certainty that the secret is otherwise safe.

I have enough confidence in Marcus's smarts to know that he cleaned up after himself well, and left no trace that he was ever there. I would suspect that the two bad guys will simply have disappeared. Carmine Desimone is not the only one who will never be found.

To reveal what transpired would be to expose Marcus to legal jeopardy. I totally believe his version of what happened, but the cops and a subsequent jury might not be so trusting.

Marcus killed two guys, both arguably in

self-defense, that were going to kill Sam. They deserved their fate, and while it might be a revealing commentary about my character, I have no remorse about it at all. Zero.

I call Sam and he comes right over. I tell him not to ask Marcus anything, that I'll share Marcus's story with him. One thing we don't need is another Marcus soliloquy.

Sam thanks Marcus and hugs him. Judging from his reaction, hugging is not Marcus's preferred type of interaction, at least not with another male. If I've ever seen a more uncomfortable human not in the process of undergoing a rectal examination, I can't remember when.

You don't tug on Superman's cape, you don't pull the mask off that old Lone Ranger, and you don't hug Marcus Clark.

"She was my best friend. I think about her and miss her every day." The witness is Sandy Ellerbee, Karen Solarno's sister. She made for a very effective witness in the first trial, and is likely to be the same in this one. She also looks very much like Karen looked, and the jury will certainly know this from the pictures they've seen.

Dylan spends half an hour questioning her about their relationship, and their closeness as siblings. He is doing so for two reasons. First, it humanizes the victim and gets the jury to like her, which in turn makes them want to punish the creep that killed her. Since Joey is the only "creep" they have the power to punish, he'll just have to do.

Second, convincing the jury that they had a really intense relationship will make it more credible when she starts relating the things that Karen told her. Since they reflect negatively on Joey and positively on the possibility that he might have killed her, that works perfectly for Dylan.

Finally, Dylan gets down to business. "Were you aware at the time that your sister was having an affair with the defendant?"

"Of course; we discussed everything. I was upset about it."

"Why?"

"Well, for one thing, she was married. I wanted her marriage to work. And I didn't like the things she said about him."

"The defendant?"

She nods. "Yes. She said he was trying to control her, to make her leave Richard. And she said she was afraid of him, that he had a bad temper."

"What did you advise her to do?"

"To end it as fast as possible." She starts to cry. "And she listened, and that's why she's dead."

"Do you need a minute?" Dylan asks. He would just as soon she take an hour, so that the emotion of the moment could have maximum impact on the jury.

"No, I'm sorry. I'm OK."

"Did you speak to your sister after she ended the relationship with the defendant?"

"Yes. She said it was the hardest thing she had ever done. She said the look in his eyes was frightening, that he was crazed. He swore at her, and told her she would be sorry for what she did."

"So she was afraid?"

Ellerbee nods. "Yes, very. She knew what he was capable of, and his family . . ." She lets the sentence trail off, so that every juror can finish it in their mind. And then she starts to sniffle again.

Dylan wisely chooses that moment to turn her over to me. Ellerbee has the jury's sympathy, and she probably should. For me to get up and attack her will annoy them. Unfortunately, annoying is who I am and what I do.

"Ms. Ellerbee, when your sister told Mr. Desimone that their relationship was over, and his eyes were all crazed and wild, how did she defend herself?"

"What do you mean?"

"Didn't he attack her in his enraged state?"

"No."

"So he just walked away? He didn't grab her, or shake her, or anything?"

"He may have."

"She wouldn't have mentioned that to you?"

She's in a slight trap; she doesn't want to say that it didn't happen, but she's gone to such lengths to paint her and her sister as such close confidantes that she can't admit the possibility that it could have happened and gone unmentioned.

"I think she would have," she allows.

"I think so, too," I say, and Hatchet sustains Dylan's objection.

"How many affairs did your sister tell you that she had?" The jury has heard previous evidence that she had at least five, so this is not breaking new ground. It also puts me in the delicate position of looking like I might be trashing the victim, never a good thing to be accused of doing.

"I don't recall the exact number," she says.

"At least five?"

"Probably. She was trying to find herself."

"And each time you suggested she end it and go back to her husband?" If she says "no," she looks like she countenanced adultery. "Yes," and then telling her to dump Joey had nothing to do with Joey himself.

"Yes."

"Do you know if she told Richard about this affair, or about any of her affairs?"

"I don't think she did."

"Because Richard could become violent?"

"He was not a violent man."

I look puzzled. "Didn't she ever confide in you that she called the police three times

306

in four years because of domestic violence?"

"They had gotten past that."

"But she was afraid that Mr. Desimone was going to hurt her, maybe kill her, because he was violent, and so was his family?"

"Yes."

"Did she report this fear to the police? Maybe get a restraining order?"

"I don't believe so."

"Did you report it? Because you were afraid for your sister's life?"

"No. I wish I had."

I've gotten what little I'm going to get from her, and don't want to look as if I'm badgering, so I let her off the stand. Hatchet adjourns for the day, but I tell the bailiff that I need to talk to Joey in an anteroom.

Joey is getting to know me pretty well, and once we get out of earshot of the bailiff, he says, "What's wrong?"

"Joey, what I am about to tell you I know secondhand, but I believe it to be true."

"OK."

"Your father has been murdered."

His look is of a man punched in the gut by Marcus. "No . . . that can't be . . . I just talked to him the other day."

"This happened since then. I believe he was murdered by someone who worked for him, a man named Bruni. Mr. Bruni is no longer alive himself."

"But no one else knows this? It hasn't been in the news."

"I have special access. Joey, you can try and reach your father, but I'm afraid you'll find that I'm right. I'm sorry."

He's very upset; the most since I've known him, and we've been through some pretty tough times together.

We talk some more, and I ask him not to mention this to anyone. Finally I say that I have to leave, though I don't tell him that I'm heading to the airport to fly to Washington, D.C.

To become a lobbyist.

I'm not really becoming a lobbyist, but I'm in a lobby. I'm in the Madison Hotel in Washington, and I'm twenty minutes late for my meeting. Which seems to be OK, because the person I'm meeting with is even later. It must be a Washington thing.

"Andy?" I look up and there is a woman I assume to be Carolyn Greenwell, the assistant undersecretary of state for Latin American affairs. I got to her not because I have great connections in government, but because Willie and I adopted out a golden retriever to her brother, who's a dentist in Teaneck.

Six degrees of Andy Carpenter.

"Yes."

"Sorry, I've been waiting for you in the bar," she says. "In Washington, if you're meeting someone after ten in the morning, assume it's in the bar."

"Sounds like my kind of town."

We head into the bar and order drinks. I'm looking around to see if I recognize any members of Congress. They're sort of my heroic role models, in that they do even less work than I do. But nobody looks familiar.

We start by talking about her brother's golden retriever, who we named Bumper because he keeps banging into people in the hope that he can goad them into petting him. She met him when she was in Jersey for the weekend. "What a great dog," she says. "I would love to get one, but I live in an apartment."

I explain to her that apartment living is fine for dogs, as long as they're not high energy, and they get taken on a lot of walks. I suggest an older dog for her; when it comes to placing dogs in homes, I can't seem to stop selling.

"So, what did you want to talk about?" she asks.

"Colombia, Peru, Venezuela, and Ecuador."

"What a coincidence, I'm going to Peru on Saturday, and then on to Ecuador."

"Why?"

"Somebody's got to, and the president is busy." When she sees that I don't fully get the Washington humor, she adds, "No special reason, other than we like to visit our embassies on a rotating and consistent basis. This week I drew the Peru and Ecuador straws."

"You don't seem pleased about it," I say.

"You ever try and find a Giants game on TV in Peru?"

"You're not a Redskins fan?"

"God forbid; I'm from Jersey," she says. "But don't mention that around here. What do you want to know about those countries?"

I explain to her that I'm working on a case involving organized crime, and that one of the main players has been making frequent trips to the countries I mentioned, including being in Peru right now. "And I have reason to believe that something big is happening."

"What's his name?" she asks.

"Simon Ryerson."

It doesn't seem to register, so she takes out a notepad and writes it down. "Any idea what the big thing might be? Drugs?"

"I think it might have to do with arms trafficking."

"Why?"

"Some of the players have trafficked in arms in the past, using boats. And those countries have large coastlines."

"You think the arms are going into, or out

of, Peru?"

"Don't know."

She thinks for a while, then asks, "And this big thing that might be happening, you mean really big?"

I nod. "Really big."

She frowns. "Doesn't make much sense. Those countries get most of their arms from us anyway, and have relatively small armies. They certainly don't produce much, so I can't see that they're exporting them."

"What about drug cartels?"

She nods. "They certainly exist, and they are and want to remain armed, but how much do they need? They're not invading other countries. So could they want to bring in arms? Yes. Enough to fit your definition of big? I don't see it."

"Is the drug trade substantial down there?

"Very. For example, Peru is the second largest producer of cocaine in the world; more than two hundred metric tons a year. But they've become better at interdicting, with our help, and the traffic has slowed down remarkably in the past year. The problem is the political will."

"Here or there?"

"There. The drug trade is woven into the fabric; people depend on it for their livelihood. They have for centuries. But like I say, unless they're getting better at hiding it, we've slowed it down a lot."

"Somehow it's got to be arms."

"I'll ask around when I'm down there," she says, and when she sees me react, she says, "Discreetly, of course. Without mentioning your name or situation."

"Thanks. If you find out anything helpful, there's a golden retriever in it for you."

"Bribing a government official in the bar of the Madison Hotel?" she asks. "You're an old Washington hand already."

Ryerson knew there was a problem when he got off the plane at JFK. Waiting to meet him was Tommy Iurato, who was not smiling.

"Where's Costa?" Ryerson asked.

Iurato looked around at the people nearby, within listening distance, and said, "We'll talk in the car."

Once they got in the car, Iurato said, "Costa is probably dead."

"How?"

"I don't know," Iurato said. "But I've tried to reach him a bunch of times, and can't get him. So I went to his house. He wasn't there, but his blood was."

"What does that mean?"

"There was blood spatter, and a pool of it on the floor. My best guess is someone took a bullet in the head, and chances are it was Costas's head. But there is another candidate."

314

"Who might that be?"

"Bruni. He's nowhere to be found."

Ryerson paused to think things through, to piece together what might have happened. "Bruni have any reason to eliminate Costa?" he asked.

"Not that I know of. They were pretty tight. But even if he did, why would he disappear? He's been waiting for the payoff," Iurato said, and then added pointedly, "We've all been waiting for the payoff."

Ryerson nodded. "And if Bruni did it, why get rid of the body?"

"So maybe Bruni is dead as well."

"Somebody good enough to handle Costa and Bruni at the same time? You have any idea who that might be?"

Iurato shook his head. "One guy could never do it. And I don't know who would want to."

"People loyal to Carmine?" Ryerson asked.

"Carmine's dead. He had nobody left when he was alive. And dead? No chance."

"Another family?

Iurato shrugged. "Always possible, but it really doesn't fit."

Ryerson had a feeling that it had something to do with Carpenter, but didn't bother saying so, because it wasn't logical.

Carpenter was a lawyer defending a client; killing two dangerous men wasn't really part of the job description.

There was always the chance that something happened that made Bruni decide to kill Costa. Ryerson's fear was that whatever it was could conceivably have convinced Bruni to go to the feds and tell what he knew. That would be a disaster.

"What do you want me to do?" Iurato asked.

"Do whatever you can to find out who did this. Someone must know something. And we need to know if Bruni is alive."

Iurato realized what he was thinking. "There's no way Bruni turned; don't worry about that. If he's gone, then he's gone for good."

"OK; keep me posted on every detail."

"I will. I also think it would be a good idea to move things along."

"I will handle the timing," Ryerson said, not wanting to give Iurato the satisfaction of agreeing with him, even though he did.

There were a few more arrangements to be finalized on the U.S. side, and he had to get the final plan signed off on, but none of that would take very long. They couldn't afford to let it take very long.

If only it would start to rain.

The most important moments in a trial are often not seen by the jury. That is because it's one of the judge's main responsibilities to screen what they see and hear, lest they be prejudiced. It's the "you can't unring a bell" theory; once the jury hears something they shouldn't have heard, the trial is forever tainted.

If the damage is great enough, a mistrial is the result. Judges basically prefer nuclear war to mistrials.

So if there's something that's borderline as to whether the jury should be privy to it, judges let it be known that they want to hear it first, before the jury. Hatchet is extremely vigilant about this, and lawyers who cross him on it are never heard from again.

Today is an example of this, and it's clearly the most important moment of the trial for our side. Our defense is predicated on the theory that Richard Solarno was the intended victim, not Karen. We have to show that Richard had other enemies, dangerous ones, and that he was himself involved with criminal activities.

But we have to get Hatchet to let this stuff in, and it will not be easy.

The law on this is simultaneously simple and complex. Basically, anything that is relevant to an issue on trial can be submitted as evidence. However, evidence may be excluded if its probative value is substantially outweighed by the danger of unfair prejudice, confusion of the issues, or misleading the jury.

Based on all this, if I were a fair-minded, impartial individual, which I thankfully am not, I would probably not let the evidence in. I think the probative value is limited, and the chance of prejudice of the jury is great.

But there are two factors working in our favor, and one leads into the other. First, judges have substantial discretion over matters like this, and appeals courts are very respectful of that discretion. It is only when "abuse of discretion" is found that appeals courts will intervene, and that is very unlikely to happen here.

The other factor helping us is that judges like to bend over backward to help the

318

defense in evidentiary matters, and this time that will be even more true than usual.

Once Hatchet granted us a new trial based on Dylan's withholding the threat information from the Montana police, it would seem unlikely that he would then prevent the jury from hearing about it. And if the Montana information comes in, then the rest should follow.

The issue is far more important to us than to Dylan. Dylan probably thinks he can survive it, but it pretty much represents our entire case. We need to muddy the water, and this is the only mud at our disposal.

So with the jury tucked safely away in the jury room, Hatchet convenes the hearing to discuss the potential admission of the evidence. Dylan is about to wrap up his case, and we will then immediately start presenting ours. If Hatchet turns us down on this evidence, it will be a short presentation.

Hike has filed a persuasive brief, and Dylan has responded in kind. Hatchet has had a week to familiarize himself with them, so he's up to date on the facts. This hearing is to present oral arguments, though it's certainly possible that Hatchet has already made his decision.

"Your Honor, for six long years, while my

client sat in a prison cell, the state failed to follow a crucial track in their investigation. They were aware of this obvious line of inquiry, as has been made clear. But whether or not they were aware of it, the relevance of that evidence is obvious. We need to be allowed to pursue it and the jury needs to be allowed to see it."

Dylan stands to respond. "It is a fishing expedition, Your Honor. That line of inquiry has now been investigated, and proven fruitless. There is absolutely no evidence that Richard Solarno was the target of the killers, or that those he did business with did him any harm."

"Your Honor," I respond, "Mr. Campbell has used as a lynch-pin of his case that my client had issued a comparatively veiled threat aimed at Mr. and Mrs. Solarno. We dispute that he did, but if Mr. Campbell felt that went to motive and supported his case, then a threat from someone else is equally relevant. If other people, people with guns, had a motive to kill Richard Solarno, then it is obviously something the jury should hear about in detail."

"Many people have enemies," Dylan says. "Murder victims have them as well. But for threats to become admissible, there needs to be independent, corroborative evidence

that the threats were acted upon. That evidence exists in the case of Mr. Desimone; it does not exist elsewhere."

"The state did not look elsewhere," I say. "Just because they made no effort to find it does not mean it doesn't exist."

Hatchet obviously feels this subject has been beaten to death, because he says, "What about the organized crime connections that Mr. Solarno had?"

"That has almost no probative value," Dylan says, "and would be extremely prejudicial. Mere association with criminals, if true, is completely insufficient in the absence of other evidence."

I shake my head. "Mr. Campbell has turned mentioning my client's family into a cottage industry, as if an accident of birth made it more likely that he was guilty. Clearly, having done illegal business with these people, as we will demonstrate Mr. Solarno did, is far more significant."

We go back and forth for a while, and I have the feeling that Hatchet is tuning us out. I'm nervous about this; if he rules against us we're going to have a very short defense case to present.

"I'm inclined to allow the evidence," Hatchet says. "With the caveat that if it goes too far afield, I'll stop it immediately." He

turns to me. "It will be your responsibility to make sure that doesn't happen."

I take a quick look at an annoyed Dylan before I say, "I'm on the case, Your Honor."

I am unsuccessfully trying to discipline myself. I've been spending a great deal of time focused on the Desimone crime family in general, and Simon Ryerson in particular. The problem with that, although I think something major is going down with that group, is I have absolutely no concrete evidence that it has anything to do with the Solarno murders and Joey Desimone's trial.

I certainly have circumstantial evidence of it, at least in my own mind. My reopening the case has provoked major repercussions; Edward Young and I became murder targets, Nicky Fats and probably Carmine became murder victims, and Sam was kidnapped.

But in the eyes of the legal system that information has no chance to be admissible in this trial. I have as much chance of telling our jury about Simon Ryerson as I have of telling them about UFOs.

I am a lawyer defending a client; I am not

Columbo. It might be challenging to find out what Ryerson is up to, and certainly rewarding to somehow thwart it, but it's not my job. Unless I have some reason to believe that following that trail could impact this trial, it's simply not something I should be spending my time on.

Unfortunately, discipline has never been my strong suit. My instincts tell me that if people are going to such great lengths to stop me, I should go to even greater lengths to persevere. I would describe that as admirable, yet strangely most people consider it annoying and obnoxious.

Among those who've used those words to describe me is Cindy Spodek, with an occasional "irritating" and "maddening" sprinkled in. When I call at her FBI office in Boston, it takes almost ten minutes for her to come to the phone.

When she finally picks up, I say, "I've been on hold for ten minutes."

"And?"

"What if I had an imminent terrorist attack to report?"

"Do you?"

"No."

"Whew," she says. "We dodged that bullet." Then, "What do you need, Andy?"

"This time I'm calling to help you."

"I'm sure."

"No, really. I've got some information that I believe is important, and I want to share it."

"So share."

"I want to meet with a local agent. Your top local agent, tomorrow after court. Seriously, Cindy, it's important, and I believe it's time sensitive."

I do have an advantage here. Cindy trusts me, and knows that I would not be wasting her time. "Tell me what it's about. I'll need something to get someone down there to see you. You may not believe this, but I'm not in charge of every agent's schedule."

I don't want to tell her too much, because although she's a friend, I'm going to want to trade, which means I need to keep stuff to trade with. "It's about Simon Ryerson and Carmine Desimone."

"Who's Simon Ryerson?"

"I'll hold that for the meeting."

She sighs, loudly for effect, letting me know I'm not playing the game. "And what about Carmine Desimone?"

"There is no Carmine Desimone."

"That's a little cryptic for me."

"I'll make it clearer at the meeting."

She pauses a moment to absorb this.

Then, "Stay by the phone."
Twenty minutes later, the meeting is set.

Lieutenant Chris McKenney didn't want to go over his testimony in advance. He said that they didn't do it that way in Montana, that he would just get up and tell the truth. "I don't really need to practice telling the truth," he said.

I had explained that it wasn't so much to practice the truth, as much as it was to make sure the testimony went smoothly, with no surprises.

"I won't be surprised," he promised, before telling me that he didn't want to come in for that long; his duties in Montana were too pressing.

I'm a little concerned about his approach, especially since as a police officer he is rarely called on to testify for the defense. He might not be thrilled to be in that position.

"Lieutenant, how did you come to hear the name Richard Solarno?" is my first question once he's sworn in as a witness.

He takes the ball and runs with it, and it's all I can do to keep up. He speaks accurately and concisely, describing the arrest of the militia group in Montana, the investigation that led to the discovery that Solarno was providing arms to them, and their threats when they thought he cheated them.

"These threats concerned you?" I ask.

"Well, sure. They weren't getting the guns to hunt possum; these were dangerous people. If they say they are going to kill a person, it has to be taken seriously."

"So you took action to protect Mr. Solarno?"

"I was about to, when I found out he had been murdered, and someone else was arrested. Although I had no evidence that anyone from Montana had done it, I certainly had a duty to report it to the investigators."

He goes on to explain that he wrote a letter to Dylan, and followed it up with a phone call. He reads the letter, as well as his notes from the call. There could be no doubt that he is telling the truth.

"Do you know if your report was ever followed up on?" I ask, even though the jury already knows it wasn't.

"I don't know," he says. "I know I was

never contacted again about it."

I turn him over to Dylan, who asks, "Lieutenant, did you have any information then, or do you have any information now, which would lead you to believe that someone from the militia group in Montana ever did anything to cause Mr. Solarno any harm?"

"No, sir."

It's the only question Dylan asks, and it's a damn good one.

I get up for redirect and ask one question of my own. "Lieutenant, you said you didn't find any evidence that anyone from Montana murdered Richard Solarno. Did you look for any?"

"No, sir. I figured that was being done on this end."

Nice job, lieutenant, you definitely didn't need to practice.

Different lawyers have different styles in presenting their cases. Most prosecutors like to build them brick by brick, starting at the beginning. They often tell the story chronologically, as it transpired in real life, and in the subsequent investigation.

Defense attorneys can have differing approaches. Sometimes they attack the prosecutor's case in the same order it was presented, or sometimes they might go after the lesser evidence first, and the bigger stuff last. Or vice versa.

I have no set way that I do it; I go by instinct, and often it depends on the way I feel the jury reacted to the prosecution's evidence. In that sense for me it's more art than science, though in real life I usually pick science over art ninety-nine times out of a hundred. The only exception is when I'm pretending to be touched by art so that Laurie will think I'm sensitive.

In this case I've decided to take a scatter-shot approach, to bounce around from place to place, exposing holes in the prosecution's case wherever I can find them. So my next witness is completely different from my first. I call Father Thomas Manning of the St. Johns Episcopal Church in Elizabeth.

First I take Father Manning through the story of his life. He has pretty much spent all of his sixty-two years serving his religion and his community, and for the last eleven years has run a community outreach program for troubled teenagers.

If that résumé doesn't make him likable and believable to the jury, he also has a completely charming way about him. He employs self-deprecating humor, and clearly doesn't take himself too seriously.

"How long have you known Joey Desimone?" I ask.

"Nine years."

"How did you meet each other?'

He proceeds to describe how Joey came in one day and volunteered to help out with the kids in the program. It was at a time that the program was understaffed and underfunded, so his help was welcome.

"What did he do there?"

"Anything we asked. Washed dishes, played ball with the kids, taught them to read, you name it. There was nothing he wouldn't do to help, but mostly he was a mentor to the kids."

"Did the kids know who his family was?" I ask.

"Yes. And Joey would help them understand what was right, and what was wrong. I never heard him say anything bad about his family, but he showed the kids there was another way. And that the other way was better."

"Did he donate money as well?'

Father Manning nods. "Ten thousand dollars every New Year's Day. Still does it to this day. It keeps us going."

"How did you react when Joey was arrested for these two murders?"

"Well, I was shocked, of course. And I felt for the victims, and I prayed for them. And

I also felt for Joey, and prayed for him as well. But . . ."

He stops, as if not sure whether he should finish the thought. Since I know what the thought is that he might not finish, I press him on it. "What were you going to say?"

"But I guess most of all I felt outraged, that this could happen to an innocent man."

"So you don't believe Joey to be guilty of this crime?"

"No, sir. I would trust Joey Desimone with my life, and the lives of my family."

Dylan stands to question Father Manning, a task I don't envy. This is not the guy you want to attack in front of a jury.

"Father Manning, first of all, I think I speak for everyone when I thank you for your service to the community," Dylan says, an obvious attempt to make me nauseous.

"You're welcome."

"Father, do you know the details of the murders, and the investigation that the police conducted?"

"No, I don't. Well, just what I read in the papers."

"So you're not aware of the evidence that has been presented so far during this trial?"

"No, sir."

"Do you know where Mr. Desimone was at the time of the murders?"

"I do not."

"You weren't with him?"

"I was not."

"Father Manning, during the time that the defendant was helping you with your program, were you aware that he was having an affair with Karen Solarno?"

"I was not. We never discussed our personal lives."

"Would you have approved of it?"

I object, but Hatchet lets him answer. "I would have attempted to discourage him from continuing it."

"Would you have thought him capable of such a thing in the first place?" Dylan asks.

"The flesh is weak."

"You testified that the defendant is still financially supporting you?" Dylan asks.

For the first time, Father Manning's tone changes, and takes on a harder edge. "He has continued to donate to our program, to the children."

It was a mistake on Dylan's part to imply, however subtly, that Father Manning might be testifying because of financial considerations. He backs off quickly, and lets him off the stand.

All in all, it was a pretty good day for us. Not good enough, but pretty good.

Cindy Spodek clearly didn't have to be very persuasive to make this meeting happen. I get my first sense of that when she comes out to the reception area to greet me on my arrival at the Newark FBI office. I had no idea she would be here.

"You work in Boston," I say.

"Thanks for the info," she says. "I was coming in anyway for some Christmas shopping." Then, "My colleagues thought it was a good idea for me to be here. You have a reputation that precedes you."

"Nice to hear," I say. "Colleagues? As in more than one?"

"Yes, you're meeting with two agents, not counting me. The one who will do most of the talking is Gregory Beall. He's based in Washington. The other is Jeffrey Givens, who covers organized crime in the tristate area."

"Why such a good turnout?" I ask. If both

of these agents showed up for a meeting that I requested, something I said must have touched a very sensitive chord.

"You're a celebrity attorney," she says. "You'll probably just sign a few autographs and leave."

"Sounds good," I say.

We start to walk toward the office, when Cindy says, "Behave yourself; I'm here to make sure you don't act like an asshole."

"You think you're up to it?"

"No chance."

When I get into the office, Cindy makes the introductions, and, as predicted, Special Agent Beall takes the floor.

"You have information for us?" he asks.

"You left out the 'vice versa' part."

He tries to look bemused. "You think we have information for you? I don't believe we called this meeting."

"No, but you sure turned out in force," I say. "In lawyer-land, we call that a 'tell.' So here's the way we can work this, and jump in if you've got another idea. I'm in the middle of defending Joey Desimone on a murder charge, and I find myself with information that you're clearly interested in. But I'm not sure how the information relates to my case."

"You want to get to the point?" Beall asks.

I nod. "I'm on the way. I'll tell you what I've got, you tell me what you've got, and you tell the court whatever you develop that can be helpful to my client."

"We'll make that decision when the time comes," he says.

"That's reasonable," I say, and stand to leave. "Call me when the time comes."

"Andy . . ." Cindy says.

"Sorry, Cindy. I forgot to mention when we spoke that I wanted to meet with serious people."

"Sit down," says Beall, who is no doubt used to people sitting down when he tells them to.

"I can't remember the last time I was this intimidated," I say, still standing.

Beall doesn't say anything for a few moments, pretending to ponder what he can and can't say. There are few things less sincere in the world than agent-pondering in a situation like this; they have gotten their marching orders long before the meeting about what they can or cannot say.

"Let's get this over with," he says.

"So we agree on the arrangement?"

"Within reason. What have you got?"

"Carmine Desimone is dead."

They exchange quick looks among themselves, and Givens shakes his head slightly.

"Not possible," he says. "We'd know about it. So how about you stop wasting our time?"

Givens has instantly annoyed me with his condescending attitude. "Well, he is very dead, and you apparently are in the dark," I say. "You spend a lot of time in the dark?"

"Better than spending my time with a dog and a dying fat man. Did Nicky tell you Carmine's death was his fault also? Or just Joey being convicted?"

I look at Cindy, not pleased that she related details about my meeting with Nicky Fats to Givens. She shakes her head, but I'm not sure why she's doing that. What I am sure about is that Givens is thoroughly on my nerves.

"Is anybody here interested in a serious discussion?" I ask. "If not, let's hug and part friends."

Beall asks, "OK. How did Carmine die?"

"Not sure," I say. "But it's a safe bet it wasn't quietly in bed with his loved ones surrounding him."

"Who?"

"Not sure of that either, but one of the participants was a man named Bruni. He's unfortunately also gone to that great cell-block in the sky."

"How do you know all this?"

"That I will take to my grave," I say. There is no way I am going to tell anyone about Marcus's role in this.

Beall asks me a bunch more questions about Carmine, which I answer in varying degrees of completeness. But I don't think they are here to talk about Carmine at all, which is why Givens has given up total control of the meeting to Beall. I think the mention to Cindy of Simon Ryerson is what brought Beall up from Washington.

Finally, he says, "OK, let's talk about Simon Ryerson."

"You know, I'm a little talked out. Why don't you talk while I rest?"

He nods, obviously having expected this. "Simon Ryerson has been running arms for the last sixteen months. Mostly for domestic consumption, and we're not sure where he's getting them. But if there's a nutjob west of the Mississippi with a rifle, chances are they got it directly or indirectly from Simon Ryerson."

"But you haven't arrested him because he's branching out, and you want to wait until he makes his big move."

"Right. And we think it's South America," Beall says.

"Oh, it's definitely South America. Seven trips that I know of in the last eight months.

Colombia, Venezuela, Ecuador, Peru . . ."

"How do you know all this?" Beall asks, obviously surprised.

I turn to Cindy. "You didn't tell them about my investigative prowess?"

"I must have left that out," she says.

"He's met with some government officials in each place, but if there's a legitimate business reason for it, we can't find it."

"Don't we already arm most of these countries?" I ask.

"Their military, to some extent," he says.

"So if the United States government is already peddling arms, why do they need Simon Ryerson?"

"You may not be as bright as you think," he says.

"That's certainly possible. Think of this as your chance to educate me."

"Each of these countries has large, private entities that deal in illegal substances."

"Cartels."

"Right. And these cartels are both wealthy and violent. They are also, shall we say, resistant to government intervention."

"So they need weapons," I say.

"Weapons that we don't want them to have. And weapons that we believe are going to be supplied by Simon Ryerson. We don't know how, and we don't know when," he says. "So tell me something about Simon Ryerson that I don't already know."

"He's the new, unelected head of the Carmine Desimone crime family."

Steven Halitzky and Sam Willis should switch places. Sam is an accountant who thinks of himself as a private eye, and Halitzky is a private eye who looks and talks like an accountant, or at least the common caricature of one.

Halitzky is maybe five eight, a hundred fifty pounds, balding slightly, and wears thick glasses. He talks in a monotone, with very little expression, and always seems to be reading aloud, even when he's not.

He is the investigator that Edward Young assigned to investigate Richard Solarno, after he had reason to believe the by-then dead Solarno had been involved with arms dealing.

He is also the man Edward has in effect loaned to me, for the purposes of testifying at this trial. Edward feels, no doubt justifiably, that he was the target of a shooting to prevent him from testifying. He wants to avoid that, and is sort of using Halitzky as his bulletproof vest.

Ironically, I think the jury, or at least those members that can stay awake, are finding Halitzky to be a compelling witness. His lack of emotion somehow adds to his credibility, as does his encyclopedic knowledge of his subject matter.

His investigation of Solarno had been remarkably thorough, and the documents that Edward had provided me didn't tell nearly the entire story. Halitzky is more than capable of filling in the blanks, and by the time he is finished, I don't think anyone could doubt that Solarno was a criminal who dealt with other criminals.

When I turn him over for cross-examination, Dylan unfortunately takes the perfectly correct approach to him.

"Mr. Halitzky, in your extensive investigation, did you uncover any evidence that someone other than Mr. Desimone murdered Mr. and Mrs. Solarno?"

"I did not."

"If you had, you would have provided the police with that information, correct?"

"Correct," Halitzky says.

"Did you uncover any evidence that would tend to prove the defendant's innocence?"

I stand. "Objection, Your Honor, that is

outside the scope. Mr. Halitzky did not investigate the Solarno murders, nor did he investigate anything that Mr. Desimone did or did not do. To save time, he also found no evidence relating to the assassinations of Presidents Kennedy or Lincoln."

Hatchet looks at me with disdain. "Next time I would advise you to stop your objection at 'outside the scope.' Sustained."

Dylan nods and goes on. "Did you find any evidence of threats against Mr. Solarno by any of the people he did business with?"

I stand again, because Halitzky did not look for any threats; that wasn't the job Edward assigned him to. "Objection. Outside the scope."

"A quick-learning lawyer," Hatchet says. "How refreshing. Sustained."

On redirect I pound home the fact that Halitzky not finding exculpatory evidence on Joey, and not uncovering threats against Solarno, was of no significance since he didn't look for them.

By the time he leaves the stand, Halitzky has delivered on his two missions. He helped my case, and he kept Edward from having to testify.

Next I call two expert witnesses to counter the forensic testimony that Dylan had presented. The term "expert" is loosely used in courtroom proceedings. There are always, and I mean always, experts on both sides of every issue. If two people take completely opposite positions on issues within their supposed areas of expertise, how can they both be experts?

Basically my experts say that the gunshot residue on Joey's jacket could have been there for a very long time, months even, and that the same is true for the fingerprints on the gun.

They also say that the gun could have been fired by other people without removing Joey's print.

Dylan questions them and makes some points, and this remains in my opinion the strongest area of his case. My experts have made some headway, but as in most trials, it becomes a question of which experts the jury will believe.

Next will come the big decision, whether or not to let Joey testify. He did not do so in the first trial, in fact, only two of all the clients I've ever had have testified in their own defense. When last I checked, both of them were getting along really well with their wardens.

Joey and I have discussed this, and he wants to take the stand. It's a regret of his that he didn't do so last time. Having said that, he also promises to defer to whatever I think is best.

It's a tough one, so I head home to take Tara for a walk and discuss it with her. She wags her tail a couple of times when I mention the possibility of Joey testifying, but I think it might be because she saw a squirrel across the street.

"How about paying attention?" I ask. "If it wasn't for you trying to be the Sigmund Freud of golden retrievers, we wouldn't be in this mess in the first place. You and your therapy."

She doesn't say anything, not so much as a bark. It's a technique that all shrinks employ; Tara is just better at it than most. And now she's trying to get me to make the decision about Joey testifying, by following my own instincts.

She wants me to get in touch with my "inner lawyer."

We head home and I talk it out with Laurie. She has no inner lawyer, and therefore is more inclined to let defendants testify. She thinks the more that comes out, the easier it will be to reveal the truth. And unlike we lawyers, the truth is what she usually roots for.

There are two factors making me more willing to consider my client testifying in this case. For one thing, I think Joey can be a compelling witness. He is smart, articulate, and believable. The jury is looking to convict a monster, and Joey simply does not fill that bill.

The other consideration is that I have no illusions about how successful we have been so far. I believe that we have been effective, but the "presumption of guilt" burden that I think all defendants carry, just by nature of being charged, is a large one. And I don't think we have closed the deal yet.

"I think you should sleep on it," Laurie says.

"Why don't we sleep on it together?"

She shrugs. "That works."

The rainy season in Peru lasts for five months, and it can be relentless. Heavy downpours, often lasting for days, are commonplace.

That's what they had been telling Simon Ryerson, just as they were telling him that it should have started a full two weeks ago. But every day he got the phone call, telling him that except for an occasional drizzle and ever-present mist, the real start to the season was late in coming.

It was the one thing that could not be planned, and could not be compensated for. The rain was not necessary to execute the plan, but it was very necessary to cover the tracks, at least long enough to ensure success.

Costa and Bruni had still not been found, dead or alive, and that fact made Ryerson uncharacteristically uneasy. He still did not believe that Bruni had killed Costa and fled, nor did Iurato. Which likely meant that someone else had killed them both, which in turn meant that they were dealing with a very deadly adversary. Because Bruni and Costa were not two men who would have gone down easily.

Neither the Desimone trial, nor Andy Carpenter's investigation, were of real concern to Ryerson anymore. The investigation, while worrisome at first, had so far made little progress, and the danger time was about to pass.

As far as Desimone was concerned, Ryerson was relatively uninterested in whether he stayed in prison or went free. Although there was always the danger that Joey, if he went free, would try to avenge his father's murder.

Ryerson almost smiled at the thought. Good luck with that, Joey.

So all Ryerson could do was that which he hated to do . . . wait. There was a limit to how many times he could check things in Peru, and in the United States. There was a limit to how many times he could reassure his own nervous people that things were going to be fine, and a limit to how often he could go over the plans once the action began.

And then he got the call he wanted to hear.

It had started to rain.

Hard.

"If you still want to, then I think you should testify." I tell this to Joey in our daily meeting before the start of the court day.

He doesn't respond for a few moments, and then says, "Oh."

I had expected him to be enthusiastic, but that's not the reaction I'm seeing at all, so I ask him what he's thinking.

"Well, I'm mostly glad you said that, because I definitely would like to testify, especially if you think I should. But the fact that you think I should means you think we're in trouble."

It's an absolutely correct analysis, so I nod. "We're definitely in trouble; if I had to quantify it I would say that we have a twenty-five percent chance of winning, maybe thirty."

"Which means there's a seventy-five percent chance I spend the rest of my life in prison."

"If you testify, I think there is the potential to improve those odds. But there is always the chance that it can backfire, and that would mean disaster."

"How could it backfire?" he asks.

"Dylan could trip you up. Make you look bad."

"How can he trip me up? I'll be telling the truth."

"That matters, but not as much as you think," I say. "Cross-examination is a game, maybe even an art, and Dylan has a lot more experience at it than you do." I tap the table. "This table has more experience at it than you do."

"I can handle it, Andy," he says, and I believe that he probably can.

"OK."

We make a plan to meet after court, to go over what his testimony will be. I don't like to overrehearse a witness; we both already know what he's going to say, and I don't want to reduce the spontaneity with which he will say it. In fact, I don't call them "rehearsals," the way some lawyers do. That sounds too much like acting out prepared dialogue, which I do not want my witnesses to do.

I don't have to play for time and call witnesses to fill out the day today, since

Hatchet has notified us that another commitment is causing him to adjourn at two o'clock. That will give me time to meet with Joey, and let him get a good night's sleep.

Tomorrow will be the most important day of his life.

My witness for today is Luther Karlsson, the shrimper who worked for Solarno, and who quit shortly before his death. I start by taking him through a little bit of his career, and then on to his job for Solarno. That job was fairly simple; it was to catch shrimp, just like he has been doing his entire life.

His testimony is actually somewhat poignant, although poignancy-recognizing has never been a specialty of mine. I don't really have a way to detect poignancy on my own, so I judge it based on how other people react. If, for instance, women put their hand to their mouths, or someone gets teary-eyed, that's a sure sign of it.

But I digress. Karlsson loves what he does, always has, and it comes through in the way he talks about it. And judging by the reaction of the jurors, I think they're moved by it.

His love for his job also leads me to the obvious question, "Why did you leave?"

He describes a growing dissatisfaction, as over time Solarno Shrimp seemed to become less about the shrimping. Boats weren't being sent out at optimum times and to optimum places; the shrimping seemed to not be the most important thing to the company.

"What was the most important thing?" I ask.

He shrugs and shakes his head. "Can't say that I know."

I take him through the day that he saw the boat loaded with armaments of various kinds. It was really by accident; he heard a strange noise in the motor of the boat as it came in, and decided to take a look and make sure everything was OK. He wound up seeing a lot more than the motor.

"What did you do after you saw the weapons?" I ask.

"I told them I didn't want to work there no more."

"Why?"

"Because I didn't want to work there no more."

It makes perfect sense. In fact, I don't question him anymore because I don't want to question him anymore. Instead, I offer Dylan the opportunity.

"Mr. Karlsson, are you aware that arms smuggling is illegal?"

"I'm not sure what arms smuggling is, but

I think it's legal to own guns. I got three of my own."

Dylan smiles, a little too condescendingly. "Based on your testimony, this was quite a few more than three, wouldn't you say?"

"Wouldn't I say what?"

"That this was quite a few more than three."

"It sure was."

"And you didn't believe that to be illegal?" Dylan asks.

He pauses for a moment. "Didn't really think about it much either way."

"But you quit immediately?"

"The next day."

"Because of the guns?"

Karllson nods his agreement with that. "That's right."

"What about the guns made you quit?"

"They weren't shrimp."

It doesn't take much more like this for Dylan to let him off the stand; in fact, I think he'd like to throw him off the stand.

But the bottom line is that Karlsson did not do much damage to Dylan's case. It's been pretty well established that Solarno was dealing arms, and that's really all Karlsson could testify to. Too bad he knows nothing about the actual killer of the Solarnos.

Once Karlsson is off the stand, Hatchet

sends the jury out and asks me how much longer my case is going to take.

"We have one more witness, Your Honor."

"Who might that be?"

"Joseph Desimone," I say, and Dylan reacts.

"Well, that answers my next question," Hatchet says. He was going to ask if Joey was testifying, since if he was not, Hatchet would have to instruct him that only Joey could make that decision. He's asked the question a few times before, and I've left it open, saying that he might testify, but that we hadn't decided yet. If Joey was not testifying, he would have to verbally say so to Hatchet, and confirm that he was told his options and voluntarily declined.

Dylan is obviously surprised, both at the fact that Joey will take the stand, and that I gave him a heads-up in this manner. I could have announced it tomorrow, and claimed that we decided it tonight. I wasn't giving Dylan a break by breaking the news now, it was more an attempt to curry a little favor with Hatchet. Dylan is too good a lawyer not to have been prepared for the possibility of having to question Joey, so he'd be ready either way.

Of course Dylan, like all lawyers, believes

that any lawyer who lets his client testify is nuts.

This time they all may be right.

Technically, the Montaro Dam should be called the Montaro Dams. While it is generally assumed to be a single dam, it is actually a series of four. There is the main one, amplified over the years on a number of occasions, and then three adjacent ones, added to reduce the pressure that has increased over time.

The purpose of the dams are twofold. They divert water into large reservoirs, which the entire central area of Peru lives off of during the dry season. But most important, they stop the water from descending down into the valley below, which by any standard would be a catastrophe.

During the dry season, the dam holds back about two hundred million cubic feet of water, a comparatively puny amount. Once it starts to rain in force, usually in November, that amount rises to an average of six hundred million cubic feet. At times, the total can rise to over eight hundred million, and the dam is graded as safe under a billion.

Inspections are done on a fairly regular basis, usually twice a year, in January and September. They are conducted by Peruvian army engineers, and the last one was done the week of September 18, just three weeks before the planting of the explosives.

The rains started three days ago, steady at first, then torrential. The villagers below the Montaro Dam took it in stride; this weather was nothing unusual, and certainly no cause for concern. The dam had protected them since before the oldest villager was born, and there was no reason to doubt its strength now.

The explosives were detonated remotely. There were thirty-eight detonations in all, executed one every forty-five seconds. It was done slowly so that it would not be noticed; the explosions themselves were each relatively small, and muffled by the fact that they were underwater, and there was a loud, driving storm above them.

By the eighteenth explosion, the dam was sufficiently weakened that it was barely holding back the water. By the twentieth, it gave way, and by the twenty-fourth, all parts of the dam were breached.

It took six and a half minutes for the water to reach the first village, and another twenty seconds for that village to cease to exist. Reaching the last of the twenty-two villages in its path took another fourteen minutes, and later estimates would be that twenty-eight thousand lives were lost in that time-frame.

For the next forty minutes, in an act of irony that no one appreciated, the rain stopped and the sun came out.

Way too late.

It was fourteen minutes later that recently appointed Minister of the Interior Omar Cruz received the shocking emergency phone call he knew was coming.

Within eleven minutes after that, he had notified the president and all of his fellow cabinet ministers. The president followed his suggestion to declare the situation to be a national emergency, and to appeal to other nations and world relief organizations for help.

Due to the remoteness of some of the affected areas, it would be some time before the full scope of the disaster became known.

But one thing was certain. Peru would need help to deal with it. They would need all kinds of provisions and emergency supplies, in what would have to be a full-scale international relief effort.

They would have to come in by the plane-load.

Many, many planeloads.

The preparatory session with Joey goes very well. I bring Hike with me, and we divide the work into two parts. I take Joey through the direct portion of his testimony first. I don't ask him specific questions; I just tell him the type of questions I will ask. And Joey, in turn, discusses how he will answer in general terms, so as not to affect the spontaneity at trial.

Next I have Hike conduct a mock cross-examination, and I instruct him to come at Joey as hard as he can. Hike is actually very good at it. His mind is capable of intense focus, and he possesses an ability to detect and hone in on inconsistencies.

Additionally, the fact that Hike can be the most annoying person on the planet helps his cross-examination technique. You want the witness to get angry and frustrated, so that he might make a key mistake. Hike is easy to get angry at, and he's a walking, talking frustration machine.

But Joey holds up well; he answers the questions in a straight-forward manner, never letting himself be goaded into anger. Of course, at the end of the day he knows Hike's on our side; Dylan will be a different case, since Joey is well aware that Dylan is trying to keep him in a cage for the rest of his life.

When we finish, I say to Joey, "OK. Time to decide whether or not you want to testify."

"I thought we already decided that," he says.

"We did. But that doesn't mean you can't change your mind. So tomorrow morning will be another time to decide."

"You think I'm going to do OK?" he asks.

I nod. "I think you probably will."

Joey turns to Hike. "What about you?"

I cringe. Knowing Hike, he'll probably predict that Joey will do so badly that New Jersey will make an exception and reinstitute the death penalty for this one case.

"I think you'll kick Dylan's ass," Hike says.

Go figure.

Hike and I head back to the office, since that's where his car is. On the way, I ask, "You think this is a good idea?"

"His testifying? I do. I think it might be

our only chance."

I turn on the radio to listen to the news. I have satellite radio, so I get all the cable news stations. The trial has been a fairly big story on those stations throughout, mainly because Joey is Carmine's son. But my expectation is that announcing he will testify will ramp up the coverage significantly.

But for now, news about the trial is nowhere to be found. The networks are covering a humanitarian disaster in Peru, apparently a dam broke and the toll of human life and property is feared to be enormous.

I think about Carolyn Greenwell, the woman from the State Department that I met with in Washington. She had said she was soon going to be in Peru, and I hope she wasn't caught in the disaster.

I also wonder if the situation will interfere with whatever Ryerson is planning, since I do believe it involves South America, and he had visited Peru on a number of occasions. Since I don't know what he's planning, it's hard to even speculate on whether this disaster will impact it.

Hike launches into a dissertation on how extreme weather is going to destroy the planet, and that there's nothing we can do about it. "We're history," he says.

"Are we going to make it to the end of

the trial?"

He shrugs. "Hard to say."

"Then we'll put Joey on the stand, just in case."

Another shrug. "Might as well."

A jolt is waiting for me when I get home. There, in the living room, is the dreaded Christmas tree, freshly cut by some Christmas tree cutter, and purchased by Laurie. And there, on the dining room table, are the four million lights and two billion ornaments that Laurie will be putting on that poor tree.

For the first time since it began, I'm thankful for the Desimone trial. Laurie surely knows I'm way too busy with preparations to help decorate the tree, which suits me perfectly.

I like Christmas trees, think they look great, and love having one. The problem is that during the decorating process, Laurie becomes a tree-Nazi. She is absolutely rigid about it, especially the putting up the lights part.

We wrap the lights around it, starting at the top. If left to my own devices, I'd wrap it around a dozen times and be done with it. Not Laurie; she doesn't allow more than maybe an inch vertically between strands. Since we have an eight-foot tree, you can do the math on how long it takes.

Then come the ornaments, with those ridiculous little hooks that keep falling on the floor. Laurie has her own system of ornament-hanging, baffling to anyone but herself, and whenever I go to hang one, it's the wrong color and shape, in the wrong place.

We resolved that problem by making the back of the tree, which no one can see, my ornament-hanging domain. I don't think she's thrilled with the compromise, but sees it as a way to maintain holiday together-ness.

"You're decorating the tree tonight?" I ask.

She nods. "I think so. I'm in the mood."

"Damn," I say. "With Joey testifying tomorrow, I really need to prepare." It's not true, of course, since I already did my preparation with Joey, and I like to maintain my own spontaneity by not overdoing it.

"Absolutely," she says. "I completely understand. You go do your work."

I pretend to be disappointed, and say, "Sorry, wish I could help. But if you're in the mood, you should go ahead and do it."

She nods. "Right. You know what else I was in the mood for? Decorating the tree together, then turning on the lights and making love on a blanket, right here on the living room floor."

"I'll go get the hooks."

At moments like this, the global community really does come together. Political considerations and alliances become less important, as countries from almost all parts of the ideological spectrum step up to the plate to help the victimized country deal with the disaster. This is partly due to real humanitarian concern, and partly due to countries wanting to appear to have real humanitarian concern.

In Peru's Montaro Dam disaster, as it already was being called, the United States was assuming its standard role as the most active provider of emergency aid. The Red Cross, again per usual, was the lead agency in coordinating the effort, and most private and public help went through them.

The scope of the disaster was just barely becoming known; more than twenty thousand killed or missing, perhaps two hundred thousand more displaced from homes that no longer existed.

In such a situation, the relief efforts must be multifaceted. First is the rescue component; there were undoubtedly many people trapped but alive, and they must be found and taken to safety. Armies in the U.S. and elsewhere are well equipped for these tasks, and many governments immediately dispatched troops. Also, search and rescue divisions of fire departments located everywhere from Seattle to Miami prepared their people to fly in and help in the mission.

And then there was caring for those already classified as survivors. They had no homes, no food, no medical care or supplies, no water, none of the normal services of life. All of this had to somehow be provided in about as inhospitable an area as could be imagined.

And all had to be provided fast.

The president of the United States, speaking on camera, read a statement expressing support for, and kinship with, the Peruvian people. When something like this happened, and happened right in our hemispheric backyard, the United States would do much more than its part.

Every serviceable airport in Peru, and many in adjoining countries, readied for the onslaught. Some of the aid would be coming by sea, but air transport would provide by far the most, because time was so much of the essence.

Simon Ryerson watched it all with satisfaction. Bringing down the dam was far from the most difficult part of the operation, but without it, nothing else could be accomplished.

Ryerson never had the affliction of a conscience, but even if he did, he could have rationalized this one away. He was doing a job, he was basically a hired gun, and if he hadn't done this, someone else would have.

The result on the ground would have been the same, but someone else would reap the award.

It was, Ryerson thought, much better this way.

In my mind, there are three possible reasons for a defendant to testify. All of them apply in varying degrees to the Desimone trial.

One is if he is likable, and believable, and the jury will therefore be favorably disposed toward him. The jury has heard about Joey from everyone but Joey, and most of it has been negative. For all they know he is a surly monster, and this is our chance to show them otherwise.

Another reason is if the client can introduce some facts into evidence, facts that no one else can bring forward. It does no one any good to have a defendant simply take the stand to profess his own innocence; jurors recognize that as obviously self-serving. But in this case, Joey can for instance relate how his fingerprints got on the gun, which is a huge piece of evidence against him.

The third reason is the Hail Mary approach, in which the defendant's testimony might somehow strike a spark, shake things up, in a way to win at least one member of the jury to the defense side. I don't think our situation here is that dire, but a positive spark of some sort couldn't hurt.

The court today has an electric feeling to it, and the gallery is packed when I arrive. I'm a little surprised, because the media coverage this morning was understandably focused on the disaster in Peru.

I find it amazing how fast the various news agencies are able to get people to any place in the world. It must cost a fortune to do so, yet each one seems to undertake the operation on their own. I would think they could find a way to consolidate their efforts, while remaining competitive, but it seems like they can't.

"You OK?" I ask Joey when I see him before the start of the court session.

He nods. "I'm fine. A little nervous, but I'll be fine."

"Just tell your story," I say. "And remember, during cross-examination, don't argue, and don't get mad. Everybody's just doing their job, playing the game. You do the same."

Hike says something to Joey, which I can't hear, and Joey nods. Hike probably told him that with the end of the world coming any day now, it doesn't matter what Joey says on the stand, so there is no reason to be nervous.

I look over at Dylan, who is standing near the prosecution table, talking animatedly with colleagues. He seems tense, keyed up, as if he were about to take an SAT test that would determine his college future. I wouldn't be surprised if he has a pocket full of Ticonderoga number two pencils.

"The defense calls Joseph Desimone," I say, and we're off.

I take some time to let the jury get to know Joey, taking him through his education, culminating in his graduation from Rutgers, and then his time in the Marines. He never saw actual combat, but by the time I'm finished with him, it sounds like he won the Congressional Medal.

Dylan objects that we need to move to more relevant matters, and Hatchet agrees, so I ask, "How did you meet Karen Solarno?"

"It was at a charity dinner. At a Hilton, I think in Woodcliff Lakes. I was living in New York City at the time, so I wasn't familiar with North Jersey."

"How did you come to be there?"

"It was a benefit to raise money to fight

cancer. My grandparents both died of the disease, so my father was always working for the cause and making large donations. He had bought two tables that night."

"So you were supporting the charity, and your father?"

He grins slightly. "Actually, I was a seat filler, because no one else wanted to go. I can't say I blamed them."

"You weren't enjoying yourself?" I ask.

"Well, it was in the summer, and with all the people in the room, the air conditioner was having a tough time keeping up. So I went outside for a walk, near the pool, just to get some air. It turned out Karen had done the same."

"So you struck up a conversation?"

"Yes. I don't know who spoke first, but we were out there for about half an hour. We just really hit it off, and we made plans to meet for lunch the next week."

"Did you know she was married?" I ask.

"No. I didn't ask, and she didn't say. I guess I just assumed she wasn't, based on the way she was talking, and agreeing to the lunch."

That's how the affair began, and I don't bring out many of the details. I take him through the days that Karen told him she was married, that Richard was abusive, and that she was going to leave him.

I turn next to the elephant in the room. "It is widely believed that your father, Carmine Desimone, is the head of an organized crime family, Mafia, if you will."

"I know that," Joey says. I can see the emotion he's feeling, and I'm sure the jury can as well. What Joey and I know, but they don't, is that Carmine is dead.

"Is that an accurate description of what he does?"

"I don't know much about what he does. I know him as my father."

"But you never wanted to go into his business?"

"That's correct."

"Did you know that Richard Solarno did business with him?"

"Not at first. Karen didn't tell me until the day she ended our relationship."

"Why did she end it?" I ask.

"I'm not sure; I only know what she told me. She said that she still loved me, that she always would, but that she needed to give her marriage a chance."

"Were you angry?"

He nods slowly. "Angry, and upset, and hurt. I really loved her." He takes a moment to compose himself. "I still do."

I get him to explain the fingerprints in the

house and on the gun. When Richard was out of town, they met at her home often. Because she was often alone, she had purchased a gun, and he showed her how to hold it, put the safety on, etcetera.

"Did you ever take the gun out of the house?"

"Absolutely not."

"Where were you when the murder was committed?"

"I was home at my New York apartment the time they tell me it happened. I had a head cold, and I was in bed."

"Did you shoot and kill Richard Solarno?"

"No, I did not."

"Did you shoot and kill Karen Solarno?"

His voice cracks a little, but he gets the words out.

"No, I did not."

Dylan goes after Joey as hard as he can, and he scores some points.

He doesn't succeed in attacking Joey's basic story; Joey just does not give him an opening to do that. That story has the ring of truth, and its credibility is bolstered by Joey's admissions, that he was having an illicit affair, that he was furious when Karen dumped him, etcetera.

Dylan is openly incredulous and derisive, pointing out that no one can confirm that Joey was at home when the murder was committed, or that he was ill. He also makes a lot out of Carmine's reputation, and Joey's professed lack of knowledge of what his father really did for a living. It's not believable that Joey was unaware of Carmine's position, and I wish Joey hadn't claimed it.

But where Dylan is most successful is in using the statement that Joey made to the police against him. Joey had been foolish to have talked to them at all, but he did not know he was a suspect. Once he realized that he was, he lied about a few things, including the affair itself, and whether he ever held Karen's gun.

"I panicked," Joe said. "All of a sudden I realized that they thought I did this. I was devastated by Karen's death, and now they were implying that I killed her. I wanted them to understand that they should be out there looking for the real killer, so I tried to make them look at people other than me."

"So you were being a good citizen, trying to help the police in their investigation," Dylan mocks.

"And I was protecting myself."

"By lying."

Joey nods. "By lying."

The cross-examination takes four hours, longer by two hours than my questioning of Joey. He holds up remarkably well under the badgering, and under the pressure of knowing that any slip-up could contribute to depriving him of freedom for the rest of his life.

If I were a ringside judge scoring the day, I would probably give it to Joey by a round or two. I have no idea if that will be enough to sway the jury, but looking at the big picture, I'm glad that he testified.

Of course, it also gives me another reason to beat myself up over the first trial. Knowing what I know now, I would have let him speak up in his own defense last time.

Of course, knowing what I know now, I wouldn't have gone to law school.

The airfield in Guaranda, Peru, was geared up for unprecedented traffic. It was more than six hours from the disaster area, or at least it would have been if the roads were remotely passable. But more important, it was only an hour and a half flight to the airport serving as the hub for the relief effort.

Actually, it wouldn't take much to qualify as unprecedented traffic for Guaranda. It was mostly a private airfield, set in an area that was not exactly a hotbed of personal and corporate jets. The military also used the airfield, but that was mostly for refueling, and it was sporadic at best.

Guaranda was so rarely used that it did not even have air traffic control personnel, and certainly no customs presence. But in the current emergency all airfields were being pressed into service, so the workers at Guaranda were rushing to get it as ready as possible for the onslaught.

Leading the effort was the director of air operations for Guaranda, Carlos Manaya. It was not exactly a sought-after position, and Manaya had been in the role for eleven years. Now forty-one and not particularly ambitious, he had until recently anticipated remaining in the job until he ultimately retired.

His career path took something of a turn recently, when he secretly accepted an assignment that immediately paid him three hundred thousand American dollars, and when accomplished would pay him seven hundred thousand more. And the best part, except for the money, was that it was for doing almost nothing. In fact, all he really had to do was turn his head and look away.

Manaya actually knew nothing whatsoever about what was going on. He could make an educated guess, but really saw no reason to do so. He would just let it happen, profess ignorance if ever questioned, and collect his money.

He had no idea about the cavernous warehouse four hours to the north, or about the precious material that had been accumulating there for the past year. Or about the trucks that were waiting to carry that cargo.

To Guaranda airport.
And beyond.

"This case is not about arms dealing. It never was," is how Dylan begins his closing argument. "It's not about sinister bad guys who walk in the shadows, or nutjobs in Montana who play soldier. All of that is part of the sideshow, meant to distract you from the real issue, the real facts."

"Way back during opening arguments, before the endless talking . . ." He smiles self-deprecatingly, though I doubt an X-ray would reveal a single self-deprecating bone in Dylan's body. ". . . we told you what the case was about, and on behalf of the state, we have proven it."

He takes about five steps toward the defense table, which leaves him about ten feet away, and he points to Joey. "This case is about this man, Joseph Desimone, who was rejected by a woman. So he killed her.

"And the reason he was rejected? Because she wanted to make it work with her husband. So Joseph Desimone killed him as well.

"In the Desimone family, men get what they want, by whatever means necessary. The son learned that from the father, who learned that from his father before him. It was a way of life, and it worked quite well for them."

Dylan then launches into a rehash of the evidence. It's impressive, but not over-whelming. It's either enough to leave some reasonable doubt, or enough to put Joey away for life. And for the life of me, I don't know which.

I stand to take my final shot at convincing the jury. "I can't prove to you that Joseph Desimone did not kill Richard and Karen Solarno. I know that he didn't, but that's my knowledge, my judgment, not yours, and not anyone else's. I wish I could prove it, but I can't.

"It's very hard to prove a negative. Things have to break just right, and life usually doesn't work that way.

"But I also can't prove to you that any one of the other criminals and gangsters that Richard Solarno dealt with didn't kill him, and didn't kill his wife. I can't point to one and say, 'he did it,' or 'they did it,' because I just don't know. And neither does anyone else in this courtroom.

"That's why you're here, to make your own decision, but you do not have free rein. As Judge Henderson will tell you, you can only convict a defendant if you are certain beyond a reasonable doubt about his guilt.

"So, in the absence of proof one way or the other, all you can do is weigh the factors. For instance, you can weigh the fact that Joseph Desimone had never once been charged with a crime. Never so much as arrested, never even a suspect.

"This is no small feat, considering the reputation of others in his family. Because traditionally members of the Desimone family are suspected, and questioned, in regards to pretty much everything bad that happens in New Jersey. And sometimes with good reason.

"But not Joseph Desimone. Never Joseph Desimone. Because everyone, including law enforcement, understood that while he was a member of the family, he was never a member of the *family*.

"So we have Richard Solarno, a proven arms dealer, supplying weapons to people who wanted to purchase them in large quantities, and did not want to purchase them legally. What does this say about them? That they were just going to practice at the range, sort of like a hobby? Or that they were going deer hunting? Of course not. They wanted to use them for criminal activities; the very act of buying them was a criminal activity.

"And a member of the Montana State Police sat in this chair and told you that Solarno double-crossed his customers, that they were so angry about it that they threatened to kill him. Who would be more likely to actually have done so? People like that? Or someone like Joseph Desimone, who never committed a crime in his life?"

I launch into our assessment of the evidence that Dylan has summed up, exaggerating the success we had in refuting it. I don't take too long in doing so; the jury has heard plenty for one day, and I don't want them resenting me for delaying their naps.

"Joseph Desimone has already lost too much of his life, time that can never be made up to him. But you have the power to say enough is enough, to stand up and say that we don't take away a man's liberty in this state, in this country, unless we know that he deserves it. We need to know it beyond a reasonable doubt.

"I submit to you that the state has not come close to meeting that burden."

I head back to the table, and when I sit

385

down, Joey puts his hand on my shoulder. "Thank you, Andy. I know this can go either way, but without you, I'd have no chance at all."

The relief effort was in high gear almost immediately, especially in the United States Private citizens flooded the Red Cross phone lines with donations and responded to media appeals for canned goods and supplies by dropping them off by the tons at selected locations.

Corporations stepped up to the plate as well. Food and drug companies made enormous contributions, building supply companies followed suit, and airline cargo companies signed up to fly the goods in.

The FAA and air traffic control system also geared up to deal with the special circumstances. Flights to that area of South America were increased tenfold, so flight plans had to be quickly signed off on. Customs inspections were relaxed; there was just no way to keep up, and delay was unacceptable.

As is always the case, the true question

would be whether this would be a short burst, or was everyone in it for the long haul. How long would the rest of the world be there, helping the victims of the Montaro Dam disaster?

The media, while still covering it intensely, had subtly moved to the next phase. Not wanting to relentlessly paint only the grim picture, they were in the mode of splashing news of a single survivor found in the rubble, and parading on people to trumpet it as a miracle. They were desperate to find a feel-good story in the middle of a feel-awful situation.

Among the many hundreds of airplanes landing daily from the United States and around the world, two in particular were carrying food rations. They were huge cargo planes, and the desperately needed rations could feed and provide water for ten thousand people for one week.

The planes landed at the Lima airport, but such was the chaos there that they were on the ground for four hours before anyone paid attention to them, fourteen hours before the unloading process began, and almost thirty-six hours before they were empty.

The pilots rested for much of this time, since they had a long trip back to the States, where they promised to load up again and be back.

But once they took off, the trip wasn't quite as long as advertised. Rather than flying directly back to the United States, one of the planes reported engine trouble.

The two planes, professing a desire to stay together, diverted to a small airport in Guaranda, one stretched beyond its very modest limits by the impact of the ongoing crisis.

The report of engine trouble was bogus, and ultimately was not necessary, as no competent authority was available to pay attention to them anyway. They could have radioed in that they were diverting to the moon, and they wouldn't have been paid any mind.

Once on the ground, they simply waited for new cargo, cargo from a warehouse four hours to the north, cargo that had been accumulating there for over a year. It would take a full day to arrive, and then another to load.

And then that cargo would be on its way to the United States.

I don't have the slightest idea what the verdict will be.

Hatchet gives what I consider a fair charge to the jury, though I'm not pleased that he twice advises them that beyond a reasonable doubt does not mean beyond any doubt.

They look serious and intent on what Hatchet is saying, but I simply have no clue as to what they're thinking. It could be, "We're going to right an injustice and get this guy out of prison," or maybe, "I only wish we could give him a needle in the arm."

Usually I have a feeling one way or the other. That's not to say I'm right; in fact, my feelings are wrong the majority of times. But I'll have an expectation, based either in logic or hunch. This time I don't.

One thing that won't be different this time is my behavior, as I make the transformation from lawyer to lunatic. While waiting for a verdict, I become ridiculously superstitious, and the rituals seem to increase with each trial.

For instance, I will only get out of bed when the digital clock is set to an even number. I'll only make right turns in the car; if I have to go left I make three rights instead. I won't mention the word "verdict" to anyone but Tara, and if the phone rings, I'll only answer in the den. I was in the den when I got the call telling me there was a verdict in the Willie Miller case, so that has become my lucky phone room.

I may have mentioned this before, but I have serious mental issues.

Laurie handles me masterfully during these times; she stays as far from me as possible. She's there if I want to talk to her, but I never do. While waiting for a verdict, I don't want to be with anyone, including me. Unfortunately, no matter where I go, I always seem to be around.

I watch television with the remote in my hand, fingers poised on the buttons. I don't want to see any coverage of the trial, especially not legal pundits predicting the jury's decision. So instead I see a lot of coverage of the disaster in Peru.

During times like this I walk Tara maybe twice as much as usual. The weather doesn't matter; in fact, I think Tara's favorite thing is to walk in the snow. If Tara is nervous about the verdict, she's hiding it well.

I make it my business in situations like this to see my client every day. I can't imagine how they can handle the pressure. I'm crazed, and my life is going to go on relatively normally no matter what the jury decides. The defendant may not have a life.

Joey is holding up well. He asks me what I think the verdict will be, and he tells me he sees it as a fifty-fifty shot. I tell him I have no idea.

Then he asks me if I think the verdict will come in quickly, and I tell him I have no idea.

Then he asks me if a quick verdict would likely be good, or if a long one is more in our favor. I say I have no idea.

Then he asks me what Laurie and Hike think, and I tell him I have no idea if they have any idea.

It's possible that my visits aren't that helpful, but I really have no idea.

The call Ryerson was waiting eighteen months for finally came. It was simple and to the point.

"They're in the air."

He didn't have to ask if the cargo was on board, or if there were any problems for him to deal with. The caller would have said either of those things unprompted if that were the case.

Absent a plane crash, very little could go wrong now.

As soon as the call disconnected, Ryerson called Tommy Iurato and told Iurato to pick him up immediately. Iurato was there forty-five minutes later, and he and Ryerson then headed out to Teterboro Airport.

The guard at the gate was expecting them, and he waved them out to the tarmac. They parked fifty feet from the private jet that was there waiting for them, engine running, and the pilot already in the cockpit.

There was no real hurry, except a psychological one for Ryerson. He wanted to be there when the cargo planes arrived, wanted to watch as they were unloaded. He had worked so long and hard on this, planned so meticulously, that he just wanted to see it come to a satisfactory conclusion.

The flight plan to St. Louis called for them to be in the air for three hours and forty-five minutes. They were gone for twenty minutes, when Ryerson noticed that there were no lights below them, and in the moonlight it almost seemed as if they were above a vast expanse of water.

There are very few oceans between New Jersey and St. Louis, but it took a moment for Ryerson's mind to compute what was happening. By that time Iurato had grabbed him and was breaking his neck.

Iurato told the pilot he could go back to Teterboro. The original plan had been to drop Ryerson's body into the ocean, but Iurato had received different instructions two weeks ago.

The body would be found, and Carmine Desimone would be blamed.

I'm watching the local morning news.

It's safe; I know I can watch it for as long as I want, secure in the knowledge that I won't be forced to see anything of consequence. My mind can get lulled to sleep by weather and traffic, with a few robberies thrown in.

There will be no news of the trial, and I won't have to see any more depressing pictures from Peru.

But suddenly, in the middle of all this comfortable banality, I'm looking at the face of Simon Ryerson, and below it is the legend of "Breaking News . . . Prominent businessman found slain in park."

Two things immediately come to mind, equally silly. First, I want to point at the screen and say, "Hey, I know that guy!," even though I really don't. Second, I wonder why TV newswriters feel compelled to use words like "slain." Who talks like that? I'm in a profession that deals with murders and murderers all the time, and I've never heard anyone outside the media use the word "slain."

My mind belatedly clicks out of idiot mode and into normalcy. I need to analyze what this could mean to Joey's case. I'd had no way to get Ryerson's name before the jury; Dylan successfully argued lack of relevance, and Hatchet was correct to agree with him.

So I have to figure out if this can somehow give me an opening. Even when a case has gone to the jury, if some extraordinarily compelling evidence is discovered, they can be brought back in to hear more testimony.

In the field in which I have unfortunately and sporadically chosen to work, very little surprises me anymore. And I am not particularly surprised that Ryerson has been killed, since I'd learned that he had eliminated Carmine Desimone and effectively taken over the family.

Mafia chieftain, for all the power that the office provides, is not a safe occupation. If they call you "Don" something, and your first name isn't Donald, you need to watch your back. If you're a crime boss applying for life insurance, you should lie about your occupation, because otherwise the premiums themselves will kill you.

It's quite likely that someone was getting revenge for Carmine, and maybe for Nicky Fats. Or it could be another coup in progress, with another boss moving in.

But what does surprise me is that the body was found at all. No jogger in the park stumbled across Jimmy Hoffa, and no one is about to find Carmine Desimone. Yet Ryerson was found in a place that made the discovery inevitable. Whoever did it wanted the world to know that it was done.

I have no way of knowing whether the killing means that whatever major operation Ryerson was working on has been completed. It's likely that either it has, or he is no longer integral to its success.

It also makes me wonder on some level if what he was doing could have had something to do with the situation in Peru. Two things are true. One is that I do not believe in coincidences. The second is that I had gone years without hearing the word "Peru," then I learned that Ryerson was going there, and now a disaster there is all over the news.

Having said that, I have no idea how a dam failing and destroying lives and property could benefit Ryerson financially. Of course, what I haven't learned about him could fill books. For example, I know that he's a businessman, and I know the breaking-news writers called him a prominent businessman, but I, and probably they, don't have the slightest idea what his business is.

All we really know at this point is that he was "slain."

Sam Willis calls with the news that his hacking efforts have alerted him to the fact that Tommy Iurato is flying to St. Louis tomorrow morning. He's flying first class. "Don't these people ever fly coach?" Sam asks.

"Crime pays, big guy." The St. Louis trip is interesting to me, since we had earlier learned that Ryerson had made some trips there in the past year. But for my purposes, I don't view this as a big deal; if there's a connection between Iurato flying to St. Louis and Joey Desimone, I certainly can't see it.

"You want me to follow him? I'll be careful this time; I learned my lesson."

"Sam, if you follow him, you're fired from the team."

"OK."

"Sam . . ."

"I won't, Andy. I promise."

I'm satisfied with that, so I settle down to spend the rest of the day watching television and dreading a verdict phone call. I go even nuttier in the time between hearing that the jury has reached a verdict, and my actually hearing what that verdict is. It is the most helpless feeling imaginable, knowing that the boat has already sailed, but not knowing where it's going to arrive.

CNN does a special at four o'clock on the disaster in Peru, focusing on the rescue effort. Apparently, they must have decided that constant normal coverage isn't sufficient; they have to do some "special" coverage.

I decide to watch it for twelve minutes, until the Knicks game starts. For some television reason NBA games set to start on the hour always start twelve minutes after the hour.

It's about eight minutes into the CNN special when I see the footage of planes landing in Peru with supplies, with the announcer talking over it about the huge amounts of money contributed to the rescue effort. And just like that, everything clicks into place.

Don't you love when that happens?

I call Cindy Spodek on her cell, and dispense with the usual banter. I'm sure she can tell by my tone of voice, and certainly by my words, that this is important.

"Cindy, we need to have another meeting."

"What for?"

"I know what's being done, and I know who's doing it."

"Is this about trying to get something for your client?" she asks.

"Of course. But it goes way beyond that."

"OK," she says. "Who do you need there? Givens certainly, but I doubt Beall will come in from Washington. Maybe video him in? And I'll video in as well."

"Beall is a must; this most concerns him." I think for a moment about whether I want Givens there, who annoyed me the last time with his mocking description of my session with Nicky Fats. Then with another jolt I realize what bugged me so much about it, and I say, "Givens needs to be there also. He's going to make the trade I just thought of."

"What trade?"

"You'll know soon enough," I say. "Noon?"

"Noon it is."

With the fake mechanical problem miraculously fixed, the two planes took off from Guaranda.

They were completely loaded down with cargo, almost eleven hundred metric tons' worth, which meant they were carrying far more weight than they brought in on their "relief" mission.

Tommy Iurato was on an American Airlines flight to St. Louis. He had the option of taking a private jet, but preferred the safety of a commercial aircraft.

Iurato was no fool; he understood that betrayal and murder represented business as usual in this operation. He knew it especially well since he had frequently been the instrument of that betrayal and murder.

Iurato was not exactly sure how he was going to play it, but he would not be the next victim, of that much he was certain. He would likely take the promised payoff

and disappear forever, but if he didn't get
what was due him, he would make sure that
others were the ones who disappeared forever.

"It's about drugs coming into the country. That's what Ryerson was doing," I say. There's something surreal about the meeting. I'm talking to three people, but Agent Givens is the only person in the room with me. There is a large-screen TV taking up almost an entire wall, and it is divided into two panels. Cindy Spodek is in one, from her Boston office, and Agent Beall is in the other, from Washington.

"Ryerson is dead," Beall says.

"Doesn't matter. He wasn't the key guy."

"And you know who the key guy is?" He sounds rather skeptical, probably thinking that I'm trying to maneuver to serve my own self-interest. He's right, but that doesn't mean I don't have news that he needs.

"I know who he is, I know where the drugs are coming from, I know how they're getting here, and I know where they're going."

"So you called the meeting," Beall says. "Tell us."

"First I want to hear what you know. Or more accurately, what Agent Givens knows."

"What are you talking about?" Givens asks.

"The last time I was here, you were acting like an asshole, which I suppose in and of itself is not that unusual an occurrence. You said something that bugged me, but I didn't know until this morning why it did."

"I'm waiting," he says.

"You asked me if Nicky Fats told me that Carmine's death was his fault, or just Joey getting convicted for hitting Solarno."

"So?"

"So I thought Cindy probably told you about my conversation with Nicky Fats, but she couldn't have. Because I never told her that Nicky told me Joey's conviction was his fault. I've never told anyone that."

"Or maybe you did," Given says.

I shake my head. "No, I didn't remember it myself until this morning. It wasn't the important part of what he said to me. What I focused on was that Solarno was a crook, and that Nicky knew it."

"So?"

"So how did you know what he said about Joey?"

He thinks for a moment. "I'm not at liberty to say."

"Well, you'd better get at liberty in a hurry, or I've got nothing to say about anything else. But you know what, I'll get you started. Jerry McCaskill told me that one of the main reasons you guys have been able to get inside and break up the crime families is intensified surveillance." I don't have to tell him that McCaskill had his job six years ago; he would certainly know that.

"You coming to the point?" Givens asks.

"Yeah. I think you knew what Nicky said to me because you heard every word of it. I think you had his room bugged."

"What if we did?"

"Then I want the tapes from six years ago, as well as the notes agents took from those tapes. I want to know if there's something on there that clears Joey Desimone."

Even as I say it, I am experiencing a terrible realization, one which makes me want to get out of that office as soon as possible.

"I don't know if they exist," says Beall, taking over. "But if they do, they're yours. Now tell me about the drugs."

"I have your word?"

"You have my word," Beall says. "I'll get people started on it immediately."

"Cindy?"

She nods from the screen. "His word is good, as is mine. And you have them both."

I nod. "There's an air cargo company called Coastal Cargo. They flew at least two planes into Peru with relief supplies; I saw them on television."

"So?"

"So they're flying back loaded with drugs. It can't be arms; there couldn't be enough to make all of this worth it. I googled it, and each of those planes can carry six hundred metric tons. I don't know what the hell a metric ton is, but it's got to be heavy. Twelve hundred metric tons of drugs would be worth an absolute fortune, even if the drug was aspirin.

"Carolyn Greenwell told me that drug trafficking has been way down for a year; she thought it was due to government efforts. But it's because they were waiting for this, so it could all be done at once."

If Beall is skeptical about this, he's hiding it well. "Who's behind it, and where is it going?"

"It's going to St. Louis, as is Tommy Iurato."

"Who is behind it?" Beall asks.

"That I'm not yet ready to tell you." The truth is that I'm not positive that I'm even right, but I'd bet on it. Actually, I am betting a lot on it.

He gets angry; I can't say I blame him. "This is bullshit."

I nod. "Call it what you want, but we're doing this my way."

There's a lot to learn, and little time to learn it.

I call Jerry McCaskill and ask if he'll be free to meet me in two hours. He says that he won't be in his office by then, but can meet me for a cup of coffee if I'd like. We agree to meet at a diner on Route 4, about ten minutes from the George Washington Bridge, and another fifteen from Alpine, which is where I'm going first.

Edward Young has also agreed to meet with me right away. He's at his house, and certainly didn't sound thrilled to hear from me. It's a reluctance he's had ever since his car got shot up and his driver killed.

His house is certainly impressive, a sprawling ranch style, with large, endless manicured lawns on rolling hills, as well as a tennis court and swimming pool.

Edward lets me in himself, though I see two bodyguards watching him do so. I have no idea if he's added the bodyguards since the shooting, or if his wealth caused him to have them before, and right now it really doesn't matter.

We head toward a den in the back of the house, though the bodyguards stay in the living room, near the front.

Once we get there, he says, "I thought we had an agreement." He's referring to his giving me the documents showing Solarno was involved in criminal activities, with him getting in return my promise not to call him to testify.

"We did, and I stuck to it," I say. "The trial's over, and I didn't call you."

He nods. "True enough. Have you gotten a verdict yet?"

"No, anytime now."

"So what can I do for you?"

"Another trade," I say.

He seems puzzled. "I've got nothing to offer you, and I can't think of anything you have that I want."

"I definitely have something you don't want."

"What might that be?"

"I have the knowledge that you are in the process of executing the largest drug deal in history." I have no idea if that's true, but it's got to be close. "And amazing as it seems, that's just the beginning."

"What are you talking about?"

"I'm talking about you probably causing the dam in Peru to collapse, making you a mass murderer. I'm talking about you taking twelve hundred metric tons of drugs out of that country, whatever a metric ton is, and flying them to St. Louis. I'm talking about you having Carmine Desimone, Simon Ryerson, and a bunch of other people, including your driver, killed. I'm talking about you giving new meaning to the word 'shithead.' "

If he's worried, he's hiding it well. He's just learned that the most important secret of his life, one he has literally killed thousands to protect, is not a secret anymore. But he is a man used to getting what he wants, and I can tell that he thinks this will be more of the same.

It turns out that he gives new meaning to the word "unflappable." "That's quite a speech," he says. "And what do you want from me?"

"Information on who killed Richard and Karen Solarno."

"I have no idea who killed them."

"I think you do," I say, though I really don't think that at all. Basically, this is a shot in the dark, and it's not going well.

"You're wrong," he says. "But maybe I can trade something else."

"You mean money?"

"I mean more money than you've ever dreamed of. I mean one hundred million dollars."

"I dream in euros," I say. "Sometimes shekels."

"You're mocking me?" he asks, showing a flash of anger.

"I'm telling you I want information that clears my client."

"How do I know you haven't spoken to the authorities about this?"

"You don't, but I haven't," I lie. "All I want is information, and then we can go on with our respective lives."

He reaches under his desk, and seems to press a button. Then he walks toward the closed door, and says, "I'm afraid your respective life is about to be shortened."

He opens the door. His back is to me when he does, so I can't see his face, but I wish I could.

Because standing there is Marcus Clark.

I'm wearing a wire, so I tell the agents it's okay to approach the house. They had not been happy with the arrangement, but they would have come in with such force that they'd have been seen, and I never would have had the chance to question Edward about the Solarno murders.

Marcus had assured me that if he hid in the backseat, and we parked close enough to the house, he could ensure my safety. As insurers go, Marcus makes Allstate look like a mom-and-pop operation.

The fact that Edward had no information, or at least none he shared with me, did not come as a surprise. It was worth a shot.

Once the bodyguards are revived, they and Edward are taken off in one of what seems like twenty thousand FBI cars that have shown up, carrying twenty thousand agents. If the government is serious about dealing with the national debt, they can carve out a big chunk by making FBI agents carpool.

"We're going to need a statement," Givens says, after the bad guys have left.

"OK. Here's one: I'm out of here."

Actually I wish I could stay and chat, because I'm not at all looking forward to my next stop, which is at the diner to meet Jerry McCaskill. The former agent is waiting for me at a table when I arrive.

"So this is a matter of life and death?" he asks, slightly amused. I had told him that to get him to see me right away. "A little lawyer hyperbole perhaps?"

"I should have said 'life in prison.' "

That surprises him, and removes the amusement from his eyes. "What can I do for you?"

"When we talked last time, you told me about the surveillance you guys were doing over the years, to break up the Mafia families."

"I remember."

"You also said that you didn't follow Joey Desimone's trial, because you were out of town on an assignment."

"So?"

"And you also said that the evidence showed that Joey was guilty."

I can see in his eyes that he's figured out where this is going.

"Tell me why you're here, Andy."

"I think you also had the surveillance back then, and I think you were completely familiar with it. That's why you knew the evidence without following the trial."

He nods. "That's correct."

I dread asking this question, because I really dread the answer. But I have to ask it. "Will you tell me what I need to know?"

He thinks about it for a few seconds, which feel like a few years. Finally, he nods slowly.

"Joey Desimone killed Richard and Karen Solarno."

"Are you sure?" I ask, knowing full well that he is.

"Beyond any doubt, reasonable or otherwise. The tapes prove it."

"Why didn't you give them to the prosecution?"

"Because it would have blown the surveillance. Now the bad guys have learned not to talk when we can hear them. But back then they felt like nothing could touch them. We were making too much progress to give up the secret."

"So you would have let Joey walk?" I ask.

He nods. "But fortunately he didn't."

"There's always a next time."

"Uh, oh. What's wrong? Is there a verdict?" are the first words out of Joey's mouth when he sees me.

"What makes you think something's wrong?" I ask.

"Well, for one thing, you're never here this early in the morning unless court's in session. But mostly it's the look on your face. You don't depend on someone for your life and not know their moods."

"You did it," I say.

"Did what?"

"You murdered Richard and Karen Solarno."

He doesn't seem shocked by what I've said, and pauses for a few moments, as if carefully weighing his response. "How did you figure it out?"

"That doesn't matter."

"Actually, to be precise, I murdered Richard Solarno. Karen was self-defense. She was trying to kill me."

"Why?"

"Probably some misguided revenge because I had just killed her husband."

"I meant why did you go there that day? Why did you do it?"

Another pause. "OK, I owe you this much . . . I owe you a lot more. Richard Solarno was a lying scumbag who thought he was bulletproof. He thought he could cheat people like my father. Whether I did it or not, he was going to be killed. The phrase is 'dead man walking.' "

"So why you?"

"I was making my bones, Andy. I was entering the business. I was joining my father," he says, before pausing. "And I was earning his approval."

"Spare me the psychobabble. Who am I, Dr. Phil?"

"I was also getting the girl."

"How did that work out?" I ask, trying not to sneer.

If he's insulted, he hides it well. "Not the way I hoped. She saw me shoot Richard from the top of the stairs, and she ran to her room. I went after her, but she was waiting with her gun. I didn't want to hurt her, but she was going to kill me. We wrestled for the gun, and I shot her."

"It just went off?"

He shakes his head. "No, I shot her. If not, she would have killed me, or at the very least told the police what I had done. But it was still self-defense. There was no other way; I wish there was. I loved her."

I'm not often speechless, but I have absolutely nothing to say.

"I served six years for shooting someone who deserved to be killed, and who was going to die either way. If I get out now, it's not that unfair, Andy."

Just then the door opens, and in an act of exquisitely bad timing, Hike sticks his head in and says, "Hatchet is calling everyone to the courtroom. There's a verdict."

Joey takes a deep breath; he seems to have been hit by a wave of tension. And I'm sure he has; just because he's confessed to me doesn't make this outcome any less important to him. The news of his actual guilt, while a revelation to me, is something he's known and lived with for a long time. Without any apparent effect on his conscience.

He manages a slight smile. "Well, this is awkward."

I stand up. "Let's go."

"How are you rooting, Andy?"

I don't even have to think about it.

"Guilty."

We head into the courtroom, where the gallery is starting to fill up. Dylan and his team have arrived, and he comes over and shakes my hand, a nice gesture. He doesn't wish me luck, because he obviously believes we want very different outcomes.

We don't.

Hatchet comes in five minutes later, and the session is called to order. Joey hasn't said a word to me, and sits silently as the jury is brought in. Hike is silent as well; I haven't told him what I've learned, so he's hoping for an acquittal.

Once the jury is seated, Hatchet asks the foreman if they've reached a verdict.

"We have, Your Honor."

"Please hand the form to the clerk."

He does so, and the clerk brings it to Hatchet, who looks at it and hands it back. "Will the defendant please rise." It's a command in the form of a question.

Hike and I rise along with Joey, though my first choice would be to just leave. I have a superstition that I always put my hand on a client's shoulder as the verdict is read. Since that superstition is supposed to yield a "not guilty" result, I keep my hands folded in front of me.

The bailiff starts to read, "As it relates to

count one, we, the jury, in the case of the State of New Jersey versus Joseph Desimone, find the defendant, Joseph Desimone, not guilty of the crime of murder in the first degree."

Joey mercifully doesn't turn to Hike or me to shake hands, since I'm not sure what I would have done if he did. Instead he says, "Andy, I'm sorry for you it had to end this way. But I'm very glad for me." Then, "What happens now? Do I have to sign papers or anything? Or can I just leave?"

"Don't ask me. I'm not your lawyer anymore."

I just pack up my briefcase and leave. I can feel Hike staring at me, but I don't say anything.

I also see Laurie in the gallery, and the look on her face clearly indicates her confusion with my demeanor. I just nod to her; there will be plenty of time to tell her what happened later.

Right now I just want to get out of this courtroom, and this job, and this skin, and this life.

FBI agents were at the St. Louis airport when Tommy Iurato arrived. They didn't take him into custody, choosing instead to follow him, even though they knew where he was going.

Other agents were already at the airport, watching the large hangars which held the Coastal Cargo planes that had returned from Peru. Using high-tech surveillance techniques, they were determining what they were dealing with in terms of manpower and weaponry.

Whatever it was, they would handle it.

A driver picked Iurato up and took him to the Coastal Cargo planes. It was clear that he had not heard about Edward's arrest. If he had, he would have tried to escape rather than head to the place the FBI would be most interested in.

The agents knew that Iurato was not armed on the commercial flight, but they made the assumption that the driver had given him a weapon. It was always safer to assume that, and be pleasantly surprised if it were not the case. As it turned out, that caution was warranted, as Iurato had been given a gun moments after entering the car.

When he arrived at the hangar and got out of the car, the agents moved in, using overwhelming force. Iurato made the decision not to shoot it out; he had long believed that going down fighting made no sense.

Even in the moment, he decided that he would instead use the bargaining chip of implicating and testifying against Edward Young to soften his fall. Young would be the key player the feds would be looking to take down.

Having prudently thought about this possibility long in advance, Iurato also would say that Young was the co-planner with Carmine Desimone, since there was no way anyone could know that Carmine was dead. Carmine was set up to be a possible fall guy in death, and there was no reason to abandon that idea now.

It was the largest illegal drug confiscation in the nation's history, more than two and a half times larger than the previous record holder. And it would set off a law enforcement chain reaction that would reverberate through much of South America.

"You think he did it," Laurie says, as soon as we get in the car. "I can see it in your face."

"It's worse than that; I know he did it. He confessed." I go on to tell her all that had happened.

"I heard about Edward Young's arrest just before I got to court," she says. "I figured it tied into this."

"I'm going to have to live with this. There's not a thing I can do."

"You did what you thought was right," she says. "And what I thought was right. And what Hike thought was right. It's the way the system works."

"So everybody did good, and the system worked, and a double murderer is out on the street."

She knows there's nothing she can say that will make me feel better. "Does Hike know?"

423

I shake my head. "No. I'm not sure I should tell him. He'll feel just as badly, and there's nothing he can do either."

"He needs to know," Laurie says. "You'd want to know if the roles were reversed."

I call Hike and ask him to meet us at the house. He gets there about ten minutes after we do, and I tell him straight out that Joey is guilty.

"I figured something was wrong," he says. "The way you took off after the verdict."

"Sorry. I should have told you then."

"Don't worry about it," he says. "You give any thought to what we can do?"

"I come up with nothing. Anything we've learned is covered by privilege. You know that. And even if we could tell what we know, he's off the hook for the murders."

I don't have to spell it out any more for Hike; he knows that jeopardy attached when the jury was sworn in. Joey couldn't be tried again for the murders if he went on national television and confessed to the world.

It's unbelievably frustrating for me. Right now I'd be willing to give up my legal career by breaking a confidence and revealing what I've learned as Joey's attorney. But that wouldn't even help; he is not guilty of the murders in the eyes of the law, forever.

"So we watch him," Hike says. "He's going to move into the family business, right? That's what the whole thing was about. And with his father gone, he'll fill the void. He'll do something we can nail him on."

"Joey's smart," I say. "He'll be careful for a while."

"But it won't last. And think of how sweet it will be when he makes a mistake."

It is a measure of how bad I feel that Hike is trying to cheer me up. The mind boggles.

At dinner, Laurie and I talk about it some more. I don't really want to, but I might as well, because I can't think about anything else. "I liked him," I say. "For six years I've liked him, and he's been lying to me."

"You had no way of knowing."

"Of course I did. The first jury knew he was guilty; how come I didn't? I feel like Johnnie Cochran."

"What is it that's bothering you the most, Andy? That a bad guy got off and is walking free? That you helped him do it? That justice didn't triumph? That you were fooled?"

"All of the above. But never again. I'm done. I'm going to rescue dogs full-time. Dogs tell it like it is."

"You're retiring?"

"I'm retiring."

"You say that after every case. Even when you win."

"This time I mean it." I can't help but smile. "Actually, every time I mean it. But this time I really mean it."

"You're too good at it. There are other people out there that need you. People who deserve help."

"I helped a murderer walk, Laurie."

"Just so I can prepare, how long am I going to have to listen to you blame yourself?"

"Till death do us part."

For the past week, I've been a walking contradiction. Actually, a walking and sitting contradiction, because when I'm not taking Tara for a walk, I'm sitting on the couch watching whatever sports I can find. It's an attempt to take my mind off the trial, but off-hour sports, like poker and lacrosse, do not do the trick.

I completely ignore anything having to do with the Desimone case. I turn off anything about it on the news, I refuse to take calls from the media who want comments on the case, I also refuse to take a call from FBI agent Beall, who leaves a message thanking me for my help. I haven't even been able to bring myself to send Joey a final bill.

The contradiction is that while I'm ignoring it, I'm obsessing about it. I pretty much think about nothing else, much as I would like to.

To make matters worse, a FedEx package

arrives from Agent Beall. He's making good on the trade I insisted on, in which I gave them the information about the drugs and Edward Young, in return for the tapes they had on Joey Desimone six years ago. Givens didn't want to do it, but Beall had agreed, had given his word, and he's following up.

I would rather listen to twenty-four hours of opera than five minutes of Joey Desimone plotting a murder. Not only do I not want to hear the tapes, but their very existence angers me. The FBI knew with total certainty that Joey was a murderer, but at no time did they intervene.

I haven't spoken to Cindy Spodek, though I know Laurie has. I should thank her for her help, but since I'm in my "miserable to everyone" mode, I'm not about to.

Cindy calls again tonight, at ten thirty when Laurie and I have just gotten into bed. I hear them talking for about twenty minutes. It doesn't seem to be about business, but rather some house that Cindy and her husband are about to move into in a Boston suburb.

When Laurie gets off the phone, she tells me that Cindy said hello to me. "We're going to have dinner next week. You up for that?"

"Where?"

"Here. She's coming in on an assignment. She's been traveling a lot, which has been a problem, because she and Tom are getting ready to move."

"She working on a case here?"

Laurie shrugs. "I guess so. Must be a Massachusetts case that spills over."

It's weird the way certain things can hit you. I totally was aware that Cindy traveled and that her cases took her across state lines. It's why they call it the "Federal" Bureau of Investigation, because it's national.

I get out of bed, leaving Laurie there, which is not something I'm normally inclined to do. I spend the next nine hours diving into the box that Agent Beall had sent me; I can sleep some other time.

All the tapes have fortunately been transcribed and cataloged, which makes my job much easier. By morning I have what I need, and start calling Agent Beall in Washington every five minutes, until he gets in.

"I need to see you," I say, when I finally reach him.

He tries to get me to say what I want, but I tell him it has to be in person. "I can be there by two o'clock," I tell him, and he agrees to see me.

I bring a small suitcase, which I carry onto

the plane. There are no clothes in it, only copies of the documents from the box and notes I've made from them. When I finally get to Beall's office, I put the suitcase on his desk.

He smiles. "You're moving in?"

"No, just negotiating another trade."

"The last one worked out pretty well."

"For you," I say.

"Your client got off; isn't that what you wanted?"

I nod. "Until I found out that he was guilty, which you've known all along."

"Not me," he says. "Just because the Bureau on some level had the information, there was no reason for me to be involved. It was a New Jersey case."

"No, it wasn't."

"What are you talking about?" he asks.

"You have enough information in that bag to put Joey Desimone away ten times over."

"Did you cut class in law school the day they taught double jeopardy?"

"There are at least eight phone taps in there between Joey and his father, or associates of his father."

"So?"

"So Joey was living in New York, and that's where he made the calls from."

Beall immediately knows where I'm going; I can see it in his face. But I spell it out for him anyway.

"He's on those calls talking conspiracy to murder, arms smuggling, laundering money . . . which is wire fraud . . . and he's doing it all across state lines. That's federal, and has nothing to do with the trial in New Jersey."

"So his lawyer is asking us to prosecute him?"

I shake my head. "I'm not his lawyer anymore, and I learned this information after he and I ended our relationship. And I'm not sure I'd constitute what I'm doing as asking."

"What does that mean?"

"This is going to become public knowledge. It will happen either by you bringing charges, or by me going to the media and telling them that you stood by while a murderer went free. And then the pressure will be so great that your bosses will force you to make the case anyway. So do yourself a favor and do it now."

I've got him, and he knows it. "It will take some time to put the case together."

I point to the suitcase. "Your case is in that case, and it's already together. A competent attorney, which I am not, could file it next week. But I'll give you three weeks."

"You understand it's not my decision."

"The people making the decision will see the wisdom in it. To say nothing of justice being served." I'm sure they will bring the case; I've really left them no choice.

As I'm about to leave, Beall says, "You never told me how you knew it was Edward Young."

"He told me he buys small businesses with big potential, and then hires people to run them who report only to him. Ryerson was a businessman who could run things; that's why Young brought him in. Once he bought out Solarno, he had access to Desimone. He thought Desimone's business could be run better, so he took it over."

"How did he do that?"

"I assume with money. He bought Desimone's employees; their loyalty was to the money. Times have changed."

"That still doesn't tell me how you knew about Young."

"Money was one reason," I say. "I knew that the operation had to cost a fortune to put together, and Young was the only person connected to this in any way that had that kind of dough.

"And I did some research on Young's

companies before I met him. I knew Coastal Cargo was one of them, and I saw the planes flying into Peru on television. I also found out that Iurato was heading to St. Louis. That was where Coastal Cargo was based, and where Young was from. He's a huge Cardinals fan. Those were major co-incidences, and I do not believe in them."

"Nice work," Beall says. "But you didn't know for certain. And there was that shooting; his driver was killed."

I shrug. "I figured he set that up to divert attention from himself, so he would look like a victim. But the bottom line is that when I came to you, I wasn't absolutely positive I was right. But if I was wrong, I was wrong. I had to take a shot; I was defending my client."

I leave Beall's office confident that I accomplished my goal, and that they will file charges.

And Joey Desimone will go down.

With a different lawyer.

Who probably won't visit him in prison.

"I thought I'd never see either of you again," Harriet Marshall said. She's petting Tara as she talks, still using that reverse pet that Tara is not crazy about, but allows her to do.

I'm not sure whether Harriet is talking to me or Tara, but I decide to do the answering. "I told you we'd be back," I said. "I'm glad it's not in the hospital."

We're at her house, in Fair Lawn. She was discharged from the hospital awhile ago, and is doing great.

"Me too," she says. "I saw you on the news. I told everybody I know about it."

"Have you been getting out a lot?"

She nods. "Some, and people come over all the time. Family and friends. But that's not the only way I talk to people anymore, not since my nephew gave me a computer. Are you familiar with e-mail?"

I smile. "Vaguely."

"You won that case, right?"

I nod. "I did, but the client is going to go back to jail. The FBI filed charges against him yesterday."

"Does that upset you?" she asks.

"I'm OK with it."

"You know, bringing Tara to see me in the hospital really helped. It reminded me of my Sarah, and of happy times."

"I'm glad to hear that," I say. "Tara makes me happy every day."

"Do you think you could help me find a dog of my own? They're telling me I could live for a long time, and I'll make arrangements for the dog to have a home with my daughter if I don't."

"Absolutely. I know a place where there are dogs just waiting for a home like this, and a friend like you." Willie and I just rescued three mellow, senior dogs, any one of which would be perfect for this home.

"When could we do that?"

"How about now?"

She smiles and pets Tara again. "Now is good."

ACKNOWLEDGMENTS

A while back, when I wrote *Play Dead*, I was accused of name-dropping, simply because I thanked a bunch of famous people. I stopped doing it for a while, because I didn't want to look like I was showing off, but that stops here.

My relationships with these people help define me; they reveal who I am. Like it or not, I walk among the stars, and I'm not afraid to admit it.

So a heartfelt "thank you" to those mentioned below. I am proud to call all of you close, personal friends:

Barack Obama
David, Butch, and Hopalong Cassidy
Kelley Ragland
Kelly Ripa
Clarence and Marlo Thomas
Kim Kardashian
Kim Jung Il

The entire Jung Il family
Woody and Gracie Allen
Marv Throneberry
Marv Albert
Albert Schweitzer
Cynthia and Richard Nixon
Margaret Thatcher
Andy and Cherry Garcia
Doug Burns
Anne and Barney Frank
Too many Baldwins to mention
LeBron James
Marilyn and James Monroe
Kramer
Daniel and Jenny Craig
Robin Rue
Denzel and Martha Washington
Matt Martz
Ratzo Rizzo
Adlai Stevenson
The Williams family — Robin, Serena, and Tennessee
Andy Martin
Andy Warhol
Andy Carpenter
Jodie and Bananas Foster
Bruce Springsteen
Hector DeJean
Jenny and Senator Joseph McCarthy
Charlie Sheen

Charlie Chan
Lawrence and Elizabeth Taylor
Wolf Blitzer
Rod Blagojevich
Earl and Sigourney Weaver
Hyman Roth
Gunther Toody
Emma and Fred Thompson
Beth Miller
Harrison and Betty Ford
Vladimir Putin
Barth Gimble
Mel and Althea Gibson
Elizabeth Lacks
Warren Harding
Aretha and Benjamin Franklin
Debbie Myers
Peyton Manning
Meg and Private Ryan
Ernie Bilko
Roy Hobbs
Bruce, Spike, and Robert E. Lee
Scott Ryder
Neil and Hope Diamond